Seduce Her Heart

By

Diana Manos

1st Books - rev. 09/06/02

1

The tall man in sunglasses was watching her again. Carla Redfern nervously glanced at the tables sprawled out along the outside café on K Street. The sounds of the street blurred together. Even the early summer sun on her face wasn't taking away the darkness she was trying to keep at bay.

"He's here," she said to Amy. "Back table."

Amy nodded over Carla's shoulder. "Here he comes."

The man walked past, out onto the sidewalk without so much as glancing at them. He stood for a moment as he adjusted his glasses, his gold pinkie ring flashing in the sun. Then in long strides, he rounded the corner of Connecticut Avenue, blending into the throng of other dark business suits.

"I'd say you've been watching too much T.V.," Amy said.

Carla realized she was gripping the sides of the table, and removed her hands to her lap. "Tomorrow, I'm telling you, Amy. No matter where we go for lunch — he'll be there." Her eyes were riveted to the faces going by.

"I think this is about breaking up with Todd, if you want to know my opinion," Amy said.

"I don't want to know your opinion." Carla realized even as she said it, she was being harsh. But she couldn't allow herself the luxury of letting Todd cross her mind.

###

"Name?"

"Carla Redfern"

"Spell it."

"C-a-"

"No, Redfern, Miss." Spell it.

It was probably a mistake to come here.

Carla followed the officer down a dingy corridor. She stepped around a man in tattered and rumpled clothing slumped against the wall, snoring loudly.

"Don't mind him," said the officer as he poured runny tar into a plastic cup. "He's a regular." He held the pot up to her. "Coffee?" Carla shook her head.

The officer directed her into a room barely large enough to surround a desk covered in papers. Papers fell off the desk onto the floor and she crunched onto them as she took a chair. The officer seated himself on the other side of the desk.

"So. You claim there is someone following you?" The officer was scribbling on a form of some kind. "What does he look like?"

"Caucasian. Dark glasses, black hair. Wide shoulders."

"That sounds like quite a few people out there." The officer chuckled.

Carla crossed her arms.

"What makes you think you are being pursued?"

"*I keep seeing him!*"

The policeman looked up and tried to contain himself. "Listen, Miss. The D.C. police force just doesn't have enough manpower to check out every instance of someone's..."

"Paranoia?"

"No. That's not what I'm saying, here... It's just that we need more evidence."

"How about my carcass in a gutter behind my apartment? Would that satisfy your need for evidence?"

"I can see your frustration here. But I suggest if you have any money you hire a bodyguard or a private investigator. Maybe they can track this down for you. I'll keep your records on file, and if you can give us more to work with, we can assign an officer to check this out." He stood up and extended his hand to her, but she didn't take it.

The officer scratched his head as he watched her go from the doorway of his office. "Come on, James," he said to the man at his feet. "Time for you to hit the road."

Carla's apartment building was of similar size to the ones lined up and down Connecticut Avenue — about ten floors, housing hundreds of people. When she first moved to Washington, this one particular building had stood out to her because it was set back from the street a little, surrounded by a lush lawn and tall trees. It had given her a feint reminiscence of her childhood home on a wide boulevard in the Chicago suburbs. Nobody wants to rent on the first floor, the landlord had said when he showed her the only vacant unit in the building, a small studio apartment. But Carla didn't mind. She had to have the place. Now this man in black situation was beginning to make her wish she'd rented in another building, on an upper floor. She checked the piece of wood jammed in the window for added security. It was tight.

Curling up in her oversized chair with a good book, Carla felt calm for the first time all day. The cinnamon candle she had burning made her think of her grandmother's apple pie, and her skin was still warm from her long hot bath. With her feet up on the coffee table, she thumbed through the pages in her book looking for the spot where she'd left off the night before.

The phone rang like a shot in the dark causing her to jolt. She reached over to answer it. The smooth voice washed over her completely.

"I thought we'd agreed you wouldn't call," Carla said.

"We did." There was a hint of mocking sensuality. He had no respect for rules.

"Well?" She hoped he'd hurry up with it.

"I have to see you. Something harmless. Lunch maybe?"

Carla was silent.

"You still there?" Todd asked.

"Yes."

"You want me to call you back after you think about it?"

"No. I don't need to think about it."

"I'm out of town next week," he said, insinuating she'd like to reschedule.

"No." She winced, regretting the word, but leaning on it.

"Well, my cell phone is about to cut out. I have to go."

Carla was feeling she should do something to soften the blow, but was disconnected before she could.

Sleep wasn't going to happen tonight. Enough was enough, she thought. Impulsively, she poured herself a shot of whisky, and the rising moon beckoned her over to the window. She pulled the blinds while the whiskey burned. Light beamed down on the trees in her neighborhood near the National Zoo, creating an eerie fairytale-like atmosphere. She looked out across the field behind her apartment and at the roof of the neighboring building, both glowing with moonlight. Tomorrow she would have to buy some over-the-counter sleeping medication.

An almost indiscernible motion made her glance closer to her window, even as her body involuntarily tensed. There. Standing back a little in the trees. Was that the form of a man looking her way?

She screamed out. But somehow, when she blinked, he was gone.

It was four in the morning before she finally fell asleep sitting up in the chair with all the lights on.

The Crow Bar was rocking on its hinges when Carla walked in, voices all screaming to be heard above one another. Music louder than the screamers. Smoke swirled in billows and hung in the rafters. People lounged in the leather sixties-style sofas that littered the place. She panned the room for the happy-hour party Amy had coordinated. Two guys across at the bar gave her a smile and one beckoned her over. She didn't know them and gave them a scowl as she passed through the room and went up the wide staircase to the loft-style room above.

She heard Amy's voice before she reached the top of the steps. Loaded already. It was Amy's last day at Hudson and Marshall and Carla wasn't expecting her to weather the layoff too well. She walked over to Amy who was in the process of lifting her glass in a toast, surrounded by a loud group of party goers.

"Who are these people?" she whispered in Amy's ear when they hugged hello.

"Old jobs, old loves, old connections..." Amy answered, bourbon breath blasting.

Carla reached up and smoothed a curly hair out of Amy's face. "Sorry I'm late." Carla was so far behind the curve, she probably couldn't catch up if she tried.

"No problémo." Amy said, trying to pretend she had a Spanish accent. She was beginning to slur.

"I like this place. Always have. I'm glad you picked it!" Carla screamed over the noise as she looked around. Amy smiled a look of satisfaction.

"Lots of memories here."

"No doubt about that," Carla said with a smile. "And many more to come."

"Right you are, my friend," Amy slung a heavy arm over Carla's shoulder and leaned onto her hard. Carla shuffled to hold Amy's weight without falling.

"Need help?" Carla heard the voice, but couldn't see who it was. Sounded male and sexy, but then again, it could be her imagination.

"Over here," the voice said.

Carla turned her head to look over her shoulder. The voice belonged to a tall man who appeared to be about her age. Curly dark hair. Brown intent eyes. A classically handsome face. He was standing with his arms crossed, wearing a dark sports jacket and black jeans, watching Carla with a look of curiosity as she stood holding up Amy. The two women were starting to sway.

"Sure. I could use a little help," Carla said to the Greek cowboy.

Amy had put her head down on Carla's shoulder and had literally passed out standing up. She started to crumple. "Amy, honey?" Carla lowered her gently into a large armchair next to them. "I'm worried about her. She needs to get home. Are you one of her old friends? I'm Carla."

"I know who you are," the dark-eyed stranger said.

Carla laughed. "You're kidding! How would you know who I am and I wouldn't know who you are?"

"Easy."

"Let's hear it."

"She didn't want you to know about me."

"And what reason for that would there be?"

"Jealousy."

"Don't you think you flatter yourself too much, Mr...?"

"Spanos."

"Mr. Spanos, don't you think that's rather arrogant to say to the lifeless remnant of a mutual friend we have here?" She looked down at Amy. She was drooling!

"Oh my gosh, Amy.... Amy?" Carla gently grabbed Amy's face in one hand and jiggled her. No movement from Amy. Carla looked up at Spanos. "Do you have a handkerchief?"

"Always." He reached up and pulled a crisp white folded square from the inner pocket of his jacket.

"Not many men your age carry these," Carla said as she leaned over and wiped Amy's bottom lip and then her whole face. Amy snorted and let her head fall onto her chest. Carla stood up and swung her long hair behind her back before looking intently at the man next to her.

"And you know all about older men?" he asked with a taunting look.

"Listen, Spanos. What's your first name?"

"Michael."

"Of course."

"What does that mean?" His eyes crinkled at the corners as he smiled widely. A very nice smile, she thought to herself.

"You look like a Michael, that's all."

He nodded, thinking that one over.

"Hey. This party is breaking up and I don't even know anyone who's left here. Can you help me get her into a cab?"

"My pleasure." Michael leaned over and gently put one muscular arm under Amy's neck and one under her knees and carried her like a baby against his chest. Carla followed him down the steps, through the smoke, past the laughing faces and voices, and out onto the street.

Michael gently placed Amy onto the back seat of a cab and closed the door. "Thank you. You're very nice to save a lady in distress."

"Well, I haven't really done that. But I could."

"What do you mean?"

"Save you." He smiled.

"Me? I don't need saving."

"Not what Amy tells me."

"You gonna get in lady, or what?" The cab driver yelled in a New Jersey accent.

"Let me escort you." He looked at her in earnest.

Carla bit her lip. The cab driver was glaring at her. "Okay," she said. "But only because Amy knows you."

Michael smiled as he got into the front seat and slammed the door. "3701 Wisconsin Avenue." The cab sped out into traffic.

###

"So. You always caretake your friends?" Michael asked Carla as they sat across from each other at Amy's small kitchen table with their hands wrapped around coffee mugs.

"Is that an accusation, or a compliment?"

"What do you think?"

"Why don't you tell me who you are and how you know Amy, seeing as Amy can't speak for herself until tomorrow, and then again she might not even want to."

"I live across the hall."

"I find that hard to believe," Carla said.

"Right out that door." Michael gestured in the general direction.

"And Amy never once mentioned you. Not once. In literally thousands of clocked hours between us talking about men?"

"You find that hard to believe?"

"Yes," Carla said, as she sipped out of her mug, eyes on him.

"She said that about you."

"What?"

"You're a skeptic."

"Why were you two talking about me, anyway?"

"She always tells me about you. She talks about you all the time. You're her best friend, I would venture to guess."

"And when did you two have all these talks?"

"While watching TV, eating dinner. She came to my house. I came to hers. Keeps the lonelies away."

"The lonelies?"

"You laughing at my lonelies?" He pouted in a way that made him look like a very handsome giant baby.

"No. I just can't picture you lonely. Not someone like you."

"A compliment?" He smiled as if he'd just won a round.

"No. It wasn't a compliment." Carla got up and sloshed her coffee into the sink and spun around. "Listen, I've got to get going. Do you think she'll be okay? I mean, can I leave her here alone, asleep and drunk?"

"I could crawl in bed with her, would that make you feel better?"

"That's not funny."

"She'll be fine. I'll be right across the hall." He wrinkled his forehead at her. "Where do you have to be on a Friday night at ten o'clock?"

"Home."

"Expecting company?"

"You know, you have some nervy questions for a total stranger," Carla said.

"I'm not a total stranger. Not really. Don't want to be, anyway."

Carla stood back and looked at him. He wasn't kidding. His expression was totally serious. Carla wrote a quick note to Amy on the pad by the phone.

She stood up and looked him in the eye. "Michael. Once again, I thank you for your help. I'm leaving now. And, may I escort you to the door?"

"You don't want to leave me alone in here with Amy?"

"No."

"You don't trust me?"

"I didn't say that."

"You didn't have to."

"I'm sorry. It's just that, she's passed out cold, and I really and truly have never heard your name mentioned by her."

"I understand." He gathered his jacket and put his cup gently into the sink.

"I'm sorry to be hard nosed about it."

"No. A lady can't be careful enough in this day and age."

Carla pulled Amy's door shut behind them as they left, and turned to look at Michael as they stood in front of his door across the hall. "Michael Spanos" it said in gold on a little panel above the eyehole. He smiled as she noticed it.

"See? I wasn't lying."

She lowered her head and her blond head of hair fell down around her shoulders. She quickly pulled it back from her eyes with one hand and pulled it to the side.

"You have really long hair. It's very pretty."

"Thanks," she said, now looking down.

"If you want to give me a call sometime, I'd like to take you out for a drink or something." He gave her a business card from his pants pocket with a casual gesture.

Carla frowned, but reached out and took the card. She put the card into her jacket pocket without looking at it.

Carla knew he was watching her all the way as she walked down the hall. When the elevator rang and opened, she heard him gently close his door.

2

Carla was fairly sure that a man had been following her since she got off the Metro. It wasn't the man in black. *Was everyone following her now?*

She first noticed a tall, slim figure with a black windbreaker, smoking a cigarette. His hair was brown and slicked back. He was leaning against the newsstand outside her office as she crossed the street. And she was certain she saw him again at the back of her subway train.

She rode to the Tenleytown stop and she gritted her teeth to prevent herself from looking back again to see if the man was following. This was getting ridiculous. She darted up the alleyway parking lot to the Fresh Fields food store and entered the bright hazy light of people bustling after work through aisles of fresh organic foods. Carla grabbed a small hand basket and made her way down an empty aisle as quickly as she could to the back of the store. If he were following her, maybe she'd lost him in the crowd. She stopped at the fresh meat counter and asked the butcher to cut her a fresh steak, a New York strip steak, enough for two people.

"Two hungry people, or two light eaters?" the butcher smiled as he asked.

"Huh? Excuse me?"

"Lady. You want twelve ounces each, or more like six?"

"Make them the best cuts you can. No fat."

"Ma'am we don't have fat on our New York strip."

"Ok. Fine. I'll take twelve ounces." She glanced behind her. Was that a glimpse of the tennis shoe man at the front of the store? The butcher handed her the meat wrapped in white paper.

"Thank you," she said as she reached up to get it.

"Here you go," said a deep voice. A thin hand came from beside her and pushed the meat closer to her on the counter. She looked up, and *it was him!* One of his teeth was gold as he cast her a dark smile.

She started to move away, but the man grabbed her coat and yanked her hard. She felt a sharp point press into her side, under her jacket. His hot breath was in her ear. He had a rancid smell. "You scream, lady, and I'll split you open like a trout. I ain't got nothin' to lose."

Where was the butcher? Carla cranked her head around to see the white doors to the butcher department swinging. No one was in the aisle.

"Now walk toward the front door, and do it like nothing is wrong, or somethin's gonna be real wrong, get my drift? You'll be dead before the crowd even figures out what happened."

Carla tried to wrench from his grasp, but he held her tighter. Something about his face seemed unstable. She was breathing faster and harder, but everything around her seemed to be happening in slow motion now. The man turned to look at her and laughed, showing his gold tooth again. He looked like an image from a hard rock video. Sounds were echoing, and blood was rushing to her head.

She was being "escorted" out the front of the store. "Let go of me," she said through clenched teeth, trying to yank herself away from him. He only grabbed her upper arm tighter and squeezed.

"I don't think you're in the position to make demands," the man said, nodding a greeting to a couple passing by with their car keys jangling. The knife was still in her side. He grabbed the package of meat and flung it into the bushes. "I have a car and driver just up here waiting for us. Gonna take a little ride." He chuckled.

Carla waited until they were out of the parking lot and walking along Wisconsin Avenue in the midst of the pedestrians before she let him have it with the pepper spray from her coat pocket. She aimed straight for his eyes. He let out a roar and doubled over.

Several people stopped and stared as Carla tore herself away from the man and bolted across the street causing a driver to screech his brakes and honk loudly as he almost hit her.

She bolted to the library dead ahead, feeling like she couldn't pull the heavy glass doors opened fast enough. There was a small ladies' room up the stairs. She took them two at a time, ripped open the bathroom door, turned and bolted it. She dug through her purse for her cell phone and called the police. She crouched down and hugged her knees. She was fairly sure the man hadn't seen her dart into the library. She tried to think of someone else to call. She was still puffing hard from her run.

Her hand fumbled mindlessly in her pocket onto a business card she'd left there. She pulled it out. It was crinkled up and a little tattered. "Michael Spanos. Private Investigator," it said. She dialed the number with her hands shaking.

"Hey, when I didn't hear from you, I figured you weren't going to take me up on my offer." Michael's voice sounded jovial.

"Well, I'm going to take you up on something, but not what you think." Carla was trying to sound calm, but her voice was shaking.

"You in trouble?"

"Locked in a bathroom, just got away from a man with a knife hunting me in Tenleytown."

"You're not pulling my leg, are you? Amy says you can really joke around."

"I know this sounds crazy, but..." She was biting her lip so she wouldn't cry.

"Fair enough. Where's the bathroom?"

"Friendship Library on Wisconsin, across from Fresh Fields."

"I know where that is."

"I'm on the second floor. The man had me at knifepoint on the street, but I peppered him and ran. Now I'm hiding here and I'm afraid to come out."

"I'll be there in ten minutes."

Carla turned off the phone and took a deep sigh. She sat listening to the footsteps and murmurs of library patrons outside.

It took Michael only five minutes to get there.

"Thought you'd have your cape on," Carla said as she opened the door to him.

"Couldn't find a phone booth," he said with a laugh. Then he got serious. "You're not hurt?"

"No." She winced when she gently pressed on her upper arm.

"Come on. I've got my car out back."

Carla hesitated.

"Don't worry. Anyone comes near you, I'll gladly let my self control out of its cage," Michael said with a smile. He led her down some back steps to the back door of the library where an elderly librarian was waiting to let them out with a key.

"Thanks, Maureen." Michael winked as they stepped out of the back door onto a side street sidewalk. Carla was busy looking to the right and to the left.

"Maureen?" she asked, as Michael opened the door to his Camaro. A shiny black one, with red interior.

"That's my gal, Maureen," Michael said, as he closed Carla's door and locked it. "Buckle up," he said. "This car is 1985, doesn't buckle you up automatically." Carla was in a daze, looking out the window and feeling confused. Michael reached over and buckled her in, tugging the belt snug. Carla sank back in the bucket seat. Soon they were moving through traffic, weaving and turning. She noticed he checked his rear view mirror often.

"What if someone is following us?"

"I seriously doubt that," Michael said, focusing on his driving, picking up the speed, heading north to the beltway. "But just in case." He opened his jacket to show her a gun tucked into the inner pocket.

Carla smiled feebly. Guns. Cops. All of this was crazy. She felt like she'd landed a part in a *Godfather* movie. It was time she got off the set.

"Hear that sweet baby purr?" He looked over with a proud smile.

"I guess," Carla said. She knew nothing about engines.

"Totally rebuilt it. This car could blow the doors off of just about anything out on the road today." Michael laughed.

Carla feigned a smile. She was wondering where he was taking her, what the plan was, how she'd sleep tonight.

"I'm taking you to Baltimore, to a hotel managed by my friend," he said, as if he could read her mind. "It's a great place overlooking the harbor."

"But I have work tomorrow."

"Call in sick."

"Will the police ever come to the library, I wonder?"

"I called them. Told them we didn't need them. We'd file a report later."

"You've got all the bases covered, looks like."

Michael smiled. "Now sit back and relax, little lady."

Carla realized her hands were in fists on her lap. She let them loosen. Michael reached over and turned on the radio.

"You like country music?" he asked.

"Maybe." She didn't know much about it, but it was the least of her worries at this point.

It was the same at the hotel as it was at the library. Doors seemed to open automatically. No registration at the lobby. Michael merely picked up a key and they went straight up to the room.

###

Carla felt like a different person after taking a long shower and soaking in the tub. She wanted to wash the memory of the knife attack off of her. When she stepped out of the dressing room into the plush expanse of a room at the Baltimore Harbor Renaissance Marriott, she saw Michael sitting by the window at a small table eating peanuts and drinking coke from a can, his feet propped up on the other chair. A brilliant combination of oranges, pinks and purples glowed outside behind him overlooking the harbor. He turned to appraise her standing there in a thick terrycloth hotel robe and a towel wrapped around her head like a turban.

"Nice." He popped another peanut into his mouth.

She walked tentatively over to the chair opposite him.

"Sit down," Michael said. He kicked the chair out with his foot. Carla was looking around for her clothes.

"I'm having the hotel clean your suit. Thought it might make you feel better."

Carla turned from looking at the sunset to look directly at Michael. "That's nice of you. But…"

"But, you're afraid I'm going to leave you with nothing more than terrycloth between us?"

"Something like that."

"I bought you something to wear to dinner while you were in the tub."

"You're kidding."

"No. Not kidding," Michael said chewing peanuts. "I hope I guessed the right size. The lady downstairs helped me." The Marriott was situated over a giant five-story mall, totally enclosed in glass. Carla had seen it on their way in.

"What size did you guess?"

"Why don't you try it on and see?" He nodded over to the closet. "I want to take you to dinner downstairs in the hotel restaurant. They have amazing crab cakes. The best in Maryland."

The dress was simple but beautiful. Carla held it up. It was tea-length black satin. It looked like it would fit perfectly. "Do you think it's a good idea for me to go out of this room? I thought we'd get room service or something."

"I think it will be fine. The restaurant manager is giving us an exclusive table. Besides, I'm certain no one trailed us from D.C."

Carla started to laugh. "I don't see how anyone could trail us at the speeds you were going."

Michael raised his eyebrows at her. She noticed his black leather cowboy boots for the first time.

"I feel funny taking this dress, staying in this room and …all of this," Carla said. She looked down nervously.

"You'd feel funnier dead."

"You know what I mean."

"You can relax, little missy. I never mess with clients."

"Comforting," Carla said. She walked over to the mirror to look at herself with the dress. No harm in looking, she thought. She turned slightly from side to side to see. The dress gently whirled. It was cut with quality.

"You can't resist it, can you?"

"I should."

"I figure it's the least you can do for calling me on such short notice. And, I won't even mention how you ignored my invitation to take you out over a month ago." He paused. "Normally women don't ignore me."

She looked him over. That was totally obvious. Muscles bulging through his shirt. Trim waist. She tried not to think about the rest of him.

"Well, I'm not your typical woman."

"To say the least."

Carla smiled and walked back to the closet and hung up the dress. "So, are you going to retire to your room so a lady can get dressed?"

"No."

Carla looked at him sternly. "What do you mean, No?'"

"I'm staying right here tonight." He reached over and patted the bed next to him. "You think I'm going to leave you alone after that goon came after you today?"

"You really think this is that serious, that I'm not safe alone?"

"I take pointy sharp knives very seriously."

Carla slumped down on the other bed across from him, feeling weak in the knees.

"Do you have anywhere out of town you can go until I figure out what we're dealing with? Any relatives out of town?" Michael asked.

Carla looked out at the Chesapeake Bay. The restaurants all along the inner harbor were lit up and festive. People were strolling along on the wide wooden dock. Bay taxis were busy loading and unloading passengers to ferry them back and forth across the water to other night hotspots.

"I have an old friend on business in San Francisco."

"Is she reliable?"

"Yes, he is. Should I call him?"

He handed her the phone then folded his arms again and sat back. Carla glared at him. "I'd like to call him alone, if you don't mind."

Michael stood up and plunged his hand into his jean pocket as casually as if he were going to pull out a stick of Juicy Fruit gum, but instead he pulled out a small revolver and lay it on the table in front of him. "Keep this close," he said.

Carla reached over and touched the gun.

"I can get you to the Baltimore airport first thing in the morning," Michael said. "Tell your friend, the sooner, the better."

3

Her flight was late getting into San Francisco. Carla looked around her as the plane was descending. An airplane was like one giant crib rocking in the sky with a cargo of adult babies all tucked in for their naps. Over-achiever Joe, sitting next to her wasn't napping. He was busy clicking away on his laptop and making in-air phone calls. She figured people like him were the loneliest people of all because they obviously feared just an hour or two with their own thoughts, in silent reverie over the puffy clouds. If they didn't keep the working frenzy rolling while lapping the country from coast to coast, would they lose a sense of who they are? She thought of Todd and how he flew coast to coast all the time, working for Senator Goldsmith. Always on the phone, always at work.

Todd wasn't anywhere to be seen as she worked her way out into the buzz of the waiting area. *What is my plan B? Call a cab?* She started to panic, but then she spotted him. He was leaning on a column across the way. Tie loosened, smiling.

When she got to him, he didn't make a move to hug her, but reached up and tossed a small piece of her golden hair over her shoulder. She dropped her overnight bag at her feet and reached up to put her arms around his neck. His lips found hers within seconds.

Carla climbed into the cab first and Todd slid in after her. His shoulder touched hers and it was warm and comforting. She leaned her head on it.

"Tired?" he asked.

"Exhausted."

He reached over and gently rested his hand on her thigh. "When are you going to tell me what planets aligned that forced you to come out and visit me?"

"Later," she said. She saw the cab driver cock his head a little, the way cabbies do when they are interested in what you're saying. They are privileged, like no other people on earth, to read the book of humanity day and night, Carla thought.

They pulled up to the Westin St. Francis at the heart of town on Powell Street, overlooking the grassy park called Union Square. Inside, the paneled lobby gleamed. A Frank Sinatra song could be heard drifting from the piano lounge.

Todd wove among the tables, leading her to the back corner. "That's why the lady… is a tramp…." the singer crooned. He was dressed in a gray, shiny double-breasted suit and flanked by aging jazz musicians with congenial faces. He winked at Carla as they walked past.

The large room had vaulted ceilings and full-length windows on three walls, each with red velvet curtains. Small round tables were scattered, surrounded by deep leather seats of various shapes and sizes. Intimate. Yet grand.

"Fitting lyrics," Carla said, as Todd pulled out her chair.

"You know I have a fondness for tramps."

"And lots of `em."

Todd ignored her remark and ordered them both stiff drinks, his a double. When the drinks came, despite her determination to stay removed and sane about Todd, Carla couldn't resist. The dimly lit lounge felt so private. The jazz band was perfect. The lights of the gold rush and the Wild Wild West twinkled outside, Carla imagined. It felt magic, like Christmas eve was magic when she was a child. Something was always so eerie about times she spent with

Todd – as if she'd watched them all before in a movie, or in another life, maybe.

She did her best to shake off the feeling and sipped her drink. The whiskey was smooth and took her for a loop, even after just one drink. She didn't care if Todd was a womanizer or an alcoholic – just for tonight. God knows he probably was both. Her attraction to him didn't make her much better, she thought.

Todd listened attentively as she told him of how she had suspected being stalked for weeks. How she felt watched. Then the night at the grocery store, the man with the knife, and her escape from the library. She left out the part about the new black dress that Michael had given her and the fancy dinner. When the waitress came around for the fourth time, Carla shook off Todd's order for another round and kept right on talking. She told him about work, about her friend Amy, and anything else she could think of. She liked telling him things. Suddenly she realized she'd been talking for quite a while.

"I know what you're trying to do," she said.

"Oh do you, now?" Somehow he seemed much more sober than she did, and he'd had twice the number of drinks.

"Yes. And it's not going to work," she said, her eyes drowsy.

"Whatever you say," Todd said, as he downed the last swig of his whiskey and soda and tipped the glass in a mock toast in her direction so the ice made a tinkling sound.

"Really," she asserted again, hearing her own speech coming back to her like she was in an auditorium – echoing, and a beat off.

Todd signaled the waitress for the check. "I think it's time I take you upstairs Darlin', don't you?"

Carla looked down at her drink and swirled the tiny cocktail straw around and around. "You *don't* know how things will end up." Her voice came out more harshly than she expected.

"You're right," his tone was soft. She turned her head in time to see the couple two tables over staring at her. "C'mon, little girl. You've been all roughed up," Todd said as he stood up and put his hands on her shoulders. "Let's go upstairs."

The hotel room was posh and pleasant. Carla threw herself down on the king size bed. Todd took off his tie, the silk rustling. He kicked off his shoes and went into the bathroom.

"I guess I'll have to sleep in one of your T-shirts," she said in a muffled voice, as she rolled her face into the pillow.

Todd returned to the dark room unbuttoning his shirt. He stopped short of saying something when he realized that she was already in bed.

"I wanted my own room, but there's nothing we can really do about it tonight with the hotel booked...." her voice trailed off as he lifted up the covers and crawled in beside her. He rolled her toward him and pressed his full length against her.

"We can get me my own room tomorrow..." she said, but his soft lips found hers to silence her. She wrapped her arms around him, and hugged him as if she'd lost him in a storm and had found him again. His kiss was slow and tender and he rolled her over on her back and grew more passionate with her. He kissed her like it was for the first time.

"I can hear your heart pounding," she said, when they came up for air.

"Yes," he whispered. "It is."

"Are you scared?" she asked, rising up on one arm to look him in the eyes.

"Always — of you." He touched her nose.

"I wonder what it is about us?"

"I wonder," he said, and he cupped her chin in his hand and pulled her mouth to his. His tongue probed her with persistent intimacy. He had a gentleness that she knew was really part of his true self. His soul was tender, and that was one of the reasons she loved him.

His hands pressed her closer. Soon he lifted her shirt to pull it over her head, and she let him. His hands were gently everywhere, followed by his lips. "Carla, I missed you," he said, and it caught in his throat. "Don't do this to me," he said between kisses. She wasn't listening to his words. They were lost in the alcohol swirling in her head. They were lost in the sheer passion he brought out in her. Soon she was overwhelmed with his touch, and she pulled him closer, letting him know she wouldn't stop him.

When they were spent, she pulled her head away from him, breathless, so she could look into his eyes. Hers were filling with tears. "This doesn't mean we're getting back together."

She gently sucked on his lips, first the top lip, then the bottom. He smiled with his eyes closed, submitting to her. When she stopped kissing him, he opened his eyes, blinking innocently. She put her hands on both sides of his face and looked at him earnestly. How was she ever going to be able to say goodbye to him?

"I understand that you think we don't work," he said. "And I also understand you just made love to me like a woman who can't live without me."

She opened her mouth to protest, but before she could say anything, he pulled her head onto his chest and stroked her back. She pressed herself closer and listened to the rhythm of his breathing. Soon it matched her own.

"I'm so glad to see you," he said. She wondered which had made them drunker, the toxic sweetness of the sorrow, or the whiskey.

"Just knowing you're out there in the world, it keeps me from going crazy," she said.

"I'm glad that works for you," he said softly. He stoked her silky hair in the dark a while longer. "Knowing that you're out there......It kills me."

It was early and Todd was up. Carla could smell the steam from his bathroom coming from his room and the smell of aftershave. She heard the zipping of his suitcase and the closing and opening of his dresser drawers. Was he packing? She sat up in bed and tried to think, forcing herself to wake up.

"You're leaving?" she asked, standing in the doorway between their two rooms.

"I have to go to L.A. for a couple of days. I told them at the front desk I'm keeping these rooms. You can stay here until I get back." He looked up from where he was leafing through papers on the desk and putting them into his briefcase.

"I don't care about that. I thought you were staying, that's all."

"I started thinking, I should probably head down to L.A. while I'm out here. Might be good to impress Goldsmith by handling some things for him down there."

"Why didn't you tell me last night, then?"

"Because it would have ruined your night, and I wanted you to have fun." He briskly moved his luggage off the bed.

"Why so glum? I'll be back in two days." He reached for his cell phone and began scrolling through to see the calls he had stored.

"I might not be here. I might be heading back," she said coldly. She could still feel the mist in her face last night as Todd had driven her in the rented convertible out to the Golden Gate Bridge. The mountains and fog behind the bridge had made it look like it was in the sky as they'd sat at the overlook alone for hours.

When Todd turned to get his suit jacket out of the closet and put it on, Carla quickly wiped her tears with the back of her hand. *He didn't care that she was frightened?* He was leaving just like he always did.

"I've got to go or I'll miss my flight." He was abrupt.

She stood in silence forcing him to pause. He looked at his watch while he leaned over to quickly brush her cheek with his lips. Not even a decent kiss.

After he was gone, she lay face first on the bed. The air conditioning was running too high, but she didn't reach down to pull up the blankets.

Michael's call came later that morning, letting her know it was okay to come back. "I found the thug that came after you in a listing of ex-cons in the area. He matched your description perfectly. I paid him a little visit."

"What?"

"Gave him a curb sandwich. He saw the sense in listening to what I had to say."

"Curb sandwich?"

"I put him face down with his mouth opened on the curb. Put my foot on the back of his head. Told him if he comes after you again his worse fear won't be the police."

Carla started to laugh nervously.

"I wish I could say your problems are over," Michael said. "But I'm afraid there are a million more like him to be had out there. Whoever sent him can send others."

Carla was silent.

"I feel like I'm hitting a brick wall on motives," Michael added. "The thug didn't give me a clue on who hired him. I'm not sure he even knows the name of who hired him. Which brings me to the link of your father...."

"My father? How did he get into this?"

"Well, first of all, it wasn't easy to figure that part out since you told me he was dead."

"He's dead for all practical purposes, *to me*."

"That's fine to tell people at dinner parties. But for me, your private investigator, all the information you can give me would be useful. Your father is one of the highest paid corporate attorneys in the country. Practices out of Chicago. I had to waste valuable time looking for all that stuff, Carla."

"I'm sorry."

"I just have a feeling this might have to do with one of his cases. Do you know who any of his clients are?"

"It's not like I can call him and say hi, Dad. Remember me? Hey, how's business?"

"Call him. Try to break the ice. I'm sure he'll be happy to hear from you."

"Michael, no. You don't understand."

"You're going to have a better chance at this than I am. You have to try."

"Can't we just call the police, get the police involved in this? Wouldn't that be easier?"

"No. We can't. The police won't be able to give as much time to this as I can, and they'll dismiss the case without any evidence. Then you'll be right back to being afraid again. Plus, once the police start snooping around, it's going to give whoever's doing this a head's up. I'm going to wait on that idea for a while until I've worn out all my resources."

"Now I'm starting to honestly get scared."

"Where's your friend? Isn't he helping you with that?"

"Not here right now."

Michael laughed. "Lover's spat?"

"If I didn't know better, I'd think you are jealous." There wasn't playfulness in her tone.

"No, it's just that I know I can protect you better."

The line crackled, making the 3,000 miles between them more real.

"When I come back tomorrow. I'm going home to my place."

"Like hell you are! That's an inconceivable plan."

"What do you suggest? I can't quit my job. I don't want to quit my job. And funny, they won't let me keep it if I don't come in to work."

"I know you have to get back. I was thinking you could stay with me and I could guard you to and from work."

Carla started to protest.

"Now listen, missy. Let me finish. I know what you're going to say."

"What?"

"You're going to say, no."

"Well, then I won't bother saying it."

"I think you'll change your mind after a few nights alone in your apartment."

"I won't. My brother-in-law gave me a gun."

"Oh, bully for you. Can you shoot the thing?"

"Yes. I can, by the way. I'm a good shot."

"I know you're not going to listen to reason on this. We'll work it out tomorrow when I pick you up."

###

Michael was waiting at her gate when she landed in D.C. and Amy was with him.

"Hey!" Carla squealed as she flew into Amy's arms. They stood hugging each other tight and swaying back and forth.

"I missed you *so much!*" Carla said into Amy's shoulder as she hugged her.

"This way, girls," Michael said as he led the way to where his car was parked on First street. Amy got in the front seat with Michael while Carla sat in back. As Michael pulled out into traffic, Amy turned around in her seat and said, "So?"

Carla smiled. "So?"

"So, Michael told me what's going on. I couldn't stand it after that cryptic call you gave me."

"Can you stand it better now?"

"No. But at least I know what all the hubbub is about."

"More hubbub than a person wants to know, or even care about."

"Listen, Michael and I have a plan. Right Mikey?" Amy put her hand on Michael's arm.

"Mikey?" Carla asked.

"You didn't hear that," Michael said, smiling into the rear view mirror where he could see Carla's face.

"What's yours and Mikey's plan?" Carla teased as she looked at Michael's eyes in the rear view mirror. He was grinning right at her.

Amy was more serious. "Cut it out, you two. Listen!" Amy was using her loud voice, the one that was the cheerleader in most group activities. "Carla, I'm not taking no for an answer, you're staying at my place where Michael can be right across the hall at night in case something happens."

Carla started to open her mouth and complain, but Amy silenced her. "No, No, No. End of story. No discussion. Absolutely not."

"Ames. Bullying me isn't going to work this time."

"Bullying you? When do I bully you?"

"How about on Thursday nights when you beg me to go out for a drink, just one little drink, you'll have me home early. Then you bully me to stay past midnight despite my efforts to leave, and then I am totally beat the next day at work."

"Oh, that's not bullying. That's looking out for your welfare. You would be a total hermit if it weren't for me!"

"True. That's probably true." Carla looked up at Michael's face in the mirror and raised her eyebrows as if to say, "Should I?"

"Michael, tell her she has to stay at my place."

"I can't tell her she has to do anything. She'll do what she wants, anyway."

He's starting to catch on, Carla thought. Very good.

"That's it. You're coming," Amy said. "Want us to swing by your place and get some things first?"

Carla heaved a big sigh and looked out the window.

"You're a stubborn little wench and you're going to get yourself hurt or killed," Amy scolded.

"I won't. I promise. I won't get myself killed. Just let me stay at my place a few days and if it doesn't work for me I'll go to your house."

Carla finally won the battle and Amy and Michael took her over to her place. They insisted on coming in so Michael could look around for signs of tampering.

"The place is a mess, probably. I don't even remember how I left it," Carla said. She was digging for her keys in her purse as they all three walked down the long narrow hallway of her building. Michael went in first, checking around the window for any signs of breaking and entering.

"Mind if I check the bathroom?"

"No. Go ahead," Carla said, but she remembered too late that she'd left her hand washed bras drip-drying the day she had left. One was her fancy red lace bra, the skimpy one. Michael smirked as he came out of the bathroom.

"Nothing in there but some fine-lookin' underwear," he said. Carla gave him a look of annoyance and slight embarrassment. Amy didn't hear what anyone was saying. She was squatting in front of Carla's giant CD collection arranged in piles along the floor, absorbed in looking at some new titles Carla had recently purchased.

"Can I borrow these?" She turned around and held up two CD cases belonging to alternative rock bands.

"Sure. Course you can," Carla said as she leapt over to her unmade bed and quickly pulled up the quilt just as Michael was getting ready to sit down on it. Amy was still reading the CD covers. Carla looked at Michael. He had his hand resting deliberately on her pillow, and on his face was a subtle but distinctly seductive look. He had a devilish tease of a smile on his face. Carla pretended she didn't see it.

"I'm ready," Amy said, putting the CDs in her purse. "Everything okay here, Michael? Will she be all right?"

"As far as I can tell, things haven't been tampered with," Michael said. "Staying at Amy's would be safer. But what can we do if she won't comply?" His eyes challenged Carla. "If you wouldn't mind, though, I'd like to escort you to and from work for a few days until we see if someone else is going to come after you." Carla frowned and crossed her arms.

"She doesn't like that either," Michael said to Amy, as if they were talking about their unruly child.

"Too bad! She's going to do it and that's final," Amy said, the disciplinarian. There was a silence while Amy and Michael waited to see what Carla would say. They were staring hard at her.

"All right! All right. You guys just break me, you know that?"

Michael got up from the bed and put a hand on her shoulder looking down at her in a mock fatherly stance. "I'll get you at eight-thirty."

"I'll be ready."

Amy and Michael headed toward the door. "Call us if you need anything," Amy said. "Call if you even hear one strange noise."

Carla nodded.

"Promise?"

"I promise," Carla said.

Amy led the way down the hall in her platform sandals, her curls bouncing. Michael, behind her, turned and cast a smile back over his shoulder.

Carla didn't smile back. Why did he make her feel like she was cheating on Amy?

4

Carla was jolted awake by a man's loud voice and pounding on her door. She sat up with a start.

"Carla! Wake up. Carla!"

"Hold on a second!" She groped for her robe. Through the peephole, Michael looked more annoyed than she felt.

"What happened to your alarm?"

"I can't figure out what happened. I went to bed early. But I had to take a sleeping pill at three in the morning because I kept hearing noises."

"Good idea. Dope yourself senseless and make it easier on some creep to get his hands on you."

"He'd have to break the window."

"Or, so you think."

"I'm starting to wonder if there's all that much to worry about."

"Do we have to re-evaluate this every five minutes?"

"But you already dealt with the man with a knife. He's not going to come after me now."

"True. But we still have the man in black to account for."

"Maybe there isn't a man in black stalker after all? Maybe I imagined it." Even in her own house, life wasn't pulling itself back to order.

The coffee she'd put in the machine stopped dripping and she reached over and took the pitcher to pour a cup for herself, then leaned across the table to pour some for Michael, his eyes taking full advantage of the gape in her robe.

"You just don't let up, do you?"

"I'm a red-blooded male, aren't I?

Carla closed her robe tighter as she sat down to scoop sugar into her coffee.

"Having a little coffee with that?" Michael asked.

Carla looked up at him. "Is your whole point in life to annoy me?"

"I hope not," Michael said sheepishly. They both sat sipping their coffee.

"I have to think of some excuse for my boss," Carla said, changing the subject.

"Why not the truth?"

"I overslept?"

"Yes," Michael said.

"Now you're beginning to sound like my mother."

"Mine, too. We both must have good ones," Michael said. Carla sat with a distant look on her face.

"How long has yours been gone?" Michael asked.

"How did you know that? I've never said she passed away."

"You didn't have to." There was an uncomfortable pause.

Carla pushed herself out from the table abruptly. "I'd better get ready now," she said, closing the sliding door between the kitchen and the bedroom.

"Take your time," Michael said.

The Cleveland Park Metro stop was much less crowded than it usually was during rush hour and Michael and Carla had no trouble finding a seat on the first train. It was ten o'clock and Carla had already called Janet, her boss, and told her that the power had gone out in her building last night and screwed up her alarm. She had to stretch the truth a tiny bit because Janet was the nervous type. That was an understatement, actually. But thankfully, Janet hadn't sounded mad. Instead she'd been all too excited to get Carla back in the office to crank out a stack of new brochures, reports and documents the agency needed written a month ago.

At the Farragut North stop, Carla got off and headed for the escalator. Michael trailed at her heels.

"Are you going to walk me all the way across the street? I figure I can take it from here, in broad daylight."

"Might look safe to you, but hey, if we had to bank on your definition of safety, we'd all be in trouble wouldn't we?"

"Fine. Walk me across." She added sarcasm of her own. "Shall we hold hands?"

Michael looked thrilled. "Let's" His hand felt strong and gentle at the same time. He smelled great. Aftershave? Cologne? Carla shook her head to clear herself of it.

"What were you thinking of?" Michael pressed.

"Nothing," Carla said. "Nothing at all."

They rode the elevator and got off together, Michael looking both ways in the hall. He seemed so fanatical and silly to her. She pulled the glass door opened to her office suite and smiled at the receptionist as she walked in. When she turned back, Michael nodded and pointed at his watch. He was reminding her he'd be back in that spot at five o'clock to pick her up. She nodded. He winked and was gone.

"Who was *that*?" Mary Anne the receptionist asked. She sat rapidly working a wad of gum with her small jaws.

"Oh nobody," Carla shrugged as she sifted through a huge stack of phone messages that had been left in her message tray during her absence.

"Doesn't look like *nobody* to me," Mary Ann continued.

"Believe me," Carla said, looking up briefly. "He is." She went back to looking at the messages, frowning at a couple of them.

"I'll be at my desk all day," Carla said, when she finished reading. She scooped up the package of magazines and other bulk mail bundled together with twine that sat waiting for her at the end of Mary Ann's desk.

"I almost forgot. Janet wants to see you in her office immediately." Mary Ann blew a small pink bubble out of her mouth and sucked it back in. "Wear protective clothing. She's crazed today."

She headed back to Janet's office and gently knocked on the door. This day was shifting to a steep uphill grind.

"Come in, Carla. Come in," Janet said, looking over the top of her reading glasses. She was wearing a dark, gray suit that fit tightly on her tall, slim form. Her desk was almost swallowed by stacks of papers and folders. It seems they had gotten higher, if that were possible, while Carla had been gone for two weeks. Janet's speckled pepper-and-gray buzz haircut looked freshly shaven. This is what Carla and Mary Ann jokingly referred to as Janet's "Annie Lenox look." A good look for a rock singer, perhaps. But on Janet, it meant trouble. The Annie Lenox phases were the worst to endure. During those times, Carla sometimes doubted her normally staunch dedication to the job.

"Carla, I'll be frank with you," Janet said. "I hope this recent interlude of absence has been caused by, well, let's say matters of utmost importance to you." Her bony fingers tightly gripped a stack of paper. Carla noticed a new ring that looked like a real ruby on Janet's forefinger. It was hard to tell from where she was standing. Wasn't that an artsy and unconventional touch for Janet to wear it on her forefinger? I'm impressed, Carla thought.

"—because frankly, this organization can't tolerate half-commitments from its associates. Do you understand?" Carla had missed half of what Janet had said, but she caught the brazenly annoyed tone in her voice.

"Yes. I'm reading you loud and clear," Carla said, as she shifted the package of mail to her other hip and leaned on the door jam to the small office. "I can more than assure you —"

"Forget explaining," Janet cut in. "I understand it is significant, and that's why I have been agreeable. But now,

I am really in need of your extra dedication. You will probably need to pull ten-hour days the rest of the week for us to meet some of these deadlines."

Carla tried hard to stifle the moan that almost escaped her lips. "Yes. I was planning on that," Carla lied.

"That's the correct answer," Janet said as she readjusted her glasses and continued reading whatever it was she was holding in her hand. Carla turned on her heels out into the hall and headed back to her office.

"Hey, lady!" It was Harold. "Where you been?" Harold was such a sweetheart. His wrinkled face always radiated kindness.

"What are you doing with that cane?" Carla asked, as she gave him a hug.

"Oh, my arthritis is acting up again. It's nothing'" Harold said. "You going to be working on my teen summer camp brochures, first, this morning, Carlotta?" he asked.

"I don't know if I can," Carla said as she whisked into her office and sat down at her desk. "I wish I could, for you, Harold. Honest," she said. "I'm swamped, though. I guess I'll have to start with whatever Janet has scheduled for me." Harold stood in her doorway as Carla began to leaf through the pile of projects that had appeared on her desk in her absence, each with a purple sticky note filled from top to bottom with tiny hand-written instructions from Janet. "This will need extra attention," one started out. "This is needed as soon as possible," another said. But the one under that said, "Make this your top priority!" And still another said, "See me about this one. It needs special attention."

Carla wanted to scream. The hardest part about this job was fighting off the insanity that sooner or later sucked you in like a vacuum.

Just then her intercom buzzed. "It's Janet," Carla mouthed silently to Harold. Harold nodded and resumed his slow progress down the hall. She picked up the phone. "Yes?"

"Carla, find that dossier from Philadelphia on Crime Prevention on American Campuses and bring it in here to me," Janet said.

"Right on top of that," Carla said. She knew she wouldn't be able to get a lick of writing done until Janet left for the evening. She clenched her teeth as she dug on her desk for the folder Janet had requested. But Carla knew looking on her own desk was futile. It was most likely on the bottom of the most recent stack of papers surrounding Janet's desk. She'd have to look for it with Janet prattling about messing things up and getting her unorganized. How is that possible? She also wanted to set it straight with Janet that she was a *writer*, not a secretary or a butler. But that would certainly hit deaf ears. Carla felt a wave of familiar apathy about this job hit her dead on. She was sorry she ever missed this job at all the past few weeks. Her hopeful anticipation of losing herself in her work today — so she could forget her other troubles — started their long plummet.

###

It was five o'clock and Carla was nowhere near finished with half of what she needed to get done for the day. She paged Michael and her phone rang back immediately.

"Yes, missy?" His cheerful voice said. "I'm almost there to pick you up."

"Don't call me that," Carla said. She was in a mean mood.

"Bad day?"

"Don't even ask."

"You're calling to tell me you need more time," Michael said.

"You're a mind reader."

"No. Just good at math. Take one part Carla, plus two parts seven-days'- worth of work piled up, and what do you get?"

"Very funny."

"How long do you need?"

"Michael, I really don't know. I feel overwhelmed. I'm going to be here for a while. I can't even tell you how long."

"All right," he said matter-of-factly. "Why don't you page me about twenty minutes before you're ready to leave? And I'll zip over and get you."

"It might be really late," Carla said. "Why don't you just let me handle getting home by myself tonight."

"Are you crazy?"

"No, I'm not. I just can't breathe with all this supervision. It's making me nuts."

"I promise not to supervise you when I come to pick you up. How's that?"

"You know what I mean."

"More than you know," Michael said. There was a small pause. Carla thought to herself, sometimes he said the most likable things.

"Listen," he added. "I'm not kidding. Please call me to pick you up."

"All right, Michael. I will. I have to go. I have to get back to work. I'll page you when I'm ready."

"I'll be waiting," he said.

###

Carla didn't even notice what time it was until Thomas Gray, the executive director, stuck his head in her door. "You still at it?" he asked. "It's nine o'clock."

Carla was broken out of her working trance. "Hi," she said with a smile, looking up from her desk. "Yes. I'm trying to get a handle of some of my new projects."

Thomas smiled. "I'm the last one to go, so I'll set the alarm system for you on my way out."

At 9:45 Carla typed the period on the last sentence of the project and picked up the phone to page Michael.

Ten minutes later, no answer. She wrapped up a few more things on her desk, then paged again. "Damn, him," she thought after she waited another five minutes. She was exhausted and starving. Her feet were screaming from the pumps she'd had crammed on them all day. Even though she'd kicked the darn things off several hours ago, her feet still ached to the bone and a nickel-sized blister was bulging and sore on her right pinky toe.

She got down on hands and knees and found her shoes under her desk, then got up and sat back in her desk chair with a sigh. She stuffed her feet into the shoes, one by one, and winced as the blistered toe felt the squeeze of the leather.

"I don't have the energy to wait here for him," Carla said out loud. Exasperated, she leaned back in her chair. She'd been so busy working she hadn't noticed a thing around her until now. Suddenly the office seemed too quiet. Eerie and creepy. Aside from the light on her desk, the only light in the entire suite was the glow of the emergency door exits dimly lighting up the dark hallway outside her door. A police car went by outside, sending spiraling red lights swirling on the wall across the hall.

Carla picked up the phone and paged Michael again. "Where is he?"

She really didn't want to wait for him, but it was later now and she was actually starting to want him to escort her home, to be honest. She stayed by her phone, hoping he'd call, while she straightened some papers on her desk. Then she walked around the corner and put the completed brochure on the chair in Janet's office next door. She knew Janet would love it. She was smiling with satisfaction as she walked back to her own office. She stared at her phone, willing Michael to call.

Just then she heard a small click out in the hall coming from the front door reception area. Must be Michael. Maybe he didn't call. Maybe he just came on over instead. She slung her purse over her shoulder and turned to head out of her office.

Click. She heard it again.

"Michael?" Her voice echoed in the darkness.

"Michael? Is that you?"

Something in her gut told her it wasn't Michael. A chill started at the back of her neck and went down her whole spine.

She reached up and silently turned off her office light, then put her purse down and peeked her head slowly out of her office. She looked in both directions down the hall and didn't see anything.

Her heart was racing wildly. She was not about to go out into the entryway and see what was making the clicking sound. She looked across from her door at the alarm signal panel on the opposite wall. It was on green for "unlocked," not the red for "locked" she'd seen earlier when Thomas had left. *Someone had disarmed it!*

It was totally silent in the office, except for her heart pounding louder now, threatening to betray where she was. Surely, a co-worker would turn on lights, make more noise.

It wasn't someone from the office. She knew that.

Carla prayed silently. She was frantic trying to think of what to do. She stood frozen in place.

Soft footsteps on the hall carpeting became audible as someone came slowly through the entryway and closer to her office. Fear sent a wave of nausea through her. *I'm going to die.* Her palms were sweating.

She couldn't think straight. *What should she do?* She pressed her body flat against the wall next to her doorway inside her office and listened as best she could. She heard the footsteps. Yes. They were footsteps. They were walking slowly, she determined. Very slowly. One step in front of the other. She held her breath.

She strained to tell which way they were going. They were going down the hall away from her office. Then they stopped. She was paralyzed. She couldn't move.

The footsteps were walking again. This time they were coming closer.

Carla reached quickly across the space in front of her to her desk and put her hands on the heavy bronze paperweight of Lincoln's bust. She squeezed both hands onto it tight and held it above her head as she stood by the doorway. Blood was roaring in her ears. She heard the steps again, and this time, they were just outside her door. Through the crack she could see it was a man in a black suit. *The one with sunglasses who had followed her!* When he stepped into her office, Carla slammed the Lincoln down on his head as hard as she possibly could. She heard her own voice discharge an "oof" sound. She heard the corner of the heavy paperweight hit the skull of the man. She felt a warm spew of blood and heard a moan and a loud thud as the man's body went down. He hit his head hard on the edge of her desk.

The rest was a blur because Carla was scrambling hard down the hall. Running and pushing her legs to go. They wanted to collapse on her. She made them go. She was grabbing the sides of the walls as she stumbled and pushed herself forward. She pressed the bar of the emergency stairway into the stairwell and slipped into it, all within a matter of seconds.

She reached down and yanked off her shoes, then stood shaking for a brief second trying to decide which way to run. She started running up the steps, taking them two at a time. Up two flights, then three until she was on the top floor. She squatted at the top in the stairwell and hugged her knees to her chest, trying to control the involuntary shaking that was overtaking her body.

After a brief while she heard the emergency door open three floors down and she heard the man swear and start heavily down the stairs. *"Bitch!"* the man said. *"Bitch! If you're in here, I'm going to kill you!"* he roared and it echoed in the stairwell.

The man started to lumber down the steps and pause. Carla heard him going down again. She waited until she could barely hear him. She knew there was an exit door into the alley at the bottom of all eight flights.

Carla leaned over the railing and couldn't see anything but the emergency door lights in the stairwell. She tiptoed fast down the steps, silently, hugging to the wall until she came to her office door. She fumbled the code to open the door as fast as possible and entered silently when the door clicked free.

She ran straight through the office and out the front door to the elevator. She hesitated a second. *Wait! Maybe he will expect me to come down the elevator when he finds out I'm not at the emergency exit,"* she thought. She wished she could think of something to do. Damn, damn. What to do?

She looked all around the lobby. She knew she was running out of time. The elevator that stood opened in front of her suddenly closed and proceeded down. She watched it go down the floors in the lighted panel above the elevator door, "seven, six, five...." She was panicked.

Then she saw Hudson and Marshall's door across the hall. She could hide in there. Amy had told her the emergency code plenty of times so she could meet her when she worked late. What was it? What was it? She scrambled to the front of Hudson and Marshall's. She punched in several choices of numbers. Wrong. She tried again. Wrong. She heard the elevator returning back up, rattling in the shaft.

Oh my God! She couldn't get Hudson and Marshall's door opened. They must have changed the code.

She rushed back over and pushed rapidly several times on the elevator call button. Lucky. An elevator opened immediately.

It opened and it was empty.

She jumped on and pushed the "close door" button over and over. The doors weren't closing fast enough.

"Ding" She heard the bell to the other elevator door just as her doors closed.

Her elevator was racing down. The doors opened. She was running like a mad woman. She saw the night security guard out of the corner of her eye slumped at his post, unconscious. She raced to the front door of the building, slipping on the waxed floor in her slippery pantyhose feet. She yanked it opened to exit onto K Street. She looked both directions. Two men with trench coats and brief cases were walking together about two blocks up, too far away to get their attention. No one else. The street was deserted. There were no bars or restaurants opened on this whole block to attract night business. It was dark.

She ran to the corner and rounded it. Just then an orange cab came barreling down 17th Street in her direction. *Oh God, please don't let him have a passenger. Please!* She waved her arms wildly in the air.

The cab driver stepped on it and came fast toward her and jolted to a stop next to her. She grabbed the door just as she looked back and saw a dark figure stagger around the corner of the building like a Frankenstein. She jumped in and slammed the door.

"Drive!" she told the cabbie as she ducked down. "Drive fast! Turn on the next block and go fast. Someone's chasing me!" The driver believed her and hit the gas. He took the corner on two wheels, just as a bullet rung near the back end of the cab and she and the driver heard the shot reverberate in the deserted street.

"Shit!" the driver said. "I *knew* I should give up night routes."

Carla was in the back seat curled up on her side. "Take me to the police," she managed to make her voice say.

"'Nuff said." The driver was a large black man with huge shoulders. "No messing with this shit."

When she got to the police station, she realized she didn't have her purse and she couldn't pay the driver. "Don't worry about it. You take care now," he said as she was getting out.

"Wait," Carla said. "Can you come in and be a witness for me?" She leaned on the opened door, sticking her head into the cab.

"Listen. I didn't get paid and I almost took a bullet. Got you here safe. That's all I want to do for tonight."

"I understand," Carla said. She managed a small smile.

The cab driver gave her a nod. Carla slammed the door, and he sped off into the night.

When Carla walked through the doors to the police station, she realized she had bloodstains trailing down her arm onto her skirt. Her skirt was torn and she was carrying one shoe. She stood blinking in the bright lights, shivering.

5

Amy and Michael were worse than over protective parents. They appeared almost immediately at the police station after Carla got there. They were frantic. By ten o'clock when Carla hadn't paged, Michael had gone to her office, probably minutes after the incident occurred. He had found the office opened, the man's blood all over Carla's desk, and no sign of Carla. He had found the injured front door guard, barely breathing, suffering from a blow to the head and had called the police. That's when, to his relief, he had found out that Carla was there.

He and Amy had been waiting for Carla at a bar on 15th Street. All Michael could figure was the building probably had a dead zone for pagers because it was on a basement level. He was furious with himself for not being more careful about the pager. Carla had never seen him so unsettled and angry.

But she didn't have time to worry about Michael. She was so grateful he was there, and Amy too. Amy wouldn't think of being left behind, Michael told her. Carla couldn't imagine how she would have made it through the unbearable process of being questioned by the police, trying to remember a description of the man, filling out paperwork, without her friends. It was awful and exhausting.

By the time Michael and Amy brought Carla home to Amy's apartment, it was one a.m. and all three of them didn't even question whether Carla should be at Amy's or not. Carla was so stunned she didn't have the energy to argue about anything. Carla felt like she was in a trance as Amy helped her take her bloody and torn clothes off and got her into a warm bath. After Carla bathed, Amy helped her into a soft nightie and tucked her into her own bed. The soft light coming from the small pink lamp on Amy's bedside table made the room glow like a little girl's bedroom, Carla thought. She felt like a little girl. Totally helpless and dependent. Her mind was numb and blank. She rested her head back on the fluffy pillows of Amy's bed.

"Here," Amy said. "Take this." She helped Carla sit up and handed her a little white pill and a glass of cool water. Her golden bracelets sparkled in the lamplight as she handed Carla the glass.

"What is it?" Carla sat blinking down at the pill, then up at Amy.

"A tranquilizer," Amy said. "You're in luck. I have one left."

"I don't want to take a tranquilizer," Carla said. She wasn't going to take some strange prescription of Amy's. This was a ridiculous idea. She handed the pill back to Amy.

"Trust me. It'll help you sleep," Amy said, pushing Carla's hand away.

"But what if I'm asleep and something bad happens and I can't wake up." She knew her thoughts were being processed and coming out as if a child had said them.

"Nothing will happen," Amy said. "Michael and I will be right here. We will wait until you are asleep. Michael says he'll stay in my living room tonight on the pullout sofa so you won't be afraid. And I'll sleep on my guest cot right here by you. Okay?" Amy patted a little cot all set up for sleeping, with pillow and blanket. When had Amy done all this? Carla wondered.

"Will Michael have a gun?"

"Michael always has a gun."

"Will he listen for noises?"

"Of course," Amy said. "Now take the pill before I grab it and take it myself."

Carla stared at Amy and realized that she might be serious about that. And suddenly the idea of being drugged to sleep seemed a good one. She swallowed the pill with a long drink of water and collapsed onto the pillows. Amy tucked the covers around her tighter and reached to turn off the light. The room was lit dimly from the glow of a nightlight in the adjoining bathroom.

Carla grabbed Amy's arm. "Ames?"

"Yeah."

"Thank you," Carla said. "Thank you for everything. How can I even tell you how much you've helped me?"

"Sweetie. Don't worry. I'm here for you." Amy leaned down and hugged Carla, rubbing her back and rocking her back and forth a little. "Don't worry," she said stroking her hair gently. Carla couldn't take the physical contact. It was bringing all her emotions to the forefront. She had held back the tears all night and now they were coming. She shook in Amy's arms as the sobs released.

"It's okay, honey," Amy crooned. "Let it all out."

"I'm sorry," Carla said. "I'm so sorry to drag you into this."

"Hey. What are friends for? Hmm?" Amy pulled away and gently laid Carla back on the pillows. She wiped her hair from around her face and handed her a tissue from the box on the bed stand. Carla wiped her eyes and honked as she blew her nose into the Kleenex.

"I just don't get it!" Carla said.

"I know," Amy said. "It's so strange."

"It makes me feel so nervous now. Someone really and truly is trying to kill me. This can't be a fluke. I have to admit that to myself now. If you could have seen this guy, felt the evil…"

"Don't think about it right now," Amy said, patting Carla. That Xanax is going to kick in like a charm in a minute and you are going to sleep like a baby. Just let Michael worry about how to get through this safely. It's his job. And, hey, now you have the police finally believing you. I'm sure they'll be able to get you back to a normal life soon."

"I hope so," Carla said. "I feel like a prisoner," she sniffled. "My life is being robbed from me."

"Not for long," Amy said. "We won't let it be for long." Carla loved how Amy could be so firm in what she said. Everything she said sounded so convicted. To hear Amy declare something was as if it were already come to pass.

"Now, sleep," Amy said.

"All right," Carla said. She was beginning to feel incredibly drowsy. Her body was very heavy. She felt it sinking into Amy's soft bed.

"Everything okay in here?" Carla heard Michael's voice coming through a tunnel. She opened her eyes and saw him standing in the doorway.

"She's good," Amy reported. "I zonked her senseless with my very last tranquilizer."

"Good idea," Michael said. "I think," he said quizzically. "I hope you didn't zonk her too hard."

"Oh, no. She'll feel great in the morning. You don't get hangovers from these," Amy said authoritatively

"Good to know," Michael said. Carla felt like she was in the hospital and the doctor and nurse were talking over her chart.

"Night, kid," Michael said. And now she heard his voice closer. It was by her ear. She turned her lazy head toward the sound of his voice and opened her heavy eyelids a crack. There he was. Right there. Hi, Michael, Carla thought. She felt a heavy hand pat her shoulder.

"Night," she heard her voice whisper. "Michael. Thank you," she managed to say as her eyelids went down involuntarily and a gentle wave of warmth and comfort snuggled her as she drifted off.

"Don't worry about a thing," Michael said.

###

The next morning Carla awoke to the sound of knocks on the door, the smell of fresh coffee, the TV, and the phone ringing. Ringing and ringing. She rubbed her eyes and the disappointment ripped through her as the memory of what happened the night before blindsided her. Amy wasn't in the cot, which was now folded up and in the corner. There was a ton of sunlight barreling into the place.

"I hope you're rested," Amy said, popping her head in the door. "You're going to need all your energy to beat the press off with a stick."

"They got the story?"

"Check this out." Amy slapped the *Washington Post* onto Carla's lap. "Crime Prevention Organization Staffer Allegedly Attacked by Gunman While At Work: Crime Prevention Fell Through The Cracks This Time, Police Say."

"Damn," Carla said. "Of course those journalist grub hounds would see the irony in this story."

"Grub hounds from the *Times* and the *Post* have been calling you since seven this morning."

Carla groaned. Has Janet called? Thomas Gray?

"They've all called," Amy said, rolling her eyes.

Carla smiled. "Only *you* could keep these people at bay." Having Amy for a friend was like having her own personal bouncer. More than once Carla had been grateful that Amy flanked her side when persistent drunk guys wouldn't take a hint to go away on a Saturday night at the bar.

"Well. Even my powers have limits," Amy said. "I'm glad you're awake now because I'm running out of defense tactics."

Amy handed Carla a portable phone. "Here. You should probably start with Janet. She sounded like she was about to have a coronary."

"She sounds like that on a *good* day," Carla said. "I can only imagine how this situation must have her bowels in an uproar."

Amy laughed.

"I wonder if I still have a job?"

"I'm sure you do. You have to. I mean, how can they fire you for being attacked?" Amy said.

"Doesn't seem fair. But what about this is fair?" Carla began dialing her work number.

"Janet Wolfman, please," Carla said.

"Carla! Is that you?" It was Mary Ann. "*Holy shit*! Are you all right?"

"I'm okay, I guess."

"This place is crawling with cops, and they are going to interview all of us one by one. They can't figure out how someone knew to get through our alarm system."

"I'd like to know that myself," Carla said.

"My God, Carla. I can't imagine what you've been through," Mary Ann continued. "I can't imagine how you got away from that guy. Everybody here is talking about how brave you were."

"I wasn't brave," Carla said. "I was scared to death."

"There is blood all over your desk, all over the rug. You should *see* the place."

"I don't really want to right now."

"I know. I know," Mary Ann said apologetically. "Here. Let me put you through to Janet. She thinks you're in the hospital being treated for shock."

"Must be what Amy told her." Carla had to smile at that one.

"Please talk to her before she drives us all out of our minds."

"Okay. Put me through."

Carla was surprised how little Janet wanted to talk about the actual incident. In her usual business-like manner, Janet wanted to focus on the plan from here on out. Carla would take another week off, using the last of her vacation. After that she could work from home until the police said it was safe for her to return to the office. Janet would send a UPS shipment of several boxes to Carla, filled with projects she should work on.

Yes. The report she completed the night before and had left on Janet's chair was excellent. No. The Federation had not released the story to the *Post*. She didn't know *how* they got it. No. Thomas Gray didn't want Carla to be quoted in any publication. Was this clear? Zero quotes, in zero publications. Carla was to refer all press questions to Thomas. He would be the only spokesman. She then told Carla to get some rest, and she was only too happy to get off the phone.

###

"All right, then," Carla said as she walked into the next room to find Michael and Amy sitting at the table eating a cherry breakfast strudel.

"You still got a job?" Amy asked as she licked icing off her fingers.

"I can't believe it. The old crow is letting me work from home," Carla said. "I've only been begging to do that for years. I guess the blood got her attention."

"Blood is so annoying," Michael said.

Carla poured herself some juice from the fridge and sat down next to Michael at the table.

"Hungry?" he asked, pushing the strudel her way.

"No," Carla said, as she sipped the juice. "And by the way, Amy, that pill you gave me, whatever it was, gave me the weirdest dreams."

"Better for you to have dreams, my dear, than to lie awake all night listening for hatchet men."

"Yeah. You're right," Carla conceded. "Michael, did you really stay here to protect us, or did Amy just feed me a line to shut me up?"

"No line. I stayed right here. Probably will again tonight."

"I'm glad," Carla said. She leaned over and put her head on Michael's shoulder. "What a living hell."

"You said it," Amy said.

"Michael, if only your pager had worked last night. Maybe this wouldn't have happened...." Carla said, her voice trailing off with her thoughts.

"I have been torturing myself with that all night, and this morning," Michael said. "That is inexcusable on my part."

"Well, you can't control everything, Michael," Amy said. "Some things just happen. Bad luck just happens. Hey, I know!" Amy suddenly had a bright idea. "Let's do something to get our minds off of all this."

"Like what?" Carla said. "We can't go anywhere."

"We could rent a dirty movie?" Amy said with a devilish grin.

"No thanks," Carla said. She wasn't sure if Amy was kidding or not. She didn't put it past her.

"I'm not in the mood, and I'd hate to waste it," Carla said with a smile. Amy and Carla both knew that Carla had never watched a porn movie in her life. Amy had teased her to no end when she couldn't get her to go to the local male strip club for one of their friend's bachelorette parties.

"Some good hot porn is a terrible thing to waste," Michael said, giving Amy a wink across the table. "But who needs it with you two women around anyway?"

'Oh, Michael!" Amy laughed with exaggeration. "Such a Casanova. Isn't he, Carla?"

"A regular Don Juan," Carla said dryly. She was thinking how this tiny apartment was going to close down on her within a matter of hours and she wondered how she'd keep herself from going insane.

Lieutenant Dirkson was well-meaning, dedicated and evidently wanted to be good at his job, Carla decided as she sat in Amy's living room discussing the case with him and answering more questions. Amy and Michael had gone to Carla's to get her clothes and things, and to pick up some groceries. Dirkson stopped by because he wanted to talk to Carla privately. The case was getting national media play since the *Post* had picked up the story, and the D.C. police wanted to keep things low key and let the media die down a bit, he explained.

"We're always getting a bad wrap," Dirkson said.

"I understand."

"I thought I'd save you the hassle of coming into the station and come on over and see you," Dirkson added. "Several reporters have been hovering around the precinct in hopes of catching a glimpse of you. Had a few photographers with them, too."

He shook his head. "Don't these reporters get that when they interfere like this they just expose the victim to more danger?"

"I doubt they are worried about that part," Carla said. "Obviously. Think of all the high school shootings these days. Aren't more of them actually encouraged by all the media coverage?"

"It's hard to say," Dirkson said. "But maybe you've got a point there."

Dirkson said what Michael had been saying all along about motive. It most likely had something to do with Carla's father. There just wasn't anything else in her life that seemed to lend itself to exposure to something like this.

"Clearly we've established at this point that there is a pattern of danger for you," Dirkson said. *No, duh,* Carla thought. *I was in talking to you guys a month ago, but nobody believed me.*

"Two dots on a graph now," Dirkson said. "We're sending a detective in Chicago to talk things over with your father."

"No," Carla pleaded. "No, please give me a chance to talk to him first, will you?" She had to talk to him first. Police sticking their noses in would just make him clam up. She wanted a shot at seeing what he would tell her. She wanted to actually try and visit him in person. He was so elusive on the phone, she'd probably only get somewhere if she saw him face to face.

"All right," Dirkson said, he would hold off on calling detectives in Chicago, but not for long.

6

Carla sat face-to-face with her nephew Sammy as she tried to spoon baby oatmeal mixed with applesauce into his mouth. His pudgy little eight-month-old hands kept pushing her spoon away and reaching for the cheerios that were scattered across the high chair table, gently picking them up with forefinger and thumb and stuffing them into his mouth. Carla's sister Karen was making coffee wearing her old, fuzzy pink slippers and a robe.

"Maybe I can help you while I'm here?"

"Hey, don't think you have to earn your keep," Karen said as she poured two cups of coffee. "I'm just glad to get you for a whole week up here with us boring married people. Too bad it took a stalker to get you away from all those swinging singles' bars and whatever else keeps you so busy down there in Washington."

"You think I don't want to visit you? That's not true."

"Just giving you some hassle," Karen said as she shuffled over to the table with the two cups of coffee and put one down in front of Carla. She sat with her head in her hands, elbows on the table. "You got sick again this morning?" Carla asked.

Karen turned and leaned with her back against the counter while she pushed her tussled hair back out of her eyes. "Yeah. This is the part I really hate."

"Rough," Carla said. She could only imagine how hard it would be to deal with a baby and walk around all day feeling about ready to vomit.

"Not pretty," Karen mumbled. "Not fun, or pretty."

"I can't believe you're going to have two of these little nougats," Carla said as she reached over and gently squeezed Sammy's face, now gooey with oatmeal and smashed cheerios. He giggled. "You're really lucky."

"I guess I am. The grass is always greener, or so they say."

"Be honest with yourself. You know you're lucky," she said to her sister. "You wanted to have babies ever since we were little. Remember? I'd be climbing trees, and you'd be wheeling your dolls all around the neighborhood in that little blue buggy."

"Will you remind me of all this when this next one is out of the cooker?" Karen said. Sammy raised his arms and gave a little cry to let Carla know he wanted out of his high chair. "Give him a cut up banana," Karen said. "That'll keep him in there a few minutes longer so we can talk."

While Carla was peeling and slicing a banana onto Sammy's high chair table, Karen raised her head and stirred some cream and sugar into her coffee. "I hope you don't mind. I forgot to tell you this is decaf. Just imagine there's caffeine. Or, you can brew up some of the real stuff for yourself."

"No, I'm good," Carla said as she sat down and reached for the cream. Sammy was rapidly stuffing banana into his mouth and chewing with a big mouthful.

"This kid kills me," Carla said as she reached over and squeezed his plump little calf. "I love this kid so much." She beamed at Sammy who was hamming it up now with the bananas, beginning to smash some pieces and fingerpaint with them on the surface of his highchair.

"So much for the extra time with him in his chair."

"So much for it."

"I'll clean him up and get him out of his pajamas," Carla said as she stood up and pulled the highchair tray table out and lifted the little guy into her arms. He squealed with delight. "Is there an easier baby than this in all the world?" She gave him a little bounce on her hip, which sent Sammy into yet more giggles.

"He's a jolly guy," Karen said. "Got his dad's personality, thank goodness."

"That's not so bad, is it Sammy? Daddy's personality, Mama's good looks." Carla crooned at Sammy as she headed out of the kitchen and up the steps to his bedroom. "See you in a minute, Mommy," Carla said over her shoulder.

Karen put her head back down on the table and groaned.

###

Carla had been at Karen and Brad's for five days. In two more days she was expected to show up at work. She'd spent a little time talking to the Mahoneys about the incident. Both of them were concerned, but didn't seem to capture the gravity of the situation. They seemed to think Michael would get this all under control and Carla could go back to her life, no problems.

Michael had called while she was here, saying he'd let her know what the next step to the plan would be, later in the week. She was hoping it would be soon, before she went insane simply wondering how she was going to live, work, pay the rent and everything else.

She still couldn't bring herself to call her father. That was just asking too much. She wanted to talk to Karen about it, but the moments they had alone without the baby fussing, or Karen feeling sick, were few and far between all week. Carla was kept busy doing some laundry, a little grocery shopping and cleaning for her poor sister. She didn't know how Karen did it. It was hard work for her, and she wasn't even nauseated. Still little Sammy was the sweetest little bundle of joy. Carla couldn't keep her hands off of him.

Karen was happy enough to take a break in the evenings and let Carla bathe him, read to him and play with him on his bedroom floor with Legos and trucks before bedtime. His little hands would push a truck across the rug making a sputtering engine noise with his lips. Wow, Carla thought. Even when baby boys can't say but ten words, they can duplicate an engine noise perfectly. Playing with Sammy made her sit back and enjoy life, for one small moment. When she was with him, life was as tender and sweet as his soft skin. In his bright blue eyes she could see how life was supposed to feel; fresh and innocent.

Spending all this time with little Sam sure made her think about having her own babies someday. That seemed like a lifetime away for her. She couldn't picture ever getting what Karen and Brad had, a cozy little home and a family. Karen enviously thought Carla was enjoying her freedom as a single woman in the city, but she didn't know how lonely it could be. Most of the time, the loneliness was always there, like a large gray wolf with opened jaws that she tried to keep at bay. It could bite at any time, with a deep pang of pain, and if it wasn't biting, it was menacing to bite, leaving a cold chill always at the back of her mind. She didn't belong to anyone. Before this whole stalking incident began, most of the time, no one even knew where she was. She could disappear for days. Who would know? Ultimately, all she had was herself.

"Hey," Karen poked her head into Sammy's bedroom, startling Carla out of her thoughts. "You have a phone call."

"Who is it?"

"Don't know. Some guy. Must be that private investigator working for you."

"He's the only one that has the number here."

"Must be," Karen said as she came into Sammy's room and scooped him up to put him in bed.

Carla ran down the steps to the kitchen and took the call. She could hear Brad's TV down on the next level in the family room. He was too far away to hear her talking. "Hello?" she said, hoping Michael had some good news for her.

"I found you." It wasn't Michael's voice on the other end. It was Todd's.

"Where else could I be?" Carla could feel her anger come to life as she heard his voice.

"God knows where, Carla. You didn't leave me a number to reach you. You didn't leave me a note, or even a page, like you promised. I just had to figure out that you'd gone, and hopefully not at gunpoint with someone." He was silent for a moment. "I was worried," he said softly.

"I didn't think you would worry," Carla said. "You didn't seem all that concerned about it."

"So that's what this is about? Me going down to L.A.?"

"No, Todd. This isn't about that. It's about a million other things, but I don't want to talk about all of it now."

"Give me a chance to make you feel better, will you?"

"No." Her voice was solid. She sat down in the chair at the kitchen table and started doodling with a pen on the memo pad that was there.

"Carla, we always go through this. You don't know how to say goodbye very well. You always get upset."

"Bull," Carla said. "*You* don't know how to say goodbye very well, is more the point here." She started drawing dark circles one after another on the paper.

"Please. I don't want to argue about it now." His voice sounded tired.

"I don't want to argue about it at all," Carla said in a voice that meant she wanted to dismiss him altogether. She started filling in the circles on her pad, making them dark and solid, scratching deep into the paper.

"Hey. I'm just glad you're all right. I wanted to know you were safe," Todd said. Carla was silent on the other end, doodling more circles. The whole page was now filled with dark circles.

"Well, now you know. I'm safe for now," she said, not wanting to talk, but feeling so many things she *could* say, that it was virtually clogging her mind, like a logjam in a river.

"I'm sorry, Carla. I'm sorry you're upset with me and that I upset you when I went to L.A."

"Don't kiss up to me like that!" Carla said. "Just drop the whole thing. I don't care that you went to L.A. You've got business to attend to. Of course you have work to do. I understand."

"Call me when you come back down to D.C.," Todd said. "If you need my help, I'm there."

"That's fine." She intentionally softened up her voice a little, but her anger was still smoldering. "I'll keep that in mind." There was silence for a moment and Carla figured Todd was assessing that the call was futile. She dismissed him as if he were merely an annoying telemarketer.

Carla was sitting at the table drawing more circles when Karen came down the steps and into the kitchen. "Was it Michael?"

"No," Carla said, still looking at her paper.

"Who then?"

"I don't think you want to know."

"Oh?" Karen raised her brows. She wasn't one to push for information. But she knew about Todd, and Carla's quest to get over him. Carla couldn't bear to tell her sister about what happened in San Francisco. She wasn't in the mood to talk about it anyway. Karen thought she'd been in San Francisco on her own, getting out of town and away from danger. She doubted Karen would approve of the move to go out to Todd. Carla could see it now. She could have gone somewhere on her own. She could have. She didn't have to run to him like that. She'd been blinded by fear and deep down the excuse that would allow her to break her own vows and go be with him.

"Come on. Let's go out on the deck. It's gorgeous out tonight," Karen said.

Carla agreed as she followed Karen out to the deck and they each took a lounge chair and lay back, looking up at the stars.

"I love nights like this," Carla said. "June is the most beautiful time of the year. It smells so good outside."

"I know," Karen said, as she gazed up at the blurry visual impact of billions of stars.

"You guys have so many stars up here!"

"We do. It's great."

"It's so quiet up here," Carla said dreamily. "Makes me want to get out of the city sometimes."

Karen just lay there gazing.

"Looking for a shooting star?" Carla asked.

"Yeah" Karen said quietly. Carla and Karen started looking for shooting stars the summer after their mother died. It was a little thing they did to make themselves believe she was up there and sending them a message down below. Silly, they both knew. But it was one small way that they dealt with their huge loss.

"I miss Mom." Carla verbalized what she and Karen very rarely said out loud, or even liked to admit.

"Me, too."

"Sometimes I feel like if she were here, my life would be so different. A whole lot better."

"I know what you mean."

"But, she's not."

"She's not," Karen repeated, obviously lost in her thoughts. The two sisters shared the same stone sorrow about their mother's long bout with cancer and her death while they were both young. Karen was only thirteen and Carla had been seventeen, when she passed away. They had developed a tough outer shell from the loss that made all other losses seem miniscule comparatively.

"Michael wants me to call Dad."

Karen sat bolt upright in her lounge chair and turned to Carla. "You're kidding?"

"He thinks this whole thing might have something to do with one of his clients or a case he's working on."

"But you are so far removed from Dad. How could that be?"

"That's what I said, but Michael seems to think otherwise."

"Figures," Karen said in a cynical dry tone.

"That's what I said, too."

Just then Brad came sauntering out onto the deck, a cigar in one hand and a beer in the other. His sleeveless muscle shirt showed rippling muscles and a small tattoo at the top of his right bicep. His boyish looking face and mop of blond hair made him look much younger than thirty years old. "You ladies mind if I join you?"

"Honey!" Karen said. "Put that darn thing out! I hate when you do that! Did you light it in the house? Now it's going stink up the place."

"Can't a man have a beer and a good cigar once in a while?" He smiled over at Carla, as if she would back him for his treachery.

"Don't look at me. I'm out of this. I think those things stink, anyway," Carla said. Karen huffed in disgust.

"Never marry an ex-marine. Especially one that comes to pick you up on your first date riding a motorcycle." Brad stood there smiling with his cigar dangling out between his teeth.

"Hey baby, you loved it," Brad said.

Karen and Brad were crazy about each other, and Carla knew it. That look in their eyes for each other she saw sometimes, like now, was priceless. Karen said marriage was boring, but Carla thought it always looked exciting and wonderful between the two of them. They'd spend entire weekends wallpapering their kitchen together, fixing up their house. They were like the mommy and daddy robin, always building and improving the nest.

"Come on, honey! That is going to make me feel sick again and I'm enjoying my first few minutes of the day without morning sickness."

Brad reached over and squeezed her foot. "Sorry babe. Well, I can see all talking is going to stop with me out here. I'm going to go back to my wrestling match."

"Not with that in the house, you aren't," Karen said. She looked stern.

"Oh, all right," Brad said, as he found an ashtray on the picnic table and snuffed it out. "But you're making me waste a great Cuban cigar."

"Relight it when you play poker with the boys," Karen said to Brad's back as he opened the screen door and went back into the house.

"Men," Karen said.

"You're telling me!" Carla laughed back. "Don't get me started."

###

This was it. Michael was putting his foot down on this one and he was not about to budge. It was time to check out what Carla's father knew. Michael wasn't going to take no for an answer. He and Carla had been bickering about it for two days since Carla had come back from visiting Karen in Baltimore, and Carla's patience was worn to a frazzle. The whole situation wasn't being helped by the fact that she was confined to two small rooms. She had to get out of this cracker box or she would scream!

The problem came down to this. Carla was too afraid to be the first to call and bridge the gap between herself and her father. So many things had gone wrong between them in the past few years. She had been waiting for a year for him to call her. It would involve too much for her to just dial him up, and resume, as if they had a smooth relationship.

"If you ask me, you are just too bull-headed," Amy said to Carla, as they stood in her small kitchen, making dinner while discussing the problem.

"You don't know all the details," Carla said as she peeled carrots.

"I know more than you think," Amy replied as she took out some ground beef and began making patties, one for each of them. This was the first night Michael wasn't coming over for dinner in days. A nice break, Carla thought.

"You only know what I've told you, and that's not much," Carla said as she peeled the carrots harder. This topic, her father, was one of her least favorite.

"I know you are messed up because you aren't in touch with him," Amy said. And she turned to look Carla in the eyes for emphasis.

"I do just fine without him," Carla said, averting Amy's accusatory glare.

Amy shook her head. "It's *so* obvious you miss him, it's not even funny."

"Why do you think that? I never even mention him, let alone pine over him."

"It's all over your face, little Orphan Annie. You don't see your face when I hang up the phone from talking to my parents. You always look so sad, it almost kills me."

"Because you have your *Mom*," Carla said. "She can give you advice. She's in your life. You have no idea what I'd give for that."

"Yes. I know you miss your Mom. But that's an old wound. Your Dad is a fresh one."

"You don't know," Carla said. She could feel the early prickles of stinging in her eyes, the kind that if she let them, would form into tears. Carla hated how Amy was so on target about something she went to great lengths to hide from everyone, including her closest friends.

"I do," Amy said. "I do know. That's the point. And you can't deny it."

"There's nothing I can do, Amy. I like to pretend I'm the one rejecting him. But that's not really how it is. It's not up to me at all. That's the part where you're wrong," Carla said.

"Then tell me," Amy said, finishing with the patties.

"When my Dad met Alexis four years ago, he dropped me and my sister like hotcakes. He wanted us out of his way. Simple. How could he date a woman close to our age, with us hanging around? Alexis wanted all of him, and that's what he gave to her."

"It's hard to deal with," Amy said. Sometimes she was not her usual bubbly self with a happy-go-lucky solution to everything. Sometimes she totally understood that there were situations in life that were not apparently fixable and were just plain painful.

"I would give anything not to have to call my father right now," Carla said. "*Anything*, at this point."

"Michael and the cops seem to think you have to," Amy continued. She was drying her hands on a paper towel.

"I know," Carla said. "I'm wracking my brain trying to think of another alternative."

"How about you let Karen place the first call?" Amy piped up. "You said Karen has been diplomatic with your father. Didn't she go to his and Alexis' wedding?"

"Yeah. She's been good about it. Better than I have."

"See if she'll call him. She could tell him how much you both miss him and ask if you can come to visit?"

"Just like that…?"

"Well, how else?"

"What if he says no. What if Alexis says no.'"

"You have nothing to lose, really. If he says no, then the cops will have a go at him, anyway. But remember, the bottom line on this is you want your freedom back. Forget about your father for the moment. Don't you want your life back? Don't you want this case solved?"

"More than anything."

"Then lay your pride aside and just do what has to be done."

"You're right," Carla said as she finished tearing lettuce for their salad. "That's the best way for me to look at it."

###

Karen was amazing. Carla called and explained the whole situation to her. What had happened at her work a few nights before, what the cops wanted her to do. The whole thing. Karen didn't come unglued. She just listened attentively. She was always so stable under pressure.

Within a day she called Carla back to tell her she'd talked to their father and had a trip planned to visit him.

"How'd you do it?" Carla asked on the phone while she sat curled on the couch, petting Amy's cat, Midnight.

"I don't know. It just went smoothly when I talked to him. Maybe he's been missing us. I also gave him a big pitch about Sammy. He hasn't even seen him yet."

"You brought Sammy into this?"

"Carla. Beggars can't be choosers. You said to figure out a way we could see him in person. And I found the way. We are taking Sammy down to visit him. And you are bringing your new 'boyfriend.' He was very excited when I told him you have a serious boyfriend. He says it's about time."

"Please, Karen. Tell me you didn't tell him something like that!"

"He thinks you might marry the guy. I didn't tell him he's a private investigator. You'll have to invent a better profession for him."

"Karen. I can't take Michael. It will be so awkward! I was picturing just you and me going."

"Knock it off, for a second," Karen said. "Let me tell you the best part."

"Oh hooray. Tell me the part that's better than this."

"Alexis is in Europe for a month. Dad is in Florida at his new beach *house* on Captiva Island. He sold the condo on Sanibel and bought a huge, fat beach house!"

Carla was silent about this. Captiva was the single most heavenly place on earth, in Carla's opinion. They'd spent all their childhood winter vacations on Sanibel and the neighboring Captiva Island was even more remote and tropical. A perfect island getaway.

"Carla? You there? You still with me?"

"Yes, I'm here. I'm thinking." Carla conceded. She was picturing lying on the deserted beach at Captiva, getting the hell out of this apartment, and forgetting all her problems for a few days. With Michael along, maybe she could relax because he could be the one to worry about things. He could bring along his trusty gun.

"Well, don't think too long. I have to know whether Brad should take time off work."

"Brad's coming, too?"

"I thought that would help you a little with bringing Michael along."

"Karen, I'm stunned. I'm stunned and I'm amazed. What can I say? Thanks for doing all this. You are the best sister ever!"

"I'm your *only* sister! That ain't no compliment, honey." They both started laughing. "Besides. Come on! A week on Captiva? You've got to be kidding. It's a no-brainer."

"It will be fun. Like when we were little."

"Yeah. Who knows? Maybe we will even have a good time with Dad?"

"I'm not going to cross my fingers on that one," Carla said. "But if I can find out anything about his cases, and get Michael a lead, I'll be happy."

7

"Care for anything to drink?" the flight attendant asked, breaking Carla out of her trance as she sat biting her lip and staring out the window of the plane.

"Diet Coke," Carla said looking up.

"Aw, come on. Live a little," Michael said. "Let me buy you a beer." He knocked his arm against hers in a jovial guy-to-guy way, like men do at a poker game.

"Two beers, please," he said, handing the attendant some cash.

"I guess it might help," Carla said.

"I hope so," Michael offered. "You're wound up tighter than I've ever seen you. Which actually, isn't saying much."

Carla feigned a smile. Michael really had no possible way of knowing how nervous she was. Her mind was going a mile a minute. She was going to visit her father. The whole idea was terrifying. The fear of his rejection was almost unbearable. What if she and her father got into a fight like the last time they saw each other? What if she felt uncomfortable there? How would she handle it with Karen, Brad and Michael along? She wouldn't be able to just walk out.

And speaking of Michael, what in the world was she going to do with that whole situation? How would she fake this boyfriend thing? She still couldn't believe Karen had put her into such a bad position. But then again, her father was always harping on Carla's lack of a man in her life. Carla got the impression that her father thought women were nothing without a man.

Karen had played this card for Carla to protect her, and Carla knew that was her intention. Having Michael along as a "serious boyfriend" was going to distract her father. He wouldn't be able to focus on Carla, which would be a relief. It was probably the right choice. Plus, how else could she manage to bring Michael along both for protection and for research purposes, if she didn't have the excuse of their being a couple? No, it made sense, as crazy as the thought was.

Michael of course was eating the entire thing up with a spoon. A dream come true for him. He could hit on her and tease her to his heart's content, and watch her squirm with no way to punish him. She stole a glance sideways at him. He was listening to airline headphones, eyes closed, and humming along to some country song. He seemed totally at ease. He always did. And it made her mad to think that he enjoyed how this whole arrangement was distressing her.

His teasing had begun well before the trip. On the way to the airport he had called her "sugar cakes" and "hot buns," taking this girlfriend thing all the way to the bank. Did he really call his girlfriends, "hot buns?"

When Carla had shot him an annoyed glance, he had only shrugged. "Just getting you all primed and ready."

"I doubt that," Carla had said.

"Oh, you think you're tough, don't you?" Michael had said, taking her carry-on bag and slinging it over his shoulder as they headed toward their gate. "I take it as a personal challenge to soften you up," he had said with his eyes twinkling.

"Go for it," Carla said. "The only reason you want to is because it's a form of the hunt, and men are natural predators. It's all about the hunt for them, and nothing more."

"You know. Sometimes its hard to live up to your incredibly jaded view of men."

"No actually, you're doing pretty well."

"And the care and nurturing of your well-being I've provided? That counts for nothing?"

"I'm paying you for that," Carla said, dismissing it. She realized she was in an incredibly bitchy mood. The tension created by her anticipation of visiting her father was really getting unbearable.

"Well listen, little missy. It's not like I've given you an invoice yet. I'm not really seeing any cash."

"You want me to write you a check?" Carla was ready to rumble. She fumbled for her purse.

"No. That's not what I was saying."

"What, then?"

"I'm saying that perhaps, just maybe, if you are capable of grasping the concept, I'm doing this for you because I want to, it's not just a job for me."

Carla was silenced. She was acutely aware of how unfair and unkind she was being. Michael didn't deserve the brunt of all her anger and fear related to her father.

"Listen. I'm really crabby right now," she said. "Just ignore me." It was as close to saying she was sorry as she could get with him.

"No. I'm not going to," Michael said. His eyes were very bright in the sunlight streaming in through the terminal window. "I'm never going to ignore you." Michael reached over and rubbed his big hand along her silky arm. "Hey," he said. "Take it easy."

"I'll try," she said with a soft smile. "It's really going to be tough, though."

"You might be surprised," Michael said. "Think positively."

At the Fort Myers airport, her father was the first person at the gate that she saw as she debarked the plane. He was tall, distinguished, stood with so much authority. There was a natural charm and charisma about her father that couldn't be denied. Just seeing him flooded her with a sense of pride in him, and his stature. Even when she was furious and extremely hurt by her father, she couldn't deny this one aspect of him. His natural power. Everyone was respectful of him. He dominated every scenario where people were involved. She'd seen it time and time again with her father: at work, at the country club, on neighborhood committees, talking to gas station attendants and waiters. It didn't matter. People just naturally and subconsciously surrendered to his leadership. He was also a very handsome man, and undoubtedly that had something to do with it.

She couldn't help but wonder how Michael would hold up. Very few men, in fact possibly none, could really say they'd won his approval when it came to Max Redfern. No man was good enough for his daughters and no man could fill his shoes. When she was in high school, Carla had seen her father eat boys for lunch one by one as she and Karen had brought them along on family picnics, out to dinner, or over for holidays.

Brad had held on pretty well. But that was only because he was so crazy about Karen. He had learned to turn off the subtle digs and criticism from Max Redfern for the sake of his relationship with Karen. And probably the military had helped him to deal with dogmatic and opinionated authority figures. Brad handled things pretty well. His personality said for a lot too, Carla figured.

Here's the moment of truth, Carla thought as she approached her father. His dark eyebrows were furrowed as she came closer. He wore a clean white Izod golf shirt and light tan dress shorts. On his feet were Docker shoes. She was surprised to see him without socks. He was very tan. She noticed his dark hair was speckling with some gray at his temples. He stood with his hands at his sides, seeming to wait for her next move.

"Daddy! Hello!" Carla said in an exaggerated way, hoping to relieve some of the tension they both must be feeling. And she reached up and pecked his cheek with a quick kiss.

"Hello there, Carla," he said, as he patted her on the back a few quick times. It was going to remain icy, then, Carla thought. Fine with her.

"Daddy, I want to introduce you to Michael Spanos."

"How do you do, sir," Michael said as he extended his hand. Carla knew Michael would give him a good firm handshake, absolutely essential if he hoped to fight his way into some kind of approval with her father.

"Good to meet you Michael," Max Redfern said. "I'm so glad you could escort Carla down for a visit."

Here we go, Carla thought. I hate how my father sees me. Poor, little helpless single daughter needs to be escorted down to Florida. Doesn't he get anything?

"My privilege and an honor, sir," Michael said.

This is going to be a royal ass-kissing jamboree, Carla thought. She plastered on a smile and looked up at Michael as he put his arm around her shoulder. What a sweet couple, Carla thought sarcastically. This acting charade was going to give her a pounding headache in no time flat.

"Well, let's go pick up your luggage and head on out," Max said. "We should be able to catch the sunset if we hurry. They are absolutely divine from the deck of my new house. That's one of the reasons I purchased it."

Carla's father pulled up a shiny, new silver Jaguar, complete with soft leather seats. With little effort, he loaded their luggage into the trunk. For a man in his mid-fifties, her father was very fit. She could tell he still jogged or swam daily, as he had for years.

Max gestured for Michael to take the front seat along side him. Mr. Brown-nose is making headway already, Carla thought snidely.

She sat sulking in the back seat as Max explained some of the history of the Sanibel-Captiva area and gave details on some of the natural birds and wildlife to Michael. Always full of details, Carla thought sarcastically. As long as it has to do with real estate, stocks, bonds, property. But when it comes to people, her father came up short.

"How is your work coming along, Carla? What is that non-profit you work for? Are you still with them?"

"Yes, Dad. I'm still working for a non-profit agency." Carla took care to slightly emphasize the word non-profit. "It's a crime fighting organization. The Federation to Prevent Teen Crime. It helps kids."

"That's a very nice by-product to come from your work," her father said. It was impossible to miss that he thought she was in a dead end career move.

"And you, Michael? What line of work are you in?"

Carla's heart began to race. In the haste to get ready and leave for the trip, they hadn't ironed out that detail yet, she and Michael. She wondered what he'd say and she hoped it would be good.

"Sir, I am currently studying for my entrance exams to law school and doing freelance paralegal work. I decided upon law after ending my tour of duty in the Marines."

"You don't say," Max said. Carla could tell by her father's subtle intonation that he liked what he heard.

"You sound like a man with a good head on his shoulders and one who isn't afraid to put some sweat into something. I've always found ex-military men to be fierce competitors in the legal arena."

"Thank you, sir. I hope that's the case."

"Do you have plans on what school you will attend?"

"I was thinking Georgetown."

"Excellent choice. I have a firm partner who went there. Speaks very highly of it. A tough school."

"Yes sir."

Carla zoned out as her father and Michael talked. The car skimmed across the Sanibel Island Bridge from Fort Myers over to the islands. This is where so many good memories flooded her; it was a moment of tribute. She remembered her mother and all the special times with her collecting shells. Laughing. Talking. The island itself seemed to embody her mother. A warm, inviting, nurturing place. Just like her mother had been for her.

Sanibel was just as she'd last seen in ten years ago. Exactly. Periwinkle Drive with all the shops and the big pines drooping over it. The white sand speckled with some of the Gulf of Mexico's best shell treasures. Carla soaked it all in with delight.

"Nice to be back?" her father said. He noticed her contemplative mood.

"*So nice*, Daddy," Carla said. And she meant it. It was wonderful to be back.

"My house is just up ahead," Max said to Michael as he indicated a stretch of skinny land road that went between Sanibel and Captiva. The road had maybe ten mansions on it, flanked by the Gulf in front and with the island sound behind. Each house had a long driveway that disappeared into jungle-like yards filled with palm trees of all shapes and sizes. The roofs of the big houses stood above the trees like giant ships.

"The house looks directly west. I like to have a cocktail and watch the sunset each night. It's fabulous."

"Let's do it then," Carla said. Her father was so stiff and formal. Sometimes she just wanted to ruffle up his hair a bit, grab his hands and dance him in a circle. He announced everything before it happened. It took all the fun out of things.

"All right," Max said as he rolled the car over the white rock driveway, the sides of the car brushing past thick tropical foliage and low palm leaves on its way. The house loomed up ahead in the growing darkness of dusk. Green and blue floodlights aimed on various palm trees reflected off of plants and trees. He pulled into the circle driveway with lights shining up on the majestic house, a white two-story Spanish-style stucco.

After unloading and walking in through the giant double doors, they stood in the foyer with vaulted ceiling, admiring the chandelier. There was an uncomfortable pause.

"I'll give you two a little time to freshen up," Max said. "And then we'll meet down by the deck, shall we? If you care for a swim, put on your suits. The pool is perfect for laps. I had it built with the full twenty-five meters."

"That sounds great, Daddy," Carla said. She and her father used to avidly swim laps together in the evenings, when she was younger and on the country club swim team.

"Josephine will show you your room. I had her prepare the larger guest room for you to share. Is that the appropriate thing to do here?" Carla knew that was her father's polite way of asking if she and Michael were sleeping together.

"That will be just fine," Michael jumped in.

"No, Daddy. We can have separate rooms, if you prefer." She was hoping to play on his old-fashioned view of protocol.

"Don't be ridiculous, Carla. You are grown adults. I'm not one to be a stickler for ethical mores when two people are in a serious relationship."

Carla didn't know what to do from here. She couldn't fight the room thing, or it would appear she and Michael weren't serious. And if they weren't serious, what was he doing here with her? She couldn't afford to raise suspicions.

Carla lowered her head to hide a blush. "Fine, Daddy. Thank you."

"All right then. I'll see you poolside in say, thirty minutes?" Max said, more as a statement than a question.

"Great," Carla said. This formality was killing her.

A short, pleasant looking middle-aged woman appeared in formal servant wear, nodding a greeting. "This is Josephine, my housekeeper and a great cook," Max said. "She knows more about this house than I do. So please feel free to ask her for anything." He gave her a smile intended to charm her.

"Oh, Mr. Redfern," Josephine said in a thick Spanish accent, obviously taken by Max's charm.

As soon as Josephine had closed the door to their spacious guest room, Carla jumped over and locked it. The huge king size bed was draped in a lavish satin quilt decorated in a tropical print. A huge array of pillows adorned the head of the bed, in greens and blues to match.

"You, jackass!" Carla hissed.

"What?" Michael said, raising his shoulders in innocence.

"Where do you want me to start?" Carla was so furious, she was pacing.

Michael made himself comfortable on the bed, kicking off his boots, stretching out on his back and crossing his hands under his head. His smirk just made her angrier.

"My gosh! For starters, you didn't have to get us a room together!"

"I thought you'd like it. Might keep you from being afraid?"

"Come on. You know how awkward this is going to be. You did this on purpose. Why did you have to say anything?" She was so mad she was fighting back the tears.

"Seriously," Michael said. "I wasn't trying to stress you out so much. Honestly. I thought it would keep you from worrying."

Carla glared at him hard. Was this a trick? A way to get her in the same bed with him? Or was he genuinely worried about her fears?

Michael sat up and put his legs over the side of the bed, sitting forward with his big hands out in front of him. He actually looks remorseful, Carla thought. His face looks sweet. She almost wanted to believe him.

"You have to admit, the last few days haven't been that easy on you. I didn't think being in Florida was going to make them any easier."

Carla looked at him some more. Man, he was a devil. She didn't know what to think about him sometimes. He was a devil with a halo.

"And another thing," she said. She wasn't ready to drop the charges yet.

"I thought I was going to vomit in the car on the way over here, you were pouring it on so thick with my father."

"I thought I did pretty well," Michael said.

"Ok, first of all. Do you have any idea what kind of a mind you're dealing with when it comes to my father? It's a steel trap. He doesn't miss a single detail, and he'll use it against you. Do you think he's going to believe all that about law school? Georgetown? The Marines?"

Carla was working up a sweat. She had her hands on her hips looking down at him.

"I got it covered," Michael said. Smiling that goofy smile that made her furious.

"How? How are you going to keep from blowing our cover on this one?"

"Because it's all true."

"What?" She stood aghast.

"What I said. It's true. All of it."

Carla stammered and started to ask more questions, but thought better of it. She was so surprised she sat down on the edge of the bed next to him.

"Really? How didn't I know about any of this?"

"Did you ever ask?"

"No."

"You haven't really asked one single thing about me."

"You're right. I haven't. I've been pretty caught up in myself."

"Understandable."

"You certainly keep the surprises coming, though, I have to admit. More to you than meets the eye."

"And who knows? If you gave me a try, you might find a guy you could like for more than his gun," Michael said.

Carla smiled. "I don't need your gun, or anything else of yours," she said.

"Oh, I doubt that, missy. That, I seriously doubt."

Getting ready for the pool was interesting. What a long week this was going to be without any room for dressing privately. Carla went into the bathroom to change into her bathing suit she wore for swimming laps. A royal-blue one-piece racing back. She could stand to crank out a few laps tonight and get rid of some of this tension, she thought.

Michael stayed in the bedroom to change. When she came out, he was wearing dark green swim trunks.

Michael let out a low whistle. "Well look at that!" he said as if she were some kind of beauty contestant.

She crossed her arms. "Oh, grow up. Please."

But she couldn't help taking a gaze at him either, with his shirt off.

Very, very nice, she thought. The bulging muscles she'd seen under his clothes were nothing compared to the real thing. He truly was chiseled, his arms, neck, shoulders, and as she dared to glance down, she noticed his thighs, were perfectly formed and muscular. The curly black hair on his chest adorned full pec muscles. She was always prone to be weak for a nice chest on a man.

To maintain control, Carla suddenly busied herself with fixing her hair in the mirror. She brushed it from top to its long bottom, pulling out tangles. When she brushed her hair, she had to lean to the side to let it hang down. Michael watched in silence as she pulled the shiny strands into a tight ponytail at the back of her head, then braided the long strand, and put yet another band on the bottom of it to hold it while she swam.

"I love to watch you do that," he said.

Carla didn't answer, but turned and searched in her suitcase to find her green and blue gauze knit swimsuit cover up, and slipped it on.

"Shall we?" Michael said, opening the door. She could smell that spicy soap smell on him again as she passed by him. What *was* that stuff?

"This is going to take some heavy drinking, or something to get me through it," Carla groaned. It was painstaking to make conversation with her father as things were right now between them, with all the underlying unresolved issues.

"Naw. Piece of cake," Michael said as he padded along, his bare feet slapping the large brick stones of the walkway to the pool.

"I'm glad you think so," Carla said, following him on the walkway. "Anyway, I'll be so relieved when Karen finally gets here tomorrow."

"What? And I'm chopped liver?" Michael asked with a chuckle.

###

The evening passed surprisingly well. The pool lights were on, reflecting a brilliant aqua blue color. The water looked entirely inviting as the evening was getting darker and a fiery orange sunset shown in the western sky, followed by scarlet, then lavender and finally purple.

Her father was busy mixing cocktails, but Carla wanted to swim laps first. He served Michael and the two of them sat in deck chairs talking things over as Carla slipped into the pool. The water was a perfect temperature. When she paused now and then on either end of the pool, she could hear them talking. They'd settled on a common interest in deep sea fishing. Her father had a forty-eight-foot cruiser, and he was fond of taking it out on fishing expeditions. Turns out Michael worked on a fishing boat at some point.

"I have the boat moored here, in fact," her father said. "I should take you and Carla out for a spin if you like. Delightful out on the gulf. It's very gentle."

Michael grinned wide. "It would be my pleasure to take you up on that," he said, raising an eyebrow noticeable only to Carla, as she came out of the pool, dripping wet and cold, her suit clinging. She leaned over to get her beach towel and wrap it around her.

Josephine served grilled chicken fajitas with the works and they had it by candlelight on the pool veranda. Carla couldn't think of the last time she'd had such a pleasant evening with her father. He was avoiding all the tough issues between them. The expensive wine was loosening her up, and she was starting to actually feel comfortable. They lingered over dinner and the candles sputtered in the evening breeze. As it neared ten o'clock, Carla knew her father would want to go to bed. Like clockwork, she thought. Sure enough, he excused himself and asked if they would mind if he retired early. He liked to get up early for exercising. Carla had never known her father to deviate from his strict early to bed, early to rise, schedule. "The Ben Franklin Method To Success," he called it.

After they all said goodnight, Carla and Michael sat by the pool, with their feet and legs hanging in. The evening had been so beautiful. It was hard to picture it ending.

"Want to take a walk down at the beach?" Michael said.

Carla hesitated and was quiet.

"Do I sense more of the hunt coming my way? I'm feeling the thrill," Michael teased.

Carla remained quiet.

"Little too intimate for you? Soft sand. Cool breeze. You might not be able to control yourself."

"You flatter the hell out of yourself, Michael."

"I know you're attracted."

"Don't be so sure," she retorted.

"Come on. Let's go down to the beach," he said again.

"No. I think we should go to bed instead."

"Now we're talking!" Michael laughed.

"No bed-bed, I mean. Sleeping in bed. I'm really exhausted. You can sleep on the floor, since this whole shared room thing was your idea."

"I doubt we'll sleep," Michael continued.

Carla couldn't help but feel an adrenalin rush wave over her as she thought of sleeping near him. Somehow she'd pushed that concern from her mind before the trip. So many other things to think about. But now it was looming and a definite reality she couldn't escape. This big hunk of a man, the chiseled Greek god, was going to sleep in the same room with her for a week, maybe even in the same bed if she let him. Sleeping beside Michael would definitely be more erotic than she wanted to admit to herself. A chill passed over her and she shivered.

"Don't forget, you never mess with clients, right?" She wanted to test how serious he was and she was hoping reminding him of his own work rule would snap some sense into him.

"Rules are made to be broken," he said with a wink. When was he going to stop teasing her? she wondered.

The beach was a gentle haven. Moonlight reflected from the sand and glowed on the water. Palm fronds whispered back and forth. They were breathless as they came down onto the white silent expanse of deserted sand.

"Come on, let's walk a little," Michael said.

They walked along without talking and Carla was surprised at how comfortable it was.

"Are you going to be all right?" he asked, finally breaking the silence.

"Yes. I'll make it," she smiled.

"Is it any better to be here, finally? Get it overwith? This reunion with your father?"

"I guess."

"How about you? Are you all right?" Carla asked.

"I'm fine with your father, if that's what you're asking me. He's not all that tough."

Carla continued to walk along silently. What could she say to this? He was tough *for her*. Michael seemed to be doing fine, though, she agreed.

Suddenly Michael stopped and turned to look at her, moonlight across his face. Carla couldn't tell if she was shivering from the intimate look in Michael's eyes or because of the chill evening air. He surprised her by reaching out and putting his hands on her bare upper arms, rubbing gently.

"Since you asked, I could be much more all right," he said.

"How so?" Carla asked. His touch felt comforting and seductive at the same time.

"With a confession," he said.

"A confession?"

He was suddenly so serious. "I've been wanting to get this out in the open."

Carla felt a strange pang of anticipation in her core. There was nothing she could do but look up into his eyes. He had her captivate.

"I've had feelings for you since I first lay eyes on you."

"Please," Carla said. She tried to think of how much wine he'd had with dinner. She couldn't remember him having much.

"No. I'm serious. You think I'm just hitting on. I'm not."

Carla shrugged.

"Seriously, Carla. You are the most challenging, interesting and amazing woman I've ever met, and you don't even see it in yourself."

Carla dug her toe in the sand. The palm leaves rustled in the breeze again. She could feel him boring imaginary holes in the top of her head, so she looked up. His eyes riveted immediately to hers and wouldn't let go. She was getting warmer now at the shoulders where he held her. She stopped shivering and shifted her weight as she looked at him. The silence thickened around them. Carla turned her head to look out at the moon.

"May I kiss you?" Michael asked, startling Carla to look back his way.

Suddenly her heart was pounding. Her throat was dry, so she only nodded.

When Michael leaned down to kiss her, everything went into slow motion. His hands were spread on her lower back, making her feel tiny and delicate in his grasp.

She slipped her arms around his neck. His spicy smell was everywhere.

"Wait, wait." She put a hand against his chest bare chest. She stood back from him and looked at him hard. "It's the gulf breeze, trust me. It has magical powers. It can make things like this happen!"

He laughed. "I doubt that," he said, smiling down at her hand. He gently grabbed her wrist and pulled her to him, wrapping his arms around her again. He buried his face in her hair. "It's you that has the powers."

They stood swaying in the moonlight. Carla rested her head on his chest. He smelled better than the ocean breeze itself. She allowed herself to take a deep sigh.

"Come on. Admit it. This feels good, doesn't it?" He rested his chin on the top of her head.

"What are we going to do?" she asked. Waves were gently lapping near their bare feet.

"About what? Us?" He said it so easily.

"Well, about the possibility of us, I guess."

"It's past the point of possibility, wouldn't you say?"

Carla pulled away from him. "It's a bad time for me to get involved with someone."

"Nobody knows that like I do." he said.

"But there are things you don't know." She started walking slowly along the sand where it met the water.

"You'd be surprised at what I know," he said, following calmly beside her.

"Do you know that I'm getting out of a relationship?"

"Oh that pumpkin head?" Michael was walking deeper into the water, the waves lapping at his ankles. "I know all about him. Amy told me that you already broke up with him."

"I did." Carla squinted out at the moon rising near the horizon.

"I know you still care about him," Michael said.

"And that's not a problem for you?"

"It's not."

Carla stopped and looked at him with a quizzical stare.

Michael bent down and picked up a shell, then hurled it out into the water.

"If you give me half a chance, I'll make you forget all about him."

Carla shook her head in disbelief. Her mind was tangled and tired.

"I know you don't understand," Michael said. "But it's simple. That's what love is. Feeling something so strongly you are willing to take a risk."

Carla looked down at her feet. *Did he just mention love?*

"Hey," Michael said. "We don't have to figure this all out right now. Come on. You look beat. Let's go back and get some rest."

###

Michael waited while Carla changed for bed. "This is going to get old? Don't you think?" he said with a grin as she reappeared from the bathroom. He was wearing boxers and was stretched out on the bed.

"This feels strange. Like we're a married couple or something." Carla scrubbed her teeth.

"It's not like I haven't seen you in your nightgown before. That same one in fact. You were wearing it at Amy's that night I spent the night," Michael said. "And we've even slept in the same room. Remember in Baltimore? The hotel?"

"That was different." She spit into the sink.

"It was?"

"Yes. It was two beds. I hardly knew you. And, I'd never kissed you before." She took a drink and snapped out the bathroom light.

"Come on. Hop in." He lifted the covers up high for her. "Don't worry so much."

She hesitantly crawled in and lay looking at the ceiling. The moonlight surged through the bedroom window and shadows of palm leaves danced on the bedspread.

Michael smiled. "You're killing me. I want you to know that." He was still lying on his side looking right at her, an arm propping up his head.

"This is going to be a long week. We should ask for separate rooms tomorrow." Carla turned her back to him.

"No. It'll seem too weird to your father."

"Then maybe you should sleep on the floor. We could put some blankets down."

"Also a little strange should your father come around."

Carla shifted her legs under the covers. "How did this happen? How did we get so locked into things being like this?"

"Hmm. That's a hard one. You need to know who's trying to kill you and I'm your private detective. Didn't it go something like that?"

"Not really. Not what just happened out at the beach…" her voice trailed off. She tried to make it sound sleepy.

"I think you might change your mind about the room." He pulled her shoulder so she rolled back toward his way.

"I don't think so." Her voice caught in her throat. Suddenly she was keenly aware of his bare muscular chest.

Michael wouldn't take his eyes off of her. She was aching for him so much there was a hum in her ears. She closed her eyes.

"Carla, if you'd let me…" He began to stroke her neck. "I'd kiss you here." Something earthy and primitive came from her throat and she turned her head.

He trailed his finger down her arm, softly tickling her, then stroked between each of her fingers. *How did he know that would feel so sensual?*

"If you'd only let me, Carla…" He ran his fingertips softly down the length of her neck again, this time venturing lower to the last spot exposed by her opened nightgown. Carla held her breath. He stroked the tender skin directly between her breasts. Electric delight pummeled her.

"You're not playing fair," she said thickly. She felt her cheeks go flush and she opened her eyes. He was so close to her face it startled her. His lips were moist. Eyes sensitive. He was beautiful.

She buried her face in his neck. "Michael, you're making it so hard for me to say no to you."

"I wish you wouldn't." He grabbed the back of her head and tangled his hand in her hair.

"I'm too afraid," she said.

Michael searched her face. Then he pulled her into his arms and hugged her tight. She sucked in a breath of relief. He knew her so well it was frightening.

Long after Michael fell asleep, Carla lay in the crook of his arm, poisoned with her regret.

###

It was a beautiful clear day and breakfast was being served on the veranda. Michael was trying to focus on the conversation at the table between Carla and her father. But it seemed darn near impossible. My own fault, Michael thought. I've created this hell for myself.

Her golden hair hung loose down her back. He couldn't keep his eyes off of it while she was eating. The curve of her slim neck was making him insane. She was intently eating her eggs. Not noticing him. Talking to her father. Then she looked over at him and smiled.

"Don't you think so, Michael?" she asked. "Michael?"

"I'm sorry. Zoning out here. Haven't had my caffeine." Get a grip on yourself, man, he thought. Don't be a fool in front of her father.

"I was just telling Daddy that we wouldn't mind making ourselves at home while he takes care of some business in Fort Myers and then picks up Karen and Brad at the airport."

"No. My goodness, no, we wouldn't mind at all." Michael was trying to sound more mature than he knew he typically sounded.

"I figured as much," Max said. "There's plenty to do here. If you are bored with the beach and the pool, we also have community tennis courts just up the road. You can easily walk to them."

"Thanks, Daddy," Carla said, beaming at Michael. "I'm sure we won't get bored with the beach. I want to show Michael all my favorite shells."

"That's fine, then. I'll leave you to your collecting, and I'll see you later this afternoon with Karen, Brad and Sammy. I'm anxious to meet the little man."

"Oh, Daddy, he is so precious. You'll be so surprised."

"I'm sure I will," Max said with a nod as he stood up to leave.

"See you later, sir," Michael said.

"At ease, Michael," Max winked. "You don't have to keep calling me sir." What an idiot, Michael thought. I'm going to overkill this right into the ground.

After Max disappeared and it was silent, Michael sat drinking his coffee and looking at Carla. He was soaking in every detail of her.

"I was thinking we could use this time to look for some information about Daddy's cases. I don't know if we're going to get another chance." Her voice was so businesslike.

"Good idea." Michael felt suddenly, for the first time, like he could care less about the case. He was a high school boy, with a fixation. He wanted to pick her up, and literally run her to the nearest bed, throw her onto it and fiercely make love to her until they were both exhausted.

"You don't sound too excited," Carla said. "I thought you were all pressed about this case research." She sounded slightly annoyed.

"I am," Michael nodded while he sipped more coffee. "I am."

"Well?"

He loved that demanding pout she put on sometimes. She could run the whole damn male world with that look.

"Did you want to wait until you hear your father's car leave in the drive first?" He loved teasing.

"Of course, Michael. I meant after he leaves. You know that."

"Irritated this morning?" He was egging her on. He'd actually meant to talk things over this morning with her before breakfast, but when he'd awakened, she was already dressed and gone.

"Well, since you're asking. Yes, I am," she said sternly

"Why?"

"You know why." She was fierce with those blue eyes. He could tell she was getting angrier. It was all he could do to keep himself from smiling.

"Because I'm a male predator?" he asked sheepishly.

Her chin jutted out slightly. "Good answer. How about pain-in-the-ass, seducing and unfair predator?"

"If you insist." He leaned back in the chair and smiled at her.

"You took advantage of me, Michael." She said his name as if it were a cuss word.

"I didn't exactly see you hating it." He tried to refrain himself from looking down at her breasts because that's exactly where his mind was going with this. She didn't fail to notice where he looked, and her anger only intensified.

"Come on, Carla. Don't get all crazy. Nothing happened."

"Maybe not in your book. But in mine, it was something." She was right. He had taken advantage of the situation. She was looking down now with her long hair falling around her.

"Hey," he said, reaching over and touching her chin. Sometimes she was such a little girl, it killed him. He felt an overwhelming protectiveness for her; it almost made his chest burn with pain.

"I'm sorry. Honestly. I really am, Carla. I'm sorry I pushed things." He wanted to add that she hadn't tried all that hard to stop him. But it wasn't the time to point out what she'd done. Only a time for showing penitence.

She looked up at him, intently. Her eyes studying him as she always did. Searching his eyes for answers somewhere.

"But I'm not sorry for what I said at the beach," he said earnestly. "I meant every word of it."

She continued to look at him. She was killing him with those eyes. It took all he had not to reach over and pull her into his arms. But now he had to control himself more than ever, or he'd lose her trust — which he was tottering on the edge of losing, even now.

"Please accept my apology," he said softly.

"I accept," she said after a long silence. And the look was finalizing. He read between the lines of what she couldn't say. She needed her space. It was too much to push her right now.

"Don't worry. I'll stay on my half of the bed from here on out. You can even put pillows between us."

"All right," she said softly.

She was a kaleidoscope. Constantly changing before him. He was imprisoned by her vulnerability and beauty. If only he hadn't seen the look on her face while he was touching her last night. The gentle little way she bit her lip, trying to control the play of feelings taking over her. He had seen her arousal building, and it took everything he had to control his own. He'd almost lost it.

He knew he had to get a grip on himself and he had to do it now. This was a matter of keeping her life safe. Remember? *Michael, what the hell are you doing*? He was angry with himself for losing his focus.

Carla broke his train of thought.

"Where should we start with the research?" she asked, firmly dismissing the topic of last night.

"His study?" Michael asked.

"Definitely." She stood up and looked at him eagerly. She wanted to get on the case.

8

This was killing him, leafing through Mr. Redfern's private things. Michael kept thinking of how accustomed to snooping he'd become as a private investigator, but this was a lot harder than he'd expected it to be. Something about this being Carla's father made it strange. Maybe he was getting soft.

The study was overlooking the pool. A real man's room, Michael thought with admiration. A place where a guy could enjoy the hell out of a Cuban cigar and some brandy. Dark grained paneling. Huge mahogany leather furniture. The couch was big enough to….Michael refrained from letting his mind get graphic with ideas about the couch. This Max Redfern had some fine taste, no doubt about it. Michael browsed along the wall looking at some prints of sailing vessels and nautical equipment framed in gold and glass boxes.

"Come on," Carla said. "Quit looking at stuff that won't help us." She sounded impatient. She already had her father's huge legal briefcase opened on the desktop and was gently leafing through it.

Michael busied himself looking through books on the bookshelf. "You never know where you might find a clue," he said.

Carla turned and gave him a scowl.

"You don't." Michael said again. That was true. Clues came up in the weirdest places. Like for example. This photo of Mr. Redfern and another man, smiling on a boat. Where was it taken and when? It looked fairly recent.

"Do you know who this man is with your father?" Michael asked, lifting the small framed picture up from the bookshelf. He turned it over. Nothing was written on the back of it.

"Let me see it," Carla said. Michael walked over and stood close beside her and handed her the picture. While she studied it, he gently leaned his head close to the top of her head and took a sniff of her. Mmm, he thought. Heavenly.

"Stand back a little," she said, as she elbowed him. "Do you have to be right on top of me?" She smiled, but Michael could tell her irritation level was at a peak. She was nervous doing this investigative work on her father, more nervous than he was, he ventured to guess.

"This is Dr. Warren," Carla said after a moment. "He's one of my father's best friends. They've known each other for years."

Michael gently returned the photo to its exact place on the shelf. "Dr. Warren? Isn't he that famous cancer researcher?"

"Yes," Carla said matter-of-factly. "He's an oncologist who has tried various alternative treatments to cancer with some success." She continued to read some papers in folders from the briefcase.

"This stuff is a lot of mumbo-jumbo," she said with a sigh. Then she looked up. "Why do you ask about Dr. Warren?"

"Just curious," Michael said. "I don't want to rule anything out because it's familiar to your father. There could be a connection with anything. That's what I've learned."

"And you're one of the best, so I'm told," Carla smiled. Oh, when she smiled like that. Man. He wished she'd grant him that smile more often.

He and Carla figured they had roughly two hours to search the house, if they wanted to play it safe. Luckily, today was Josephine's day off. They had the place entirely to themselves. Michael was still having trouble reining his mind in to the task. Carla had on a bright stretchy neon pink T-shirt that showed every luscious curve, and some short cut off jeans that made her rounded rear assets look amazing. She was leaning over the desk, totally oblivious to his gaze, or she'd be beating him with the nearest thing available about now.

Michael was finished looking through the bookshelf. Other than the picture of Dr. Warren, there was nothing of interest. He browsed through a stack of magazines found in a large whicker basket by the leather chair. Mostly women's magazines. They must belong to Carla's stepmother. A magazine on deep sea fishing caught his eye, and he leafed through it. He looked up occasionally as he turned the pages, to watch Carla shift from leg to leg, exposing a different angle each time to her upper thighs. Her long hair flowed down her back like gold. He was dying.

Suddenly she jerked her head up from what she was so intently reading. "Michael. I think I found something!"

Michael quickly closed the magazine and tossed it back into the pile with the others in the basket.

"What?" He was instantly at her side, leaning beside her looking at the paper she held.

"I don't know. But I think this is very interesting," she said.

Michael read what she was holding. It was a brief for the executive vice president of Simon and Simon, one of the largest pharmaceutical companies in the country. Hell, in the world, for that matter.

"Your father is representing Simon and Simon?" Michael asked.

"No. From the looks of this, it looks like he's suing them." Carla pulled the thick folder out of the briefcase and carried it over to the couch. "Let's read through this. Here. You take half."

Michael joined her on the couch and took the stack of papers she gently handed him. "Bossy little wench, aren't you?" he said.

She hardly heard him. She was pouring over the documents already. He had no choice but to join her. For quite a while they sat reading their stacks of documents, the silence broken only with the turning of pages.

After they had carefully read though the entire folder of documents, the picture became clear. The most important documents were several long depositions of executives at Simon and Simon, each denying any wrongdoing by the company in withholding new alternative medication that could help to cure cancer patients. The medication, Zanaton, was researched and developed by Dr. Warren, the depositions said. The plaintiff, Mr. Redfern's client, was an elderly woman who claimed her husband could have survived his colon cancer, if he'd been treated with Zanaton, which happened to be prescribed by Dr. Warren. For some reason, Simon and Simon had denied they carried the medication.

"Ho-boy," Michael said. "This looks like a pretty big fish."

"Sure does," Carla said as she carefully took Michael's half of the papers and put them back in exact order in the folder.

"Anything else that can rival this for interest in his briefcase?"

"Nothing," Carla said. "Everything in there has to do with this case."

Michael stared out the window at the palm leaves glistening in the afternoon sun and at the refection of the pool water dancing on the garden wall. Damn. This was controversial as hell. The media was going to have a field day with this one when and if the story broke. Really big. But how could this connect to Carla? That was the part that puzzled Michael. Without question he needed to do more research on this. Maybe take a trip up to Chicago again.

"You think you can ask your Dad about Dr. Warren. How he's doing? Or ask him what he's working on these days? Maybe we can get a hint from what he says."

"I can try, Michael. But you see how stiff he is. And, like I said, he catches everything. The last thing I want is for him to think I'm snooping on him."

"I still don't see why you can't come out and just tell him what's up with you. That someone's after you. He's your father, for Pete sakes," Michael said.

"You don't get it. There's a lot you don't get about our relationship. He's being so polite and easy on this trip. I think having you and my sister along, he's showing a softer side."

"I'll take your word for it," Michael said. He turned so he could look Carla more fully in the eyes. He could tell she was worried by the way her brow was furrowed, and she was biting her lip like she always did when she fretted.

"Don't worry," he said. "We're going to figure this out. No matter what, we'll get to the bottom of this."

"It's coming back, Michael. My fear. It's like I got to have this little twenty-four hour vacation of not thinking about it all day yesterday. And this…. this research. It's making me think about the night in my office. The man with the gun."

"I know, baby," Michael said. He knew it was a risk to call her baby, but he couldn't help himself. He didn't care what she thought. He just wanted to comfort her. She was going through hell, no doubt about it. He reached over and pulled her gently into his arms, leaning her against him, and engulfing her. She didn't put up the slightest resistance. He was surprised. They sat like that on the couch for a while in silence.

"Michael. I'm so tired." Her voice was muffled in his chest.

"I know you are." He gently played with one long strand of her hair.

"I know I shouldn't say this. But, what would I do without you?"

Michael laughed. "What do you mean, you shouldn't say that? Hey? Don't I deserve to hear some of your more positive thoughts?"

"Yes. You do deserve to," she said somberly. Michael squeezed her a little tighter. She was so serious. So quiet. She could be frightening in her pensive moods. He wondered what all went on inside that brain of hers. She had a very dark side, and when she went there, she was closed off from the world. The mood was coming over her now, and he wanted to ward it off. He wanted to see her smile again, the magical smile, and laugh like she did last night at dinner. Besides, hell, they were in Florida.

"Let's go down to the beach, you want to?" he said with a grin.

"I don't know, Michael. Last time you asked that… it got me in trouble." She ventured a smile.

"No monkey business this time. I told you that. I'm back to being your one and only private eye, best friend and confident. Honest." Michael held his hands up as if to show he wasn't hiding anything.

"Okay," she said. There. There was that sparkle in her eye that he loved. "Let's go collect shells. We have to anyway, since we said we'd do that while my father was gone."

"All right, then," Michael said. "Should we change into our swimsuits?" he raised an eyebrow.

"Not at the same time," she said primly. "I'll change first and meet you by the pool."

"Sounds good to me," he said. But inside he was aching. This grand house. Alone. *With her!* If only they could not wear suits at all. He shook his head to shake off the image of her naked breasts floating just below the surface of the water.

Carla's bikini was just like in the song. Itsy bitsy, yellow, and polka-dotted. She had been so excited showing him the seashells for which Sanibel and Captiva were famous, she had forgotten to be the prude she'd set out to be last night. Kneeling in the sand, she was busy sorting shells and arranging them in front of her. When she had gotten too hot from the glaring sun, she had peeled off her shirt and then her shorts, like a distracted child, who's busy building a sand castle.

Michael's breath caught in his throat. "Have mercy on a guy," he said.

Carla smiled and looked at him wide-eyed as she nestled back down into the sand to continue sorting the shells. "What? You've never seen a girl in a bikini before?"

"Not a girl like you," he said. He was desperately trying to keep his eyes off of her.

"See this one?" she said, as she held up a small delicate shell shaped like a cone. He knew what she was up to. Her usual. She was changing the subject. "This one is probably my all time favorite. It's called an agiler."

"Very pretty," Michael said. He could care less about the shell. "All of them are pretty." He looked at her careful display of shells on the sand.

She looked up at him and smiled. She was squinting from the bright sun. "You don't care a bit," she said accusatorily. "I can tell."

"I'd care if one was hanging from a chain around your neck," he said.

"Cute."

Michael smiled. This woman. This girl. She was beyond his dreams. He wanted to take her swimming.

He nodded to the water. "Let's go in. Want to? It's so hot out here."

She continued smiling at him with a look of speculation. He could feel the gears in her brain churning.

He reached over and gently took the shell from her slim fingers and placed it by the others. He stood up and extended his hand to help her up. "Come on. There's nothing to figure out about this. Let's go in the water."

She still knelt there, quizzically looking at him. He guessed she thought he'd try to get fresh with her in the water. She had no idea. In all actuality, he was glad the rest of the family was on the way down and that there were only two days left of this trip. He wasn't going to be able to survive this level of stimulation much longer.

"Not coming?" he asked, still extending his hand.

"No," she said. Her laugh was a true giggle. This time, she was playing with him.

"In that case," he said. "I'll have to carry you over my shoulder." And he bent down to scoop her up.

"No! Michael!" She squealed and scrambled backwards, sand flying as she went. "No!" she shrieked, as she got up and ran toward the water. She was fast on her feet, but he caught her easily and lifted her in his arms. She kicked her legs and pummeled his chest as he waded into the water with her. Soon he was in waist deep and he tossed her down into the water with a splash.

She came up with her long hair, streaming wet behind her, blinking the water from her eyes. "You rotten thug!" she said. And she splashed him.

"A thug, now, am I?" He leaned back into the water and floated on his back. The temperature was perfect. The water was clear and pale blue.

"A thug with one thing on his mind," she said with a laugh, and she dove under the water again and came back up.

"Tell me it's not on your mind. I dare you," he said. He was relaxing back in the water. The saltwater was holding him up with no effort at all.

She stood up again in the water, several feet from him. Her bikini was wet, clinging to her in a delicious way, water trickling down into her cleavage. Her hair was wet all around her like a mermaid's. She was staring at him hard. The sky and the straight blue horizon behind her couldn't compete with the color and intensity of her eyes.

"I'm not going to say," she said, and she tossed her head a little and laughed. But, he knew. He could tell. One thing he never missed was when a woman wanted him. And this was beginning to be the only woman he wanted to have. He could feel his heart hopelessly falling, and he didn't care. He floated on his back and watched as Carla swam away from him in sure, solid stokes, her thin arms sparkling with water in the sun.

South Seas Plantation, on the tip of Captiva, had a five-star restaurant, and that's where Mr. Redfern had made reservations to take them all for a late dinner. Karen and Brad had flown in late in the afternoon while Michael and Carla were still at the beach. When Michael and Carla had come back, everyone was taking a rest, so they hadn't seen them yet.

Michael stood looking in the mirror, tugging on his tie to get it snugged up right. The darn thing. He felt like he was choking. Who the hell would dress formally on a tropical island? Who in their right mind?

Just then Carla came out of the bathroom. She was dressed in a shimmering, satin turquoise dress, short and tight on her thighs. She had on delicate white high-healed sandals and her hair was in a bun, with a few ringlets streaming down. Her pink lipstick glowed as she smiled at him, sending his head spinning.

"What are you up to?" she asked as she cocked her head. He stood scowling and holding the tie in his hand. Then he lifted it as if he were going to hang himself from it. He let out a gagging sound.

"Oh, stop. Who said you have to wear a tie?"

"You said it was formal."

"It is formal. But this is an island, remember? A remote island."

"Will your father be wearing one?"

"Would it matter?

"Hell, yes."

"He'll be wearing one. But that's just the way he is."

"Then, I'm wearing one.

"Fine," she said coyly. And she twirled to leave the room, a wisp of floral perfume lingering behind her. "I'll meet you in the sitting room. I can't wait to talk to Karen."

"No, wait." Michael said as he tightened up his tie. "I'm coming."

"You look phenomenal," he said to her, as they walked down the hall, her heels clicking on the big tiles. He offered her his arm, and she took it. She felt like a princess on his arm. It was wonderful.

"There they are!" Karen exclaimed as they entered the white living room. White carpeting. White furniture. It was stark, but beautiful, Michael thought on first impression.

"At last, Michael! I've been dying to meet you," Karen said as she ran up to give Carla a big hug, and then one to Michael. He subjected himself with a smile. When she was finished with him, Karen turned to Carla for the introduction.

"Michael," Carla said with a smile. "This is Karen and Brad Mahoney."

Brad extended his big hand and gave a tight grip to Michael's. "How're doin', man?" Brad looked like he'd barely shaved. And without question, he wasn't wearing a tie. Michael suddenly felt more relaxed. Maybe he should dare to take his tie off, too? Why was he such a nervous wreck about these little details?

"Where's Daddy?" Carla asked, looking over her shoulder, slightly edgy.

"Oh, he's coming," Karen said. "Alexis called. I think he might have spent some time talking to her. Put him behind."

"Hard to believe he's not ready at eight o'clock sharp," Carla said. The two girls laughed. They looked a little alike, Michael thought. Both pretty. Same smile. But even if Karen weren't pregnant, she wasn't as slim as Carla, and she had short brown hair. She was wearing a red maternity sundress and flat brown sandals. Much more casual than Carla.

"You guys are going to love South Seas," Karen said. She had a bubbly way of talking that put Michael at ease. "It's our favorite spot. Right, Carla?"

"It is," Carla agreed with a smile and a nod.

The two sisters stood beaming at each other like they hadn't seen each other in years. They wrapped their arms around each other and sauntered over to the love seat where they sat down together side-by-side whispering and talking, and patting each other's legs. Michael was left standing with Brad.

"So, how's it going?" Brad asked. Michael knew he meant, with the father.

"Not as bad as I thought," Michael said. "Could be worse."

"Stick around," Brad said with a laugh, and he nudged Michael. Michael was liking Brad already. He felt somehow familiar.

"I'm hoping to," Michael said with a nod.

Brad caught his meaning. "Wise choice," Brad said. "She's a gem."

"Stubborn, though."

"That's putting it lightly. If you think Carla's bad. You should see Karen. She beats me black and blue."

Both girls suddenly looked up from where they were comparing nail colors with fingers outstretched. "What was that?" Karen asked.

"Nothing, honey," Brad said as he winked at Michael. "I'm just telling him what a great gal I have."

Karen smiled at him. "Okay, then don't let us stop you."

Carla looked at Michael and tilted her head back and laughed. It was great to see her so happy. Having her sister here was really making a difference for her, he could see that.

"Where's the baby?" Michael suddenly thought to ask. "I've been looking forward to meeting him."

"He's down for bed already," Karen said. "Dad hired Josephine to come over and babysit while we go out."

At the mention of his name, Max appeared around the corner in white dinner slacks, white shirt, a navy blue and white pinstriped sear-sucker jacket and a navy tie. He looked like Cuban royalty, Michael thought.

Dinner was elegant and the food was amazing. Everyone ordered seafood and each dish was more gourmet and surprising than the next. Several waiters hovered around the table, filling the water glasses each time anyone took a sip. The wine was poured with even more regularity. Outside torches flickered, reflecting off of the royal palms. Michael spent much of the night listening. He couldn't help but feel like an imposter. He wasn't really "with" the family like the others thought. He wasn't Carla's boyfriend. He was a spy. Halfway through dinner, he felt an ache hit him. He wished he were a part of this family, somehow, and he wondered if he ever would be.

Carla was so refined and comfortable eating in a setting like this. She sparkled like the diamond earrings she wore, and the small diamond pendant around her neck. Michael felt like a clumsy klutz next to her. Sure, he knew which of the five forks he should use, and in what order. Sure, he knew how to keep his napkin in his lap. But he wasn't comfortable. His family was more the bar-b-que in the back yard type. Hot dogs and potato salad on the picnic table. Michael's father was a loading dock foreman on the harbor, always wore his napkin under his chin.

Michael couldn't help but watch Max Redfern as he chuckled and asked questions of his daughters. He sure didn't seem like a man who didn't care about them. He wondered what made the girls so adamant and negative about him. He wondered what Carla had fought with him about, and why. If he could figure out some of these things, he might have some insight into her, he thought. He might understand her tough shell and her protectiveness about her heart.

After dinner they headed back home along the Captiva road in Max's Jaguar, winding along the shore where white waves crashed on the sand. Brad sat in front with Max, and Michael had the privilege of sitting in back in the company of the ladies. Halfway home, he stretched his arm out behind Carla's head, and she leaned against him comfortably. Sometimes she surprised him. She felt so soft and pliant against him. He loved it when she was able to let down with him.

When they got back to the house, Karen excused herself for bed. She said it was way past her bedtime. Being pregnant she couldn't keep her eyes opened. Max said his goodnights as well. That left Michael, Brad and Carla. Carla winced at Michael. He knew she was tired too, but Michael really wanted to hang out.

"Mind if I stay up, sugars?" he asked Carla in front of Brad.

"No, not at all," she said as she reached down and took off her shoes. "These things are killing me," she said. Her face was beginning to show some sunburn from the afternoon in the sun. "I think I'm going to head back to bed."

"Sure," Michael said.

"You two don't get into trouble now," she said, and she smiled gently and rubbed his shoulder. She looked beat. He watched as she padded away, holding her shoes in one hand and her little dinner purse in the other. She walked with her slim legs so straight and sure. Her back held tall. There was a slight sway to her hips. He couldn't take his eyes from her until she was out of sight, and when he looked back up, he noticed Brad was watching him with a smile.

"Want a beer?" he asked.

"Thought you'd never ask," Michael said.

"Come on," Brad said. "There's a refrigerator stocked with beer in the garage," he said.

"You're kidding?" Michael said.

"No, I'm not kidding. Is this Shangri-La, or what?"

Michael chuckled as he followed Brad out through the breezeway and into the garage, loosening his tie and pulling it off as he went.

When they were stretched out in lounge chairs out by the pool, cold beers in hand, Michael felt himself relax for the first time in days.

"Want a smoke?" Brad asked, extending a pack of Marlboros.

"No thanks," Michael said. "Trying to kick the habit."

"Know what you mean," Brad said as he palmed a match and his cigarette glowed in the dark.

They both sat in silence for a moment. The cold Heineken was great. The stars looked brilliant. Billions of them.

"Some place," Brad said.

"You're not kidding," Michael said. He thought he could hear his own Baltimore accent in Brad's voice.

"Where you from?" he asked.

"Me?" Brad said. "I'm from Baltimore. Near the harbor."

"You're kidding! *I knew it*!" Michael couldn't help but laugh out loud. "I knew you felt familiar for some reason."

"Went to Dunbar," Brad said, taking a long tug from his beer bottle.

"Dunbar," Michael shook his head. "Damn, they had a football team."

"I was on that team," Brad said.

"A hell of a team," Michael trailed off.

"Then you must be from Walbrook," Brad said.

"Your deadly rival," Michael said. The two men laughed.

"What year? 1988?" Brad asked.

"Yeah, man. We must have played each other."

"No kidding. You offense or defense?"

"Defense lineman"

"I was a lineman. Offense."

"You must have been the guy who broke my arm!" Brad said, and they both laughed again.

Brad held out his bottle for Michael to toast.

"To Homecoming of '88."

"Oh, yeah," Michael said as their bottles touched.

"You empty?" Brad said. "I'll go get us a couple more."

"I'm always empty," Michael smiled.

"Now we're talking."

After Brad came back with the beers and settled back in his chair, he ventured the question Michael was expecting at some point.

"So. What's the real story with you and Carla? Are you her P.I., or her boyfriend?"

"What did Carla tell you?" Michael was hoping to get any information he could.

Brad paused while he lit another cigarette.

"P.I.," Brad said as he exhaled smoke. "That's what she said, anyway."

"But you think otherwise?" Michael asked.

"Yeah." Brad nodded. "She looks interested. Definitely."

"You think so?" Michael knew he was beginning to sound too much like a schoolboy with these questions. But what the hell.

"Oh, yeah. She's a cold one. But she's warming up real good to you," Brad offered.

"Wow. If this is warm…"

"My God. She roasts men on a spit, I'm telling you. At least the little bits of stories I get from Karen, or that I overhear when they're talking."

"That doesn't surprise me."

Michael was quiet a moment. He wondered if he should ask much more about Carla. He wondered how much would get back to her. He wondered if Brad would tell all of what they talked about to his wife.

"But you seem good together, you know?" Brad nodded. He sounded genuine.

"How so?"

"I don't know. She seems calmer around you. She looks like she's in love to me, man."

"That's hard to say," Michael said. He was feeling sorry for himself again. Too many beers and he knew he had to go back to share a bed with her and keep his hands off.

Michael decided he had nothing to lose. He was going to go for the big question. "What's up with the father? Why do the girls hate him so much?"

"Aw," Brad said. "They don't hate him as much as you'd think."

"Seems pretty rough to me," Michael said.

"No. They're just hurt," Brad offered. "When he remarried a couple of years ago, he got kind of cold toward them. They felt pushed away. You know how it is."

"And the stepmother? Is she really that bad?"

"A regular debutante, but polite."

"I know the type."

"You'll see when you meet her."

"When will that be?"

"I don't know," Brad said. "Next Christmas?" and he smiled.

"I hope so," Michael said.

9

She was gone again. When he rolled over in the morning without opening his eyes, and reached over to see if she was there, he felt nothing. Just a flat bed. He sat up. How did she do that? Slipped out each morning without even waking him up. *And he called himself a private eye!"*

He stumbled to the bathroom, looked in the mirror and rubbed his hand over his beard. His head was thumping away at his temples. Claw gripping his skull. How many beers did he and Brad have? He couldn't remember. But then, they'd also had all that wine at dinner. He'd better nip this hangover in the bud before he hit that harsh sun. He reached for the bottle of pain reliever and chased a couple of them down with a tall glass of water.

After he got dressed, he went to look for her. When he went out into the house, it was empty. Not a peep coming from anywhere. He wandered from room to room. He finally found Josephine in the kitchen, cutting up a whole pineapple on a big chopping board.

"They are all at the beach," she said with a smile, waving the knife. "All of them. And the bambino." She went back to chopping. "Except for Miss Carla," she said as an afterthought. "Miss Carla not go with them. She is at the pool."

Michael thanked Josephine and went down the back hallway and out the door into the garden. He heard her voice even before he could see her. She was speaking softly as he walked up the wide garden steps to the pool, hands in his pockets. There was something about her voice. It was smoothness. He heard it right away. Who could she be talking to?

Her back to him, sitting in a chair with her legs outstretched on a stool, red toenails gleaming in the morning sunlight. She was wearing white shorts and a white tank top. He noticed her shoulders were sunburned as he came up behind her. She still didn't hear him.

"I told you," she paused. Her head was down, cradling the phone in her neck. "I'll call," she said softly. Then she must have sensed his arrival because she turned and smiled at him.

"Listen. I've got to go now." There was a long pause as she listened to something from the other end. Her face was distant and she looked out into the yard.

"I can't say. I'll have to call you," she said again.

She looked at Michael and held up a pointer finger, signaling she'd be right off the phone. Michael decided to give her a little privacy and started walking slowly around the pool, looking down into its depths and watching the play of light on the edges. He heard more muffled talking, but he couldn't make out the words. She was keeping her voice low. Then from the other side of the pool he heard her say, "me too," right before she said "goodbye" and put the phone on the table next to her.

"Good morning, Michael," she said with a bright smile. She was in an unusually cheerful mood.

"Was that pumpkin head?" Michael asked from across the pool. He didn't mean to say it so abruptly, and without even saying good morning. But every muscle in his body was tensing involuntarily.

"Pumpkin head?" she said, her head tilting to one side.

"You know who I mean." He felt angry and he knew his voice sounded it.

"Why don't you come over here so we don't have to yell," she said calmly. She was still reclining in her chair with her feet on the table. He felt incredibly annoyed by how seductively relaxed she looked. She was relaxed from talking to *him*, he thought. Her ex-"can't-let-go-of-him" boyfriend.

"I'll yell if I want to," he said raising his voice, hands still in his pockets. Even the sunshine was annoying him right now. The sound of a seagull screeching overhead was grating on his nerves.

Carla sat looking at him with a dazed look. He couldn't see the subtle play of expression on her face from where he was standing. Was she laughing at him or was she angry? Either way, it wasn't going to help matters for him, he thought. He wanted to go over and shake her.

"Excuse me, I was talking on a personal call." Her voice was cold. "Is that a problem for you? Does being my private investigator allow you access to all personal interactions I have?"

She was going to play like that, he thought. The knife was well placed, and had gone in smoothly.

"That's all I am to you?" He knew the hurt in his voice was ringing clear as the morning sky.

She was silent.

"Answer, Carla. That's all I am to you? Your private investigator?"

She got up and walked around the pool to him. She looked him in the eye. Now that she was closer he could see it wasn't totally anger that she felt.

"No," she said softly. She reached out and touched his arm softly. Her eyes looked pained.

Michael shook her hand off with a shrug of his shoulder. "Then what am I? Tell me. Tell me exactly," he said. I'm acting like a child, he thought. I'm a fool now, in front of her. No control.

There was a slight shake of her head before she stepped back a few steps and looked down. The sun shone on the top of her head. She had her hair back in a long braid. She was silent for what seemed like an eternity.

"I don't know, Michael. I told you that I don't know how I feel," she said. "I never hid that I was confused."

Michael felt boiling heat come up the back of his neck. "Confused about *him*?" he stammered. "Confused about *him*?" Each time he said the word "him," he visualized finding this guy and pounding his face into pulp.

"Confused about how I feel," she said, still with her head down. She was digging her big toe into a little hole in the cement.

"Confused about how you feel about me, compared to him?" Michael demanded. He wanted clarification. Was she confused about all men involved in this picture? Or was she just confused about the ex-boyfriend?

He couldn't control his questioning now. He threw another one out before he knew she even had a chance to answer. These were rhetorical anyway.

"Was that him on the phone?" he asked sharply, as if they both didn't know who it had been.

He was controlling his breathing. He felt like he could pound on the brick wall behind him. He knew this wasn't his better side. And he surely didn't want to show it to Carla, man-hater that she was already. But here it was, seeping out unrestrained. His jealousy was raging beyond his control and taking him by surprise.

Carla looked at him and her lips tightened. "Listen," she hissed. "I don't have to take this from you. I don't have to take twenty questions about who I was talking to, or why."

"Just admit it. Will you at least give me that? Admit you were talking to him. Your so-called ex-boyfriend."

"I don't have to *admit* anything," Carla said. "I haven't committed a crime." She stood her ground and glared at him. He could see she the anger building up in her face. Her eyes were blazing.

"Then tell me if he called you, or if you called him."

She was silent for a moment staring at him. He honestly wondered what she would do. She looked like she wanted to hit him. That would have been easier to take than her silence.

"You're an asshole," she said through her teeth. The look in her eyes held pure disdain. She turned and ran around the pool and down the steps. He thought he heard her crying, but he wasn't sure.

"Just be adult enough to admit it," Michael yelled out after her. He couldn't stop himself.

She turned around fast at the bottom of the steps and looked up at him, her long braid whipping around with her. "*You* be adult, Michael. You are the one who is jealous for no reason." And then she turned and was gone, her braid bobbing behind her.

Michael kicked the chair. He kicked it hard and it fell over backwards.

"*Son of a bitch*," he hissed under his breath. Now what the hell was he going to do? Any minute the others would be back, and he'd have this terrible look on his face and no way to hide it.

He peeled off his shirt and threw it hard onto a chair. He went to the deep end of the pool and dove in. The water was cooler than he'd expected it to be from the morning air. It rushed across his face and past his ears as he took a long dive to the bottom. When he came up, he gasped for breath and bobbed on the surface a little.

The sky was cloudless. A perfect azure blue. He turned onto his back and kicked back and forth up and down the pool. He kicked harder and harder. His breath was heaving. Water was pounding in his ears.

After a while he stopped kicking and floated silently. He looked up at the shiny green palm branches. A gray seagull came and perched on the top of the light post and stared at him.

"What are you staring at, old man?" he said to it. The seagull stared back at him with beady unblinking eyes.

God, she made him mad. He didn't know who he was mad at the most. Himself. Her. Or that son-of-a-bitch she still loved. What was it she had said about that ex- punk-ass? *"She still had feelings for him?"* Whoever he was, that scum wasn't going to keep his slimy grip on her. That's for sure. Not now. Not after her body had shown him her attraction last night.

But had her mind shown him she cared? Her heart? If he really stopped and thought about it, she hadn't ever said anything about falling in love with him. The closest she had come was in the library yesterday when she'd said she didn't know what she'd do without him. You could say that about a good vacuum, or a trusty car. You could say that about your tax accountant.

Come on, man. Get it into your head. She doesn't care like you do. You seduced her, and she responded. Big deal. You could probably fairly well seduce any woman if you wanted to.

Michael slogged over to the steps in the shallow end of the pool and sat down. The seagull screeched and took off low over the house. The pool looked like a giant diamond in the sun, random rays reflecting everywhere. Suddenly Michael wasn't so sure about what he was trying to do here. He wasn't sure at all. He put his head in his hands. *How do I seduce her heart?*

Carla had to get out of there. Away from the house. Away from him. Tears were stinging and she wanted to cry so badly, but she'd be damned if he saw her do it. She stifled a sob as she ran out to the front yard. She was trying to think of what to do. Take a jog? Too hot. The sun was already pounding down and making the place a stream bath. She walked down the drive and across the street to the beach.

No sign of her family in either direction. No sign of anyone for that matter, except a small figure in the distance walking and stopping to crouch over from time to time. A shell gatherer.

Maybe Daddy had taken Karen, Brad and the baby down to Sanibel where the waves were quieter. Or maybe they had taken a drive through Ding Darling Wildlife Refuge to look for alligators.

She was glad no one was on the beach. She needed some time. She looked behind her to make sure Michael hadn't followed her. No sign of him. Just thinking of the look on his face and his drill sergeant attitude made the blood boil in her veins. *Where did he come off?*

He put a whole new definition on jealous, and she'd dealt with plenty of jealousy in her time. She used to think it was her looks that caused it. In high school, Carla had felt as if she were a prize or an object, to be shown off or guarded. Now that she was older, she wasn't so sure if men were any different. That was one of her reasons for not committing, not getting close. That was one of the reasons she'd ended up with Todd. He wasn't controlling, by any means. And that was because he wasn't committal, just like her. But that option also had its downsides, as she knew all too well.

If she even dared get close to a man, they had a way of seeping into her skin, without her even knowing it, and before she knew what to do about it, they were trying to control everything about her – just like her father. She'd gotten out of her father's clutches and she wasn't about to sign up for more like it. She had passed up on all sorts of things just to make it out on her own, where her father couldn't have a single say in what she did. She didn't take his money, so she didn't have to take his crap.

And now Michael. *Michael!* Just saying his name made her want to scream. She was hating this ugly feeling inside of her. She wanted it to go away. She tried to focus on something else.

The beach was so beautiful. White sand. Little shells dotting along the water line. Each one looked like it was from a shell shop. Almost fake. She bent down to pick up one or two here and there. The pink and purple scallop shells always caught her eye. And the shiny olive-shaped shells were nice to hold. She saw one now and picked it up, rubbing her thumb against it like one of those soothing smooth rocks people keep on their desks for stress.

Stress wasn't the word for it. Not only was she afraid for her life. But now that she was mad at Michael, she didn't even know if she wanted him to stay on the case. If she had enough money, she could just pay him off. Despite the fact that she threw it in his face constantly, she wasn't able to pay him, except on a payment plan of some sort. Maybe she didn't really need his help after all. The police could keep working on it. And now that she had this clue about the pharmaceutical company, maybe she'd see if Lieutenant Dirkson would look into it.

She looked up at the horizon. "Here's how God draws a straight line," her mother used to say. It sure was straight all right. It made her feel that there must be an answer to everything, if this kind of exactness existed in the world. She sure hoped so, anyway.

Todd was another problem she had to figure out. He had called her this morning while she was sitting by the pool after breakfast, waiting for Michael to wake up. Everyone in the family is an early riser because of the baby, and of course because of Max's "Benjamin Franklin Plan." They'd been up and dressed and had eaten breakfast before nine, then were biting at the bit to do some kind of activity.

Carla hadn't wanted to leave without Michael. She wanted to let him sleep in. He had looked like such an angel lying there, with his curls askew. His hair got more curly when he slept, and she liked it. She knew he was up until the wee hours of the morning because she'd felt when he'd crawled into the bed, smelling of beer, feint cigarette smoke and his unique spicy smell. She hadn't let him know she was awake. She had actually been very much awake.

She had been thinking of his touch and his kiss, and wishing she could have some more of it. She was beginning to feel safer with him than she'd ever felt with anyone. She couldn't believe how honest he was with his feelings. His heart was right out there, on his sleeve. She loved him for that. She was starting to feel so much about him. He always had a kind word. Who couldn't fall for a guy like that? And especially one packaged in a Greek god's body?

But now she knew something about him she had to factor in. This green monster of his. How dare he! She wasn't his wife. She wasn't even his girlfriend. You'd think she'd have just committed the worst of all crimes, just for taking a call from her ex-boyfriend. And yes, he was her ex.

Todd had been sweet on the phone. He was missing her. Worried about her. He was hoping that the break-up was just a temporary one. They'd been through this before. But she knew it wouldn't be temporary. She had to end it with him somewhere. There were so many reasons why she had to break it off for good. She'd made up her mind about him. But he still tugged on her heart. And she thought he probably always would. A fatal attraction.

Carla sat down and curled her knees up to her and hugged them. She looked out to sea. Far out. It had such a calming effect. She took a deep sigh.

Too bad Michael hadn't given her a chance to tell him about Todd's call herself. She had been planning on it. But when he started in like that, it only made her want to keep everything to herself. And now, he'd probably never know what she really thought. He probably thought all sorts of bad things.

But how could she be responsible for what he thinks? Besides, she was crazy to think anything between them could ever work out now that she knew about his jealousy. She was not a good candidate to deal with jealousy. And it meant now that she and Michael were as incompatible as oil and vinegar. She regretted she even let herself get close to him in the first place.

###

By the time Carla came back from the beach, the sun was high in the sky. No cars in the drive. She didn't hear any water splashing from the pool, so she decided to check inside. The whoosh of cool air-conditioning felt great as she opened the front door.

Josephine was in the kitchen arranging some flowers in a vase. Carla went to the refrigerator for some lemonade. She poured herself a tall glass and chugged it down, then wiped her mouth with the back of her hand.

"Wow. I didn't realize I was so thirsty," she said, smiling at Josephine. "Where is everybody?"

"They all came home and waited for you, for very long time. Waited and waited, but baby was restless. So they all went down to Mr. Redfern's boat. Your father say he will pick you up on dock. Hurry, he say."

"Michael went with them?"

"*Si*," Josephine winked. "The nice young man went too. Very handsome," she said, and she clucked in her check.

Carla scowled. How was she going to spend the day on her father's boat with Michael. She'd have to talk to him. This was going to be horrible.

"When did they leave?" she asked.

"An hour ago. Your father say he will stay near to dock and pick you up. He wants to go over to Turtle Island."

"It's already two o'clock. I was out there longer than I thought," Carla said, as she looked at the clock.

"You supposed to take Mrs. Redfern's car to dock. It's in garage."

"Thanks, Josephine," Carla said as she grabbed car keys from the meticulously labeled key rack by the garage door. Her stepmother's "old beat up car" for driving at the beach

117

was a BMW convertible. Several years old, which made it a "junker" for Alexis, no doubt. Carla rolled the sunroof opened. She reached up and pulled her hair from the hair bands holding it firmly to her head and in a braid. She loosened it all out and swung her head from side to side to set it free and revved the car out of the drive.

Carla took the curves fast along the outside road to the tip of Captiva. No cars in sight, and she shifted up to fifth. The car hummed. Carla laughed and tilted her head back.

Her father had said to her when she left home that he had lavished her enough with the good life that she'd never settle for less. She'd find a rich man who could give her the manner of life to which she was accustomed. She'd thought he was a tiny-minded, materialistic hog, at the time. Most of the time, she didn't miss "the good life," in any way, because so much of what she loved in life, money couldn't buy. A good friendship, for one thing. To kiss a little baby. To smell the ocean. A good book. To hear great music. She didn't want for more.

But she had to admit. This island. With this house. This car. Made her have to think a little. It was a life she could easily use now and then. But it wasn't her life anymore. Visiting with her father had been nicer than she thought it would be. But she didn't feel at home. She didn't feel she was even part of her father's family. It was so hard to relate to him, anymore. He focused on entirely different things than she did. Annual symphony tickets. Gutting Alexis' lakeside condo in Chicago when he moved in, and completely redoing it, from scratch. Alexis liked to redo lots of things that were already in fine shape. And Daddy was right along with her on all of it. Always bigger and better. Always something more to have. Carla thought it was a big waste.

The marina came into view up ahead. Masts bobbing in the Florida sun. A short distance out she saw a cabin cruiser anchored. She parked the convertible and closed up the sunroof then jogged down to the dock and walked quickly to its end and waved to the boat. Arms waved back. Then she heard Karen's loud voice laughing across the water and calling her name. Carla waved both of her arms high over her head. She heard a honk come from the boat's loud horn and she heard her father start the engine to come over and get her.

When the boat pulled up alongside the dock, Michael was busy tying it off and putting bumpers between the boat and the dock. Looking all official, like a mate, she thought. He reached a hand over to help her step on board, but she declined and didn't even look him in the eye, but bounced onto the deck with sure footing.

"Hey, troops!" she called. "You guys are a busy bunch today."

"We've been busy, but where have you been?" Brad asked raising his can of beer toward her. "We keep missing you."

"I'm sorry. I kept looking for you, too, but I couldn't find you."

"Luckily we found Michael here. He didn't even know where you were or when you'd be back." Brad raised a curious brow.

Carla wondered what her father was thinking. His back was to the group as he held the wheel. She couldn't tell any emotion coming from him, one way or another. Probably in all likelihood he was just happy as a clam to be on his boat.

"Sorry. I was looking for shells and the time got away from me, I guess."

"Well, sit yourself down, pop a cold one, and get relaxed because your father is going to sail us to Turtle Island for dinner," Brad said.

"Really?" Carla asked. She looked over at Karen who nodded a sign of approval.

"Really and truly," Max said as he turned his back slightly. "I haven't been there for years. I thought you'd like to take a little trip." He looked like a real captain in white shorts, white shirt and a cap.

"Sounds wonderful," Carla said. She plopped herself down on a recliner next to Karen.

"Want a beer?" Brad asked as he rumbled through some ice in a cooler.

"No, thank you," Carla said. "You got a coke or lemonade, though?"

"Here ya go, party girl," Brad said, handing her a coke.

"Can't drink alcohol in the sun," Carla said as she squinted up at Brad. "Gives me a rotten headache."

"Doesn't bother me a bit," Brad said. "Or Michael. We've been kickin' em down."

Carla looked over at Michael who stood with one leg up on the bench, leaning on his elbow, looking out to sea, a can of beer loosely held in one of his hands. His mood was more pensive than she'd ever seen it. It almost made her worried. What if he was madder at her than she was at him? That idea hadn't even occurred to her.

As if he could read her mind, he turned his head slowly, looking directly into her eyes. They were not angry eyes, but sad and deep and heavy. He looked terrible. It made her heart ache, and it surprised her. She didn't know what to do, so she bowed her head to avert his gaze.

"Where's Sammy?" Carla said, suddenly realizing he wasn't around.

"Down below, sleeping," Karen said. "We wore him out completely this morning, swimming and on the beach. He went nuts."

"I'll bet he loved it," Carla said, with a smile.

"Little guy is down for the count," Brad said.

###

The afternoon sun was high and bright as the Algonquin, Max Redfern's forty-eight foot cabin cruiser, slipped out of the marina and out into the gulf waters surrounding Captiva and neighboring islands.

"It won't take us long to get there," Max said. "Maybe a couple of hours." He was totally absorbed in steering the boat, monitoring the speed, charting the course. Carla took off her T-shirt and shorts and laid back in her bathing suit to catch some rays. Out of complete emotional exhaustion, she must have drifted off. When she woke up, Karen was dozing under her big sunhat, and Brad was talking to Max, sitting on a stool beside him. Michael had disappeared to the back of the boat somewhere. She couldn't see him from where she was sitting.

"You'd better get some sunscreen on," Brad said as he looked over.

Carla wasn't wearing her bikini, but a slightly more modest two-piece swimming suit. Navy with white trim. She looked down to see her pale white belly now a scarlet red, as well as her arms and legs. She could feel the pain starting to set in already.

"Yes, indeed, get some of the stronger sunscreen from down below," Max added. "I think there's some in the cabinet by the sink."

"While you're down there, check on the baby, will you?" Karen said. "Michael went down a minute ago to get him up from his nap."

Carla winced as she got out of her chair. She forgot how potent this tropical sun could be. She should have been more careful. *Michael was down taking care of the baby? This was a new twist.* She made her way to the back of the boat and down the skinny passage steps to the interior. It was one big room, serving as a living room, bedroom and mini-kitchen. There was a small table for two, some chairs, a refrigerator, and a big foldout bed in the very back.

Michael was lying on the bed with Sammy beside him. Sammy was touching Michael's nose and laughing.

"Now, where is Sammy's nose?" Michael asked.

Sammy grinned and reached over to touch his own nose with his pudgy forefinger.

"Very good, little tiger," Michael said, and he put his big hand on Sammy's tummy and jiggled him a little. Sammy squealed with glee.

Carla knew Michael probably saw her come down, but he hadn't looked up or acknowledged her yet. She stood hesitantly on the bottom step and watched. She was amazed. He looked so natural with Sammy. He knew just what to do with him. Most of the men his age that she knew, without kids, didn't have a clue how to even talk to a toddler, let alone how to play with one. In fact, most single men she knew would actually avoid touching a young child or a baby.

Michael looked up with his big brown eyes. He smiled gently, but she could still see the sadness in them she'd seen earlier. No anger. Just sadness.

"Looks like you and Sammy are having some fun," she said. She walked over to the kitchenette and started opening cabinets looking for the sunscreen. She didn't want him to think she came down here just to talk to him.

"Looking for sunscreen?" Michael asked.

"How'd you know?" she said, as she turned toward him.

"Not hard to guess." His eyes took in her belly and legs.

"Yeah. Pretty bad," she said. "It's going to be worse by tonight, I'm guessing."

Michael was lounging so seductively on the bed, his big muscles bulging as he held himself up on his side. He was shirtless with jean cut offs. He looked like a carefree Tom Sawyer.

"Where did you go? We couldn't find you this afternoon," Michael said.

"I was on the beach. I took a long walk." Carla resumed looking for lotion. In the last set of cabinets above the sink, she found some at last.

"Want some help with that?" Michael asked. "I can get your back for you."

"Sure," Carla said, gingerly approaching him. She still felt so awkward about this morning. She was trying to read him. Should she just pretend it didn't happen? She was feeling very confused, now that she was looking at him and his sad eyes. The slow movements he had.

"Turn around," he said when she stood in front of him with the lotion. She felt a cold squeeze of lotion hit her upper back between her shoulder blades.

She waited for him to touch her, almost breathlessly. Why did she want to feel him touch her so badly? Wasn't she angry with him, the jealous jerk?

He began to massage the lotion into her back gently and slowly, moving from her upper back to her shoulders, lifting the straps to her suit and rubbing lotion below them, on her back. She could feel herself relaxing. The tension between them settling. She felt like she did the night he played his little touching game with her. His touch was killing her. She was beginning to feel like once he touched her, she had no choices. She wanted him in every way. The attraction between them was becoming stronger than just a physical chemistry.

She felt a small cold squirt hit her lower back, and then he was massaging gently and deeply. Long after the lotion was in, he was still gently rubbing. She hung her head with relaxation and pleasure.

"That really feels good," she said. He didn't answer, but soon she felt his hands gently on her shoulders, turning her toward him.

He continued to hold her shoulders in his big hands, gently but firmly. Just like the night on the beach. His big soft eyes were looking deeply into hers. She couldn't see anything there to hate.

"I'm sorry, Carla," he said. "I'm sorry I was such an asshole this morning"

Carla didn't expect this. She didn't know what to say. Should she apologize? But she still didn't feel wrong. She met his gaze. He was much more than her private eye. Maybe she was falling in love with him. This day without his teasing smile and his comforting company had felt so lonely and terrible to her. She was right when she had told him she didn't know what she would do without him.

"I'm sorry you were hurt," she said. "I was going to explain the call before you blew up at me."

"It's all right. You are right. I had no right to question you. I did it because…"

"Shhh," Carla said. And she held a finger up to his soft lips. She reached over and gently kissed him on the cheek. "You don't have to tell me now," she said. "Let's talk about it later."

She thought she saw a sparkle appear at the corner of his eye as he smiled a small inquisitive smile at her.

Sammy, who had been quietly watching them, suddenly stood up and lunged toward Michael who quickly caught him before he flew right off the bed onto the floor.

"Whoa there, pal. Where you think you're going?" he said, and he lifted him high above his head. Sammy laughed and squealed. Then Michael put him down on the bed on his back and nuzzled his head into the baby's stomach. This brought even more laughter on Sammy's part.

Carla watched all this in amazement.

"What are you looking at?" Michael asked. His voice was carrying that usual teasing tone she had grown accustomed to.

"You." She said. "You are like Mr. Mom."

"Four of my brothers and sisters already have kids. I'm the favorite uncle."

"You have that many brothers and sisters?"

"Six."

"Wow. You've never said. That's what probably makes you so easy-going."

"Maybe," he said taking the baby's little hands in his and helping him to jump up and down on the bed. Sammy was beside himself with laughter. Michael laughed back at him.

Carla could sense things weren't totally back to normal between them, but at least they weren't icy cold like before.

"Come on, let's take him upstairs," Michael said.

"Wait, we have to change him first."

"I already did," Michael said, and he swung the baby up to his shoulders. Sammy clung onto his hair and grinned as Michael walked bouncily toward the stairwell. There was nothing Carla could do but follow. She grabbed the sunscreen to finish putting on her lotion upstairs.

10

The afternoon cruising the islands near Captiva was mystical and removed from all-the-world. With the little bit of relief, now, between she and Michael, Carla felt like she could relax and enjoy herself. Her father seemed to be absorbing the afternoon as he anchored outside of Cayo Costa so they could float in on rafts and swim the deserted beach and look for shells. He appeared to be content that they were all together again, as a family. It was something they'd been lacking for several years now. For dinner they cruised over to Cabbage Key to eat at the quaint little inn restaurant built in 1938 by playwright and novelist Mary Roberts Rinehart. Everyone who ate there signed a dollar bill and pasted it to the wall, as was the tradition. The walls and ceiling of the place were covered with bills.

Karen and Carla searched for a bill with their name on it that they'd stuck up years ago, but they couldn't find it. Karen thought it was over the doorway. Carla thought it was more near the back window. The others wanted to get on their way, and the baby was fussy, so they had to give up looking for it.

As they headed back to Captiva in the Algonquin, Carla thought to herself, life could not possibly get any better than this.

Everyone was sunburned and exhausted, lounging about in chairs in the back of the boat. The baby had fallen asleep in Karen's arms as she sat rocking him in a lounge. From her chair next to Karen's, Carla could see his long curly eyelashes resting against his rosy cheeks. He looked like a cherub.

Michael was leaning against the rails of the ship, somewhere behind Carla's chair, near enough for her to smell his spice, mixing in with the gulf breeze. He was near enough to touch, she thought, and she could feel the strong urge to do so coming over her. The sunset out over the gulf crept in like a soft halo, displaying brilliant oranges, scarlet, deep reds, finally fading to purple.

As the boat eased its way into the marina slip, Carla's father came up with an idea that totally surprised her. He wanted to know if Michael and she wanted to take the boat out, drop anchor and spend the night.

"I thought you might like to experience the water at night from the boat. It's something Carla and our family used to enjoy years ago," he said to Michael.

How did stuff like this keep happening? Carla thought. The harder she tried to stay clear of getting intimate with Michael, the more fate itself threw them together.

Michael looked over at Carla, not sure how to answer.

She was trying to read in his eyes to figure out what he wanted to do, but she couldn't see anything there, except just plain weariness. His eyes said to her, "It's up to you."

The Mahoneys were gathering their things and debarking. Brad was carrying sleeping Sammy up over one shoulder and a diaper bag on the other.

"Oh, go on," Brad said as he waited for Karen to climb the steps to catch up with him on the dock.

"How many times do you get a chance to do something this romantic, man? Before long you'll have one of these little guys and then you can't sleep out on the gulf," he said

"Or anywhere else for that matter," Karen chimed in. They both laughed. She had now climbed out of the boat up to where Brad was standing. She slipped her arm through his and they said their goodnights, then they walked away down the dock.

Who says we're getting married and having kids? Carla thought. What was with all this assumption on her family's part?

"Here you go," Carla's father said, slapping Michael on the back. "Take the keys and keep her safe," he said with a smile. "Carla, I mean," he added with a laugh. "And the ship, of course, take care of her as well. I trust you with both." He nodded. The three of them were still standing in the main part of the boat.

"Thanks a lot, Max. I appreciate it."

"Thank you, Daddy. This is so nice of you," Carla said as she gave a hug to his stiff upper body. "Really, Daddy. You are going all out."

"It's the least I can do," Max said. "Things haven't exactly been smooth sailing between you and me lately."

"I know, Daddy." Carla said. Apologizing to him made her feel like a little girl who had broken the cookie jar. "I'm sorry I was so angry last time I saw you."

Carla looked over at Michael, wondering how he was going to survive observing this little heart-to-heart conversation. But he was busy making himself obscure. Rubbing the wheel, looking over the dials and instruments.

"Things were hard for you and your sister when I met Alexis. I understand that now," Max said. "I want to make things right, and include you more with us. Alexis agrees with me."

Carla winced at the mention of her stepmother. Somehow she didn't picture having any quality time with her father as long as Alexis was around. This visit had healed so many things between Carla, Karen and her father, but she couldn't overlook the fact that it was most likely because they had him to themselves, away from Alexis' interference.

"I read recently that step-families are difficult to blend, even when the children are much older," Carla said.

"I guess there's something to that," her father said. He got out a pipe and began pressing aromatic tobacco into it from a pouch he carried. When he was done, he lit it with the crack of a match that flared in the dark, then was gone. Carla could smell the distinctive, savory smell of pipe tobacco she had come to love when she was a child.

"I thought you quit pipe smoking," Carla said.

"Took it up again, recently," he said, with the pipe still in the corner of his mouth. "I've had some big cases that have really put some stress on me, so I broke down one night and had a pipe smoke. Now I find I can't so easily stop."

"I was going to ask you about your cases," Carla said. "Remember when you used to always tell me about your big cases?" She sat down in a chair and Max followed suit. Michael stayed standing near the ship's wheel.

"Not much to tell, actually," her father said, pulling the pipe from his mouth and letting a puff of smoke drift skyward.

"I have one lawsuit against a drug company. It's going to be a tough one, though. Drug companies have such deep pockets, and their attorneys are exceptionally good at finding obscure loopholes to get them off the hook."

Carla ventured a glance over at Michael. He was looking out at the water, but she could tell he was listening.

"Do you think you could lose the case?" Carla asked.

"I'm going to do all I can to win it," he said. "I think I might even take it all the way to court. Their attorneys have been trying fiercely to settle out of court. But my client doesn't want that. She wants to have a jury hear her story."

"Corporate cases going all the way to court are pretty rare, aren't they?" Carla asked.

"Oh, yes. But this case has potential to go into a class action lawsuit, involving a large number of people, if we can go after it the right way. The company is in some real trouble for withholding one of its new products, approved by the FDA, that can supposedly put cancer into remission. They are withholding the product, my client claims, because they can make more money off of the chemotherapy and pain killing medication on dying patients, than they can make on patients in remission."

"Do you think that's true?"

"That's what we're working on proving."

"Could this turn out to be as big as something like the tobacco settlements?"

"Well, I wouldn't say as big as that. But it could go pretty big."

"And you're the lead attorney?"

"It's all my case. It was referred to me by Ernie Warren. You know, Dr. Warren. You might remember when your mother and I used to play with him and his wife every weekend in a golf foursome. He's still one of my closest friends. He has pulled for me as an expert witness plenty of times. Great friend."

"I know Doctor Warren, Dad. He's given me a birthday present every single year since I was born. Last year he sent me a card and a little glass bird."

"Ernie's quite a guy. He was just down here sailing with me, not too long ago. We had a fine time. Splendid time. Did some deep sea fishing."

"That sounds so nice," Carla said. *Expert witness? Class action lawsuit?* Carla's mind was reeling. Maybe these were important pieces.

"Well, it's past my curfew. So I'll let you kids enjoy," Max said, getting up. "There's some cold champagne and I think some beer in the refrigerator if you like."

"Well? Should we take it out? Or would you be more comfortable just leaving it docked here and staying overnight in it?"

"I thought you wanted to sail it yourself?"

"I do," Michael said. "But if we stay here on shore, it'll give you a chance to run away, should I prove to be an asshole at any time."

Carla smiled. "Ah, I see. Thinking ahead for me. I appreciate that."

"I've been thinking," Michael said, just as Carla started to say something at the same time. They both laughed.

"You first," Carla said.

"Well, I've been thinking about why I went off the handle and made a jealous fool of myself this morning," Michael said. He stood with one leg up on a chair, an arm resting on it, leaning forward, looking at her intently.

"I'll admit I'm an overly jealous person. Not exactly my best side. I was hoping to keep you from seeing it," he said.

"I wish I hadn't seen it either, if you want to know the truth," Carla said.

"It's just..." Michael trailed off and searched for the right words. "When I heard you talking to him in that voice...I just snapped." He looked down and winced as if the memory of it was hard to take.

Carla was quiet. She hadn't thought about how her tone of voice would affect Michael. She hadn't even thought about her tone of voice at all.

"I told you I still have feelings for him," Carla said

Michael met her eyes. "Somehow I'm wanting to pretend this guy doesn't even exist."

Carla rested her chin in her hand on the armrest of her chair and looked at the sparkling water. Only a few lights from the marina were reflecting off the water. "I guess it must seem to you like I'm playing both sides."

Michael leveled his chin and looked at her hard. "It feels that way." He was steadfast, locked on her despite her urge to squirm out of the eye contact.

Michael took a deep breath. "You feel something for me, but you also feel it for this —ex man of yours."

"Haven't you ever broken up with someone, and feelings still lingered?"

Michael stood and began fiddling with the wheel on the ship.

"You have, haven't you?" Carla asked again.

"I have," Michael said. "But it's not something I like to talk about."

"Who does?"

"I'm not in contact with my person from the past, though," Michael said, turning back toward her. "And you are. That makes things somewhat different."

"Now do you see why I am hesitant to let things go any farther between you and me?"

"Yes," Michael said. "I see why." He shook his head. His broad shoulders were silhouetted in the light from the lamp on the dock.

Carla felt a wave of sympathy. She felt ashamed for what she was putting him through. But what could she do? Her heart wasn't equipped with a throw-switch. The heart takes its time. She was a victim of it, just as much as Michael was. And so was Todd, for the matter. But more than anything, she was exhausted and confused. She needed to straighten out her life. End things once and for all with Todd. Make him stop calling her. Make herself stay away from him. Then she would be more at liberty to let her feelings develop with Michael. But how could she even tell what she felt in such an arena of chaos? Michael was her protector. *Of course, she would be falling in love with him.* The whole thing made perfect, logical sense. It probably wasn't even based on emotion.

She sighed, then shivered as a wave of cooler night air stole over the boat. She wished her incredibly sordid, twisted little life would unravel into something stable so she could have some sort of peace. Right now, even without men in her life, she had much worse problems to worry about. Like how to stay alive once she got back to Washington. They had to go back in just one more day.

She sighed again. She wished there were a way to brace for the struggle ahead. She had almost allowed herself to forget about it for a minute or two, down here on the island.

"Let's take her out." Carla said. She suddenly wanted to feel the sweet escape of the water, and also to change the subject and the sad mood stealing over her. "Tomorrow is our last day. I really want to take her out, so we when we get home and everything is rotten, we can remember the good time we had."

Michael chuckled for the first time all day, and it did Carla's heart good. "Let's make it an especially good memory while we're at it," he said.

###

Michael set a low cruise speed north. As the boat hummed along over the nearly still water, most of the time Carla and Michael made small talk, or didn't talk at all. Carla was so thankful it wasn't the tense silence of earlier that day. It was the familiar comforting silence they had shared on the beach the night Michael had kissed her.

Carla watched the blackness of the sea roll by the ship, whirling into foam behind them as they headed toward the white blaze of moonlight rippling in the distance across the water. The smell of the gulf intoxicated her. The way Michael held his head into the wind as he steered the boat, she knew he shared her same appreciation.

Cruising in the dark like this made Carla think of when she was young, when her whole family would take cruises in the evening and she would snuggle with her mother and Karen under a blanket and her mother would stroke her hair and sing softly. The island where Carla was taking Michael was one of her favorite childhood spots. It had a beautiful white sand beach and water so clear you could see little schools of fish swimming at your feet. She hadn't been there since before her mother got ill.

"This is it," Carla said. "Up ahead." She pointed to a low line of trees a few hundred yards off.

"Just aim for the tip of the island to the right, and when we get closer, you'll see the cove."

Carla watched Michael's shoulders and bulging arms as he steered the ship. She wondered what he was thinking.

"Let's cruise in a little closer and anchor."

Michael cut the engine and the boat bobbed gently on the small swells coming in toward the island. They were close enough to see the beach. They could swim there if they wanted. Carla could hear small waves lapping at the island's shore. She lay back and was almost blinded by the stars.

"Beautiful, aren't they?" Michael said.

"So beautiful, it amazes me," Carla murmured. She was lying with her arms behind her head, her legs crossed, stretched out on the lounge chair.

She heard the chair next to her crunch as Michael lay down too.

"Hard to believe we are just specks on this giant canvas," she said. Michael was quiet. She looked over at him. He was blinking up at the sky.

"Shooting star," he said suddenly, pointing to a place above his head and to the right.

"Darn, I missed it," she said. "Now I don't get to make a wish."

Michael turned to his side, propped his head on a bent arm, and looked at her. "What would you wish?" he asked.

Carla was silent for a moment, thinking about it. "I'd wish that we hadn't had a fight today," she said, still looking up at the stars. She knew he was looking at her, and she wasn't ready to look at him and feel his intensity yet.

"Why?" he asked.

"I don't know. It just feels bad. When you are mad at me, it feels bad," she said. Then she turned her head to look at him, his curly hair like a halo on his head in the dim light. She could just barely see the golden-rosy tan on his cheeks.

"I liked it when we were happy together," she said again.

Michael continued to look in her direction. Carla looked up, searching for another shooting star. Then he took her hand from where it was lying on the lounge and put it in his.

"How does this feel?" he asked. "I'm not mad anymore. I never was mad at you. I was only mad at myself."

"But *I* was mad at you." Carla smiled. "But then, what can you expect?"

Michael laughed. "What *can* I expect?"

"How about this?" She climbed from her chair onto his, lying down next to him, pressing her body close to his so she wouldn't fall off. He put his arms around her and held her tight.

"Mmm," he said, squeezing her softly. "This is unexpected, but very good."

"Unexpected?" she said, feeling the full length of him. He lifted one of his fuzzy legs and put it over her to keep her from falling off the chair. "Why unexpected?"

"Because it doesn't fall into the 'men are predators' behavior category," he said, gently rubbing her back.

"I guess it doesn't," she said, smelling him, feeling him so close was causing a million pistons to fire inside her head.

His lips were suddenly on hers, soft and gentle at first, as if questioning how she felt. She crushed her mouth to his, pressing herself against him, putting her arms around his neck and grabbing handfuls of his thick hair. He ran his hands up and down her back and she felt a shiver go through her. He squeezed her tighter with his leg. They were enmeshed.

When the kiss was over, they both lay there quietly, breathing heavily and looking into each other's eyes.

"I'm falling for you, Michael," Carla said, her hands still tangled in his curls. "I'm falling in love with you and I can't stop myself."

"Who said you should stop yourself?" he asked. He gently rubbed her bare arms. His eyes still held a certain sadness and a look of questioning. He wasn't the Michael who had confidently tried to seduce her just nights before. And she knew this was her own fault.

"I say so," she said. She buried her face in his chest. "I'm afraid if I let myself, I'll lose you somehow, and I don't want to lose you."

"You can't lose me," he said. "You've got me. More than you know."

Carla searched his eyes. "Michael. What would you say if I said I want you to make love to me tonight?"

He was silent. How different this scenario was playing out from the night just days ago, when he couldn't keep his hands off of her.

"I wouldn't say anything." He was so close, she could feel his heart pounding.

Carla frowned. *He didn't want her?* It never occurred to her he'd say no.

"I wouldn't say a word," he continued in a low voice. "But I'd pick you up and carry you downstairs to the bed. Then I'd give you whatever your heart desires… and more," he said in a rough whisper. He nuzzled his nose in her ear. She could hear his ragged breathing.

Carla felt her breath escape in a rush.

"Do you want me to do that?" he asked. His voice was thick with desire.

"Yes," Carla whispered.

Michael leaned over and put his arms under her and scooped her up with ease. He cradled her like a baby in his arms. He carried her down the steps, to the cabin bed. Moonlight flooded across the pillow. This would change everything, she thought.

###

It was morning and he was naked. That's all he knew at first. Then he remembered. *Was he dreaming?* If he'd been dreaming, then it was the best dream of his life. He turned his head. No. Not dreaming. There she was. A golden angel.

Her hair flowing down around her neck across one breast and down to her waist.

He reached over and gently stroked her face. She sighed and turned her head in her sleep. They'd been up half the night. He decided he'd better get away from her before he woke her up.

He slipped on his swim trunks. The morning light was already bright, but it wasn't even nine o'clock. He sat on the ship's deck and looked out to sea. What an amazing place this was. What an amazing night. As long as he lived, he would never forget it. If he thought he'd been in love with her before, it was nothing to how he felt now. She was the one. *The one.* And he would defend that now to death. She was all that mattered to him. He wanted to marry her.

"Morning, sailor. Whatcha doin?" It was her silky voice. She was leaning on the stairwell behind him.

"Dreaming of heaven," he said with a smile.

She came softly over to him and sat by him on the end of the lounge chair.

"Dreaming of dying?" she said. "And so young?"

"No. I've been to heaven and back," he said with a smile as he reached up and smoothed a long hair from her face.

She smiled and lowered her head and her hair fell all around her and onto him.

Michael made her breakfast. Granola bars and a coke. Basically, that was all that was in the refrigerator besides alcoholic beverages.

"When do we have to go back?" he asked while they sat at the little table eating.

"I don't know. Probably by noon."

"I don't want to go. But if you say we have to… "

"You know what I want to do first?"

He smiled. "God only knows."

"Swim."

'Okay."

"Come." She stood up and pulled his hands. He followed her onto the deck. It wasn't two seconds and she dove into the water. It was turquoise and clear and beautiful. She smiled up at him with an impish grin as she treaded water, her wet hair slick. Before he could smile back, she had both pieces of her suit in her hand. They landed in a wet plop at his feet where she tossed them. She tilted her head back and laughed.

He stripped naked without taking his eyes off of her then threw a life ring out toward her, before he dove in. With a few good strokes he caught up to her, pulling her toward him, his hands on the small of her back.

He slipped his arm through the life ring. Now they didn't have to tread water. They were slippery together. He grabbed her by the back of the head, pulling her hair, gently but urgently tipping her head back to him, before kissing her. "You are amazing," he said muffled into her lips.

"Not as amazing as you are," she answered against his lips. And then she smiled. Her hands were all over him. A mermaid couldn't have taught him more about pleasure. He groaned and grabbed her tighter.

"Want to swim to the shore?" she asked. "I'll race you."

"You never quit, do you?"

She only grinned back at him.

"You're on," he said.

He let her beat him and he watched as she waded out of the water, a perfect curve to her back, water ringlets flowing down off her long hair. She found a soft spot in the sand, and lay down, leaning back on her elbows. She smiled at him as he came out of the water.

"You're going to sunburn," he said, looking down from where he stood over her, dripping water deliberately onto her belly.

"I know," she said. "We can't stay like this long."

"We could always hide in the woods," he said, sinking down beside her.

"And live like Tarzan and Jane?" she said, smiling, closing her eyes and tipping her face to the sun.

They sunbathed for a short time, and then he was feeling restless. "I think we should head back," he said.

She wrinkled her nose at him, eyes still closed. "I don't want to go back," she said. "Ever."

11

Carla and Michael laughed all the way home along the beach road. It was a beautiful clear day and they put the top down on the car. Carla's ponytail was blowing wildly. The radio was on loud. The feelings of the night before, and of the morning, were strong between them. No talking was needed. Carla smiled at Michael as she held the wheel making the curves in the road. He squeezed the back of her neck in response. Just for this moment, in the bright sun, they were together in the world, and it was perfect, Carla thought.

But as soon as Carla swung the car into the drive, she could tell something was wrong. Karen was sitting out front on the porch holding a handkerchief. The look on her face didn't look good. Daddy's car was gone.

"Dr. Warren was murdered last night," Karen said as they walked up to where she was sitting on a porch. Her eyes were puffy and red. She looked like she'd had no sleep. "In cold blood. In his own home." Karen was visibly shaken up.

"Daddy flew out early this morning to go back and help the family. The police in Chicago wanted to talk to him. He said to apologize for leaving without saying goodbye. He said to give you his best."

Michael reached over and rubbed Carla's back.

"Let's go inside," he said. "We can talk better in there."

"I didn't know what to do with myself," Karen said as they corralled her along. I was just out here waiting and waiting for you. There was no way to reach you. I couldn't sleep. Brad has been so good with the baby. I've been too unraveled to do much," she said.

Carla put her arm around her sister as they walked down the hall to the kitchen. "Listen, sweetie. You are

140

really going to need some sleep. I know this scares you because you're adding it to what happened to me, right?"

Karen nodded. "What *is* happening here? To my family? My close friends? We aren't famous or anything. Why is all this happening?"

Carla nodded over to Michael. "That's why Michael is helping me. You understand now? This never was a little thing."

"I guess I didn't want to believe you when you came to stay at my house. I just ignored the details. And when you told me about the man in your office that night, I thought you were exaggerating."

"Believe me, every day, I want to ignore the details of this situation. But it just keeps getting more and more real. There's no need for me to exaggerate anything," Carla said.

Carla turned to Michael. "Is this murder linked to my situation, do you think?"

"Probably linked to the pharmaceutical case," Michael said. "But I still don't know if it's linked to you."

Karen sat on a kitchen stool, her belly round under her maternity dress, her eyes wide and tired. She looked so vulnerable.

"Let me go talk Karen into taking a nap," Carla said. "I'll meet you in the study, in a little while."

Michael nodded. He was totally somber.

###

"Is she okay?" Michael asked as Carla walked into the study where he'd been sitting in a deep leather chair, thinking, with his feet on the big matching hassock.

"Yes. She's mostly exhausted." Carla said. "Pregnancy makes every fear worse, evidently."

"Mine are getting worse, and I'm not even pregnant," Michael said.

Carla looked around the room. None of her father's business papers were remaining. He'd taken everything back with him.

"I need to go to Chicago," Michael said. His eyes were distant.

"Who are these people?" Carla sank down into the couch and put her head in her hands.

Michael slid over beside her and pulled her close into his arms. "Come on, baby," Michael said. "You've got to stay tough. We don't know at this point if Dr. Warren's murder has anything to do with you at all. Remember I'm the only one that wants to link your father's case to you. No one else has that hunch. Not even the police."

"I'm going to Chicago with you," Carla asserted.

"Come on," Michael said, giving her a little squeeze. "Please. Consider staying at Amy's. You can rest." His eyes were firm and gentle, but they annoyed Carla. He was treating her like a baby about the case.

"Michael, be realistic. I don't want to be locked in a tower while you slay the dragon."

"Look. I'll be back within a few days. You can talk to the cops in D.C. See if they've got anything. You cover D.C., and I'll cover Chicago."

"Michael, you're not going to push me off that easily."

"Push you off? I'm just thinking about you, about what you shouldn't have to go through. About how to minimize stress."

She threw his arm off of her and stood up. "Your stress, or mine?"

"Ours," Michael said in a soft tone. He stood up too and wrapped his arms around her. "Ours, babe. We're in this together." He held her for a while, rocking back and forth. Then he walked over to the phone and made reservations to Chicago.

Carla's flight back to Washington was miserable. She sat alone by the window next to a young couple that held hands and snuggled the whole way. She put her pillow up to the window, buried her face in it, and deliberately made herself doze.

At the airport, Amy was all smiles.

"So?" Amy said smiling. "How was it?" Somehow Amy had failed to notice Carla's sunken candor.

"It was great," Carla said. "Right up to the part where my father's best friend got murdered last night."

Amy's jaw dropped. "You are kidding me!"

"Not kidding," Carla said. She squeezed the muscles in the back of her neck that were beginning to feel like giant steel chords. In the dark she could see the Potomac River as they crossed the 14th Street Bridge, heading up into the city.

"No shit, Sherlock. This isn't good."

"Where's Michael?"

"He went up to Chicago to check things out. He sentenced me to quarantine at your place again."

Amy smiled. "Is that so bad? I missed you like crazy!"

Carla smiled back and grabbed Amy's hand.

"No, Ames. It's not bad."

"I got a job while you were gone. A good one."

"That's terrific. What is it?"

"Same kind of work as my last job, only with a better law firm. I'm administrative assistant to the senior partner at Rosenberg and Stein. A twenty percent pay increase."

"Fantastic, Amy," Carla said.

"When do you start?"

"I already did. Friday was my first day."

"What day is today?"

"It's Tuesday, you beach bum," Amy said.

Carla smiled. She was so tired she could hardly keep her head up.

###

When they got back to Amy's it was too early for bed. Michael was right. Amy's place did feel safe and cozy. The two women put on their pajamas, popped some popcorn and sat on the couch to talk.

"So what happened down there? I'm dying to know," Amy asked, stuffing a mouthful of popcorn into her mouth. The garnet ring on her middle finger sparkled and matched her pale purple nail polish.

"Well, it seemed so short. The time flew," Carla said. She was stalling, sorting through what to tell.

"And?" Amy said, still chewing.

"Well, my father was very nice. Nicer than I expected him to be."

"See?" Amy said. "Didn't I tell you he missed you?"

Carla ventured a small smile. Amy pushed the bowl of popcorn her way. "Have some, please! Don't make me eat all of this alone."

Carla reached for a few kernels and put them into her mouth.

"And the case? Did you find out anything?"

"Yes. We think we got a good lead," Carla said. "Something about a pharmaceutical company getting sued by an old lady." Carla was too tired to go into the details.

"Sounds juicy," Amy said. She didn't press for more. Carla knew what her final question would be.

"So," Amy said with raised eyebrows. "How did the fake boyfriend thing work out? Did you and Michael fake it all the way?"

Carla lowered her head. She could feel a blush coming on.

"No. Are you kidding?" Carla decided an outright lie was the best thing for Amy right now. She didn't want to make her upset.

Amy's eyes opened wider. She was chewing her popcorn faster. "But you saw him naked right? Accidentally? You shared a room?"

"No," Carla said firmly, reaching for more popcorn. "No, no, no. We stayed professional the whole time. We had separate rooms."

Amy was buying it. She looked pleased. "I guess that's for the best, don't you think?" Amy said.

"Sure, it is. Yes," Carla said with a nod as she chewed. Even as she said it, she hated herself for lying to her best friend's face.

"Todd called for you two times while you were gone," Amy said. The sound of Todd's name threw a wet blanket on Carla.

"You're kidding," Carla said.

"The first time, he wanted to come over and see you. The second time he practically paid me to give him your number in Florida. He said it was urgent."

"So, that's how he got the number…" Carla said.

"You don't sound excited about it. I thought you would be."

"We're broken up."

Amy laughed. "How many times have I heard that?"

"No. This time it's real."

"Well, it's high time. I've been telling you for a long time. That guy isn't good for you."

Carla put her arm around Amy. "I know you're right. And I should have listened to you," she said.

Long after Amy had fallen asleep in her own bedroom, Carla lay awake on the pullout sofa in the front room. Her mind was whirling with the concerns about the case, Michael, her father. It was a mistake to come to Washington. She should have gone to Chicago. Maybe she should consider telling her father everything, like Michael had suggested.

###

The next day, Carla was groggily aware that Amy was dressing and leaving for work. She smelled the shampoo lofting in the shower steam and the hairspray. She heard Amy's heels click back and forth from the bedroom to the bathroom. She smelled the coffee dripping in the coffee maker. But she didn't open her eyes. Then she heard the key in the lock and it was silent except for the traffic going by outside on the avenue.

Carla sat up, rubbing her head, sitting on the lumpy sofa bed. She looked over at her stack of work that her boss, Janet, had sent, piled in two large boxes on the floor. She knew she should get up and get cracking at it. But she felt so limp and unmotivated.

###

By noon, Carla was up and showered, and had eaten some toast. A little late, she thought. But better late than never. To be honest, she wanted to just stay in bed permanently. Life for her in Washington now felt like it weighed a million pounds. It was an anvil sitting right on her head. She had enjoyed the escape to Florida, but it made the contrast to life in this spider web more severe.

Carla carried the boxes over to the table and began sorting through the projects. She buried her head in the reading material she needed to go through in order to start on the writing.

Then something interrupted her. It was someone walking loudly down the hall in the direction of Amy's apartment. It was a long hall, and whoever it was, was coming fast. Now there was a knock on Amy's door. Carla's heart leapt to her throat. She grabbed the pistol she had beside her on the desk and carried it over to the door, on tiptoes. As she walked over, the door banged again, this time more urgently.

Carla gently took the safety off the gun and pointed it downward as she looked through the peephole.

It was Todd. She sighed and leaned against the door.

"Carla are you in there?" he said.

"Yes. Hang on," she answered. She put the gun back on safety and ran it over to the table, hiding it under some of the papers. She smoothed her hair back out of her face and walked calmly back to the door and undid the chain, turned the lock opened, and let him in.

"For God's sake, Carla. I've been trying to reach you." His face looked worn and tender.

Carla stood staring at him. He had taken her off guard. She didn't expect to see him face-to-face today. She didn't have her feelings collected.

He studied her face. "Not happy to see me?" he said, sounding disappointed. "You sounded like you couldn't wait to get your hands on me when I talked to you a few days ago." He went over and plopped himself down on the sofa. Carla locked the door behind her and followed him into the room. She was too nervous to sit, so she went over to stand by the kitchen table where she had been working. She leaned against it and crossed her arms.

"Aren't you exaggerating a little, Todd?" Carla said. True, she had been friendly. As a person. As a friend. But, not dying to get her hands on him. "You should have called first before coming over here," she said briskly. "I'm swamped with work. Being out of town has put me so behind."

Todd sat back with his arms outstretched on the back of the sofa.

"You're always swamped," he said. "Come on. I came to rescue you. Let's go out for a drink. Then I'll take you back to my place. I promise to keep you safe." He winked at her.

"Don't you understand?"

"You don't mean it about breaking up. If you want more attention, I'm your man. I can give you that."

Looking at him, Carla felt regret and loss. How many times had she hoped he'd say these very words to her? But it was too late now. He sensed he was losing her, so he was willing to try harder. She felt the pining lonesomeness the heart grapples with when it knows a goodbye is inevitable. Things would never work with them. She had tried. Now that she had felt the strength and loyalty of Michael's love, it was easier for her to be strong. She walked over to the couch and sat beside him, looking him in the eyes.

"I don't want more attention. I just want us to be friends. Forever and ever."

Todd crunched his brow. "Friends? That's a new one, Carla. I've never heard that come from your lips."

"Well, it's true. It's our only option. It's the only option that won't make things hurt."

"I'm hurting," he said softly.

"I'm sorry for that," she said. "I know how it feels. Like all those times I longed for you and you were busy working; or busy with other women."

"I worked a lot, yes. But other women, no." he said.

"Todd. Please. Don't waste your breath on such an obvious lie. You and I both know you play the field."

"And you don't?" he said. "I thought that was our agreement. I don't ask questions. You don't ask questions. I thought that was how we'd worked this out."

"Don't you think that's rather sick, Todd? When you think about it? Two people, afraid to commit, and afraid to say goodbye, so they cling to each other on one side, while they work deals on the other side. How close to reality is that?"

"Closer than you'd think, Carla. That's America today."

"Then I don't want it," she said.

Todd was quiet, looking her over.

"Wait a minute. I know what's gotten into you. I should have noticed it before. That distant gleam in your eye. That rosy glow in your cheeks. It's that private eye."

Carla was quiet. She glared at him.

"It is, isn't it? I bet he got into your pants in Florida. Good man," Todd said sarcastically. "He must work fast, or else you made it easy for him."

"I don't see why you have to ask, or get ugly," Carla said, the blood starting to rise in her face.

"Can't be helped, my dear. I know you so well, as do many others, evidently."

Before she even knew what happened, she had reached across and slapped his cheek with a resounding crack.

Todd touched his cheek in dismay.

"Don't you ever make me feel cheap again," she said.

"Carla. Nothing about you is cheap. On the contrary. I doubt if any man will ever be able to pay a high enough price to have you. Certainly not me."

He stood up and they stared at each other in silence.

"Well, I'm going to leave you now, to your work. If you need me…. For anything…" he said, looking down into her eyes earnestly. "You know where to call."

Carla nodded. Her eyes were filling with tears.

"Honey, I'm home," Amy yelled, jokingly, as she walked through the door.

"Dinner's ready," Carla smiled from the kitchen.

"How nice! It's so nice to come home to somebody," Amy said, as she limped into the bedroom. "These new shoes are from hell!" she said, and Carla could hear them hit the back of the closet as Amy threw them in, one by one. She poked her head out of the bedroom, reaching up to unzip her dress from the back.

"How was your day?" Amy asked from the bedroom.

"Well, I slept a lot of it away. Then Todd came by for an unannounced visit, I took a bath and read your magazines."

"You took a bath with Todd?" Amy asked, coming into the living room wearing cutoff sweat pants and a T-shirt. She was smiling.

"Hardly." Carla was scooping tuna casserole onto plates at the table.

"Well, then. What happened?"

"He came by. Said he missed me. The same old stuff. Then we got in a big fight, and he left."

"You actually fought with him? That's something new. Usually he breaks you down. This is progress," Amy said, opening a bottle of cheap wine from the refrigerator and pouring it into juice glasses. "Sorry, I keep meaning to buy wine glasses," she said.

"Doesn't bother me," Carla said, taking a seat and sipping on the blush wine.

"Gourmet, Carla! Look at this. A candle and all," Amy said, sitting down and lifting her glass for a toast.

"So what were you fighting about?" Amy asked, taking a big bite of the casserole.

"Breaking up. Same old things," Carla said.

"He believes you, doesn't he?" Amy said.

"Not really."

"Why should he? You always run back to him. And I'm very proud this time you're sticking with it. We've got to get you out of this mess and then get you circulating. What you need is a new man."

"I'm sure that's what would do the trick," Carla said.

After dinner they watched a little TV, but soon Amy decided to hit the hay. "This job is kicking my butt!" she said. "I'm exhausted and it's only nine-thirty."

"That happens to me with every new job," Carla said. "Mind if I stay up a bit longer? I'm going to read."

"No problem. I'll just close this door," Amy said. "Have you heard from Michael?"

"No, not yet." Carla wondered herself why he hadn't called yet. He must be totally absorbed, she thought.

"Maybe he'll call tomorrow," Amy said, now in nightgown and slippers. She came over to Carla and wrapped her arms around her and squeezed her tight. "Goodnight. Thanks for the dinner," she said in Carla's ear. Then, looked her in the face and kissed her cheek. "What would I do without a friend like you?" Amy said.

"What would I do?" Carla said. Her heart felt rotten. Carla knew she'd leave for Chicago come hell or high water tomorrow. She had to. She'd take a cab to the airport when Amy was at work.

###

The noise was so loud at Chicago's O'Hare airport that Carla had to squeeze a finger over the ear that wasn't on the receiver. She had her carry-on bag at her feet. She was careful not to lean on a place where someone had pressed gum to the phone booth wall.

"Daddy?"

"Yes."

"It's Carla."

"Carla. I'm glad you called." His voice trailed off.

"I know all about it, Dad. Dr. Warren. I came for the funeral."

"You're in Chicago?"

"I just landed at O'Hare. Should I call a cab?"

"No. Let me come and get you. Can you stay the night with us?"

"Us?"

"Alexis is back from her trip."

"Does she mind?

"Why, no, Carla. I don't understand where you get these concerns and misconceived notions."

"I don't know, Dad. I guess I make them up?"

"Let's not get sarcastic or remote, here." Carla's father was as astute at picking up her innuendos as she was at reading him. "We've just had a death close enough to be a death in the family. Let's stick by each other and let bygones be bygones."

"Daddy. I'm not about to raise any kind of fuss. If Alexis says I can stay with you, that's peachy with me. Maybe we'll get to know each other better." She paused for her father to interject something, but there was silence on the line. "When is the funeral?"

"Tomorrow. That's lovely, Carla. I'm glad you will be here." Her father's voice sounded very tired and suddenly older to her.

"Me too, Daddy. The whole thing scares me." She wanted to let down and cry, but she bit her lip.

"The police say they think the incident was caused by breaking and entering. Ernie caught some people robbing him and he took a bullet when he tried to stop them."

"Horrible, Daddy."

"I feel devastated. Ernie was the best. He will be well missed." There was an audible silence where she knew her father was collecting his feelings.

"I'll wait for you at baggage claim."

"We will be right there."

Carla heaved a big sigh as she hung up the phone. It was hard enough to squeeze water from a stone talking with her father. But now she had to throw Alexis into the mix, with all the red-hot hurts still burning between them. As Carla waited for her father to arrive, she was kicking herself for being a stubborn idiot. She had to come up here to Chicago. Well, this is what she deserved. Every minute of it.

###

Todd was pacing back and forth. It had been one hell of a rough day. His boss, Senator Goldsmith, had a bill on the floor this week. A big one. No. Make that, *"The Big One."* And he was hemorrhaging votes at the last minute from both sides of the aisle. Todd had spent all day trying to salvage votes, but committees on the Democrat side had surely done their work well in the eleventh hour. It was a coup. What a nightmare.

After months of Todd working, negotiating and tweaking, possibly the biggest law to be passed under the current administration, there were signs today that the bill would likely not pass the senate, effectively throwing it back to the drawing board, never to see the light of day in this year's congress. The house had a matching bill with even less hope of passing. Goldsmith had designs on being the savior of this issue. It would be a huge feather in his cap if this one could pass, setting him up in a pre-election year as a possible presidential candidate. But that was just a little secret among Goldsmith's top staffers. Todd knew about it. Hell, yes. He heard about Goldsmith's ambitions each and every day. They were driven into his brain with an anvil and loaded onto his back as if he were a donkey. But there were reasons for Todd's patience and forbearance. He was hoping to ride in Goldsmith's wake. Maybe make it to presidential advisor one day. If not for Goldsmith, then for another Republican. And there were always hopes that this would put him in a good light in California, if Todd felt he should want to sidestep Washington ambitions and head over to state political life.

All these dreams kept Todd alive as he slaved, usually ten or more hours a day, for the past six years for the old geezer. Goldsmith had a reputation in Washington for playing hardball — with no mercy. Prestigious and eccentric as hell, Goldsmith was worse for the wear these past few days. Todd was the nearest dog to kick, and frankly, he was damn tired of it.

To make matters worse, Juanita had given him the cold shoulder for the first time since he'd met her several months ago. Of all days, she'd decided to play difficult today. Just when he could really use a soak in the Jacuzzi with her long, beautiful Spanish legs wrapped around him.

He looked out over Pennsylvania Avenue from his penthouse on the 9th floor, swirling some scotch in a glass. Expensive scotch. He'd broken into his best stuff. At least he'd allow himself this one treat for the day. The blinking lights of the city were just appearing. The Capitol building stood white and ominous in a pale lavender sky.

He looked down at the plush carpet he'd just had installed. Nice touch. He liked the arrangement of modern art he'd collected and the black and maroon motif of the entire condo. Silk and crystal. His bedroom was mirrored, high and low; and his bedspread was luxurious black satin. He knew how to make the place look pretty decent, he thought. Or so his women friends always said so.

His building was nothing to brag about, by all means, considering life in Washington. But it wasn't shabby, either. With a little help from some family money, and the hard work he'd put in for Goldsmith, he could get by. Sure. It was a little tight sometimes, with the exorbitant rent in this area. But he'd rather live well with a little pinch, than live a lesser quality of life with more money in the bank. It was contrary to his father's hard lessons on financial success, but Todd never claimed to be his father. For God's sakes no. He was his own man. Had been for years. Let his younger brother, Charles, follow in the old man's footsteps. Besides, the east coast was getting into his blood. The pulse was so quickened here, so much more vibrant than California. He lifted his heavy crystal glass to the panoramic view of the city through the full-length living room window and toasted the town. After he socked that one down, he poured himself another and drank it to Goldsmith, this time more slowly, with discrimination, enjoying the smoothness of the scotch.

If he were honest with himself, he wasn't actually drinking the scotch to ease a bad day on Capitol Hill. He had weathered plenty of days like these. No. He was hoping the scotch would deal with a much stronger problem. He was hoping to numb himself enough to get Carla off his brain. She was always there. A constant yearning despair. Despite how busy work was, despite his long hours of strain each day and his exhaustion at night, she occupied huge parts of him. And now there was no escaping. She'd gripped his thoughts like a vice since the incident at Amy's. She'd slapped him. She'd actually cracked him one. Like in the movies. He reached up to touch he face again, and he smiled.

He loosened his tie as he walked back through the long hallway to his bedroom suite. That little firecracker. He was going to make her pay for that one, he thought, as he threw his tie on the bed, pulled his belt out of his pants and peeled off his shirt. He reached into the closet for a hanger for his suit pants. She's going to pay in pleasure, he mused, as he slid out of them and hung them up. His revenge would come when she would beg him for more. She was just playing coy to fire his passion, and it sure as hell was working. He ached for more of the loving they had made over the past four years that had been unmatched, ever, in his fairly experienced love life. In fact, their relationship was unmatched in any friendship or intimacy he'd ever known, even when Carla refused him physically – which frankly was more times than not in the past year. But, sex, or no sex, the facts remained. Without Carla, he wasn't himself. Life wasn't right. The shades of the sun and the moon were wrong. Without Carla, there was no spark. His life was flat. He had to hear her voice. His only true sedative. He had to feel her complicated mind intertwine with his. When other lovers had gone home after sweaty nights of pleasure and passion, he'd lie alone, still craving Carla's touch.

He hit the speaker button on the phone by his bed, and then the redial to get Amy's number where Carla was staying. He'd been trying the number for days, with no luck. He was in the walk-in closet hanging up his suit jacket when he heard the phone ringing. Todd stuck his head out of the closet to hear better. It was a man on Amy's line.

"Hello?" The voice was deep with a city accent he couldn't quite place. A cheap, rough-side-of town, eastern accent. Pittsburgh, maybe?

Todd stepped from the closet and grabbed the phone from the bedside table.

"Hello, is this the home of Amy Goldstein?" Todd asked.

"Yes, who's this?" the voice sounded impatient and wary, not to mention lacking in couth.

"I'm calling for Carla Redfern. Is she available?" Todd said.

"It depends on who you are," the voice was clearly setting a threatening tone.

"And who might you be?" Todd was equally perturbed. But he wasn't going to lower himself to this degenerate's level. No doubt it was probably the boy who had recently gleaned Carla's attention. The private investigator.

"If you're calling for Carla, she's not here. Who's calling?"

"Todd. Todd Grisham. And you must be her bodyguard?"

"Her private investigator and bodyguard. Can I give her a message, Mr. Grisher."

"It's Grisham," Todd said in annoyance. "No. But I'd like to leave you one, if I may."

Silence.

"Don't think you can break up what we've had together for years, just because you are helping her in a pinch, and no doubt making plenty of money off of her."

Todd waited to hear a response, but there was none. The silent type, he thought. Todd had to take advantage of it. "And you're a fool to think she means anything serious by her actions toward you. She's the most unpredictable woman you will ever meet. She can make anyone feel they're the love of her life. You got me? And, and let me assure you. You're not."

"Let me assure you, Grisham, you're not, either." At this, Todd had to laugh. He'd let her get under his skin, poor chap.

"Just tell her I called, will you?" Todd used the voice he reserved for caddies and waiters.

"Tell her yourself."

"Lost your manners?"

"No, but you're about to lose your face if I run into you."

"No need to play the jealous fool. I'm telling you, man. She's nobody's girl."

"We'll see about that, Grisham. But I'd say my odds are much greater than yours, seeing as she told me herself she doesn't want to see you."

"She told me, as well."

"Then why don't you believe her and stay away?"

"Would you?"

There was a long silence. "No."

Todd had to respect the man's honesty.

"All right, then. Do as you wish. But I'd prefer you tell her I called."

"Prefer all you want, asshole." And the phone was slammed in Todd's ear.

###

"Who was that?" Amy said as she came into the living room, drying a pot from the night's dinner she and Michael had just eaten. "Was it Carla?"

"No, it wasn't."

"Who, then?"

"That asshole she calls an ex-boyfriend."

"Todd? What did he say?"

"Nothing. I couldn't hear past his stuck-up fake English accent."

Amy laughed. "I'm glad you agree with me about him. He's no good, I keep telling her." She put her hand on his arm. "Don't you have a nice friend we could hook her up with?"

Michael was absorbed in his thoughts and didn't answer. He felt his fists balling up and his shoulders tightening. He recoiled from Amy's touch. He was distracted by the sound of pumpkin-head's weak breath still in his ear, he had no patience for Amy's sympathy.

"What is it? Is it something he said?"

Amy's face pushed too close to his wouldn't let him slip into his own thoughts. "No," he said, annoyed. "No. It was nothing."

"Michael, I know you better than that. I know when you are mad, and you look mad."

Amy had sat down by him on the couch, putting her arm gently around him. Normally he would have taken her concern in stride. She was a good friend to him. But suddenly Carla's admonitions that Amy was in love with him were coming back to haunt him.

Michael stood up with a start. "Why do you have to henpeck me, huh Ames? Why can't you just let it go? Why are you are always prying into my feelings?" Even as he said it, he realized he'd never raised his voice to her, or shown her these kinds of critical feelings. Their friendship had always been warm and easy-going.

Amy sat in shock looking at him trying to hide the tears welling up in her eyes.

My God, what was he doing? Breaking this girl's heart? She'd been his best friend for the past year. He'd spent more time at her house, than at his own. He'd eaten more dinners the past year at her kitchen table than he'd eaten at his own mother's house. How had he not seen her feelings developing for him?

Michael slumped his shoulders. He felt like a heel. Amy still sat where she was on the couch. She was looking down and twisting the kitchen towel around and around in her hand. He saw a teardrop fall into her lap. She didn't look up.

"You are in love with her, aren't you?' Amy said. She still didn't look up. But her voice was quivering.

"What? Why would you ask me that, Ames? Why would you care?" He walked over and leaned against the front door. Suddenly the room was smaller than a mouse cage, and getting stuffy.

"You are. It all makes sense now. How could I have missed it?" She made no move to wipe the tears flowing down her cheeks.

"How could you see something that wasn't there?"

"It was there, Michael. It was there in the electricity between you two. I just tried to write it off as the excitement of the case. I never dreamed…" her voice trailed off and she choked into a sob but stifled it with her hand.

Michael stood at the door. He couldn't force himself to go to her side.

"Why, Michael? Why didn't you tell me?"

"Tell you what? Tell you I was attracted to her?"

"Why didn't you tell me you *weren't* attracted to *me*," she bowed her head.

This was killing him. He wasn't going to be able to take this. He wanted to throw the door open and run. But he knew he had to go over to her. He had to make himself help her through this. We strode over to the couch and sat down beside her and put his arm around her.

"I feel like such a fool," she said into his shoulder between sobs.

"Don't be," Michael said rubbing her back. "Don't be."

Amy pulled back and looked at him. Her eyes were puffy and red.

Michael got up and went to the bathroom, pulling off a long stream of toilet paper and bringing it back to her. He stood beside her while she blew her nose. She looked up at him pitifully. He knew he needed to stay and talk this out with her, no matter how miserable it was. She deserved that. He sat down again beside her, and looked into her eyes.

"How do I say this, Amy? I love you as a friend. You are the greatest. Haven't we had fun times?"

Amy threw the towel onto the floor and stood up. She swirled around and stalked to the kitchen a few steps away.

"No. We haven't. We haven't had any fun times. We've had lies." She leaned over the sink as if she might be sick.

"Come on, now, Amy. You're blowing this all out of proportion. When did I ever intentionally lead you to believe that this was going to be more than a friendship?"

Amy turned from the sink and stared at him with bleary eyes. A sob released from her chest. It was the saddest thing he'd ever seen. This was awful.

"You didn't Michael. You didn't," she said, and she fell silent. "I just hoped, I guess. I assumed," she said meekly.

"Amy, I would never ever want to hurt you. Don't you know that?"

Amy stared at him hard. "I know that, Michael. I know you wouldn't. I know you didn't deliberately fall in love with her. And maybe... if you hadn't met her, you might have fallen in love with me..."

That was it. He had to straighten this out. He had to help her see things as they really are. He got up and went over to her by the kitchen sink and put his arms around her and hugged her tight. She pressed her face into his chest and sobbed some more.

"Did you sleep with her yet?"

"C'mon Amy? What kind of question is that?" Amy was silent now, sniffing. Michael continued hugging her. Poor kid. How could he soften this for her?

She suddenly swung out of his arms and stood back from him, pressing the tattered tissue to her eyes. Tears were coming again.

"Michael, just go. I need you to go."

"Come on, Ames. Don't let me leave you like this."

"No," Amy said. She raised her voice to a pitiful wail. "You have to leave now."

She stood sniffling while Michael stood helplessly unable to do anything to comfort her.

"I'll be fine. I'll sort this through, Michael. I promise. Please. Please forget we had this conversation. Next time you see me, I'll be as good as new." She looked up at him, and the pain was so evident in her face, it stabbed Michael hard. He felt like such a heartless jerk for not seeing how she felt earlier. If only he could have prevented this for her. He winced.

"And don't tell Carla we had this conversation. At least promise me that."

Michael stood up and nodded. "I won't say a word." He didn't know what to do. He didn't want to leave her like this. He felt so protective of her. All this time, always looking out for her, yet driving a stake into her unknowingly.

"I'm just tired. This just caught me at a weak moment."

Michael nodded again. He felt miserable.

"Please let me stay," he said. "We can rent a movie. Or we can talk if you want. I don't want to leave you like this."

"You can't fix this one, Michael. Just let me have some time to myself."

He started to walk over to her to give her a hug goodbye, their usual big tight bear hug.

"No," she said, holding her arm out toward him to ward him off. "No. Don't hug me. I don't want that from you now," she said.

Michael nodded. "All right, Amy. I'll go now. But I'm not leaving this apartment as a man who doesn't care about you."

"Right, Michael," Amy said with a half-smile. She wiped another tear with the back of her hand. "I know that." She laughed a small sarcastic laugh. "I know you care about me."

Michael didn't want to go to his apartment across the hall. He went out onto the street into a drizzling rain and walked down Wisconsin Avenue for a while. The heat was building in his chest over the conversation with Todd. He needed to work somebody over but good. Yet his heart was breaking for Amy. His mind twisted in agony. And then, there was still no word from Carla. She was in Chicago. That's all he knew. He didn't know what her plans were or how long she would be staying. He hadn't realized she had gone there until he had raced back to Washington to be with her. She was staying at her father's and working on the case, was the only message she'd left him via Amy. Michael would have seen her at the funeral, but he'd opted not to attend. He was busy with the cops in Chicago, and had other leads to trace and precious little time to do it in. He cussed himself for missing her in Chicago. He'd left her countless messages at her father's since he'd returned, and even a few with the housekeeper. Carla shouldn't be out running all around the country. He felt crazed by the thought of her danger. Why wasn't she returning his calls?

What if Todd was right? What if Carla was just playing with him? What if her actions meant nothing? The doubts crept out and pricked his mind from where he kept them safely locked away. He'd felt her love, hadn't he? Or had he only felt her passion and her need to be protected? The drizzle continued and Michael hunched his back against the wetness. Carla's sudden disappearance to Chicago had him unnerved. He felt so lonely for her. Things felt out of control.

Wisconsin Avenue was unusually quiet. He walked along past a young couple arm in arm, heads close together, the woman giggling softly. He passed where an old beggar was leaning on a broken down wall. Michael dropped his pocket change into the cup the beggar held out.

"God bless," the old man mumbled.

Michael was walking faster and harder now. Sweat was building up. He was only a block from his boxing gym. It would still be opened. He went in, changed into sweat clothes at his locker, and pounded on a bag for a good hour. He pounded until his hands were red and bloody, and his muscles ached. He jogged all the way home. But even still, the sleep was hard coming.

12

Carla sat with her arms wrapped around her bent knees in the windowsill of her father's deluxe condo in downtown Chicago. She knew Alexis would have a fit if she saw her with her feet touching the polished marble sill, but the view from the twenty-fifth floor was spellbinding.

Looking east, Carla could see far out on Lake Michigan to where sailboats floated like a cluster of toys on the huge expanse of navy water. Out the north side of the dining room, she could see a spectacular view of Lincoln Park, with all of the tall buildings lined up like so many Monopoly toy hotels. Below her, tiny cars sped along on streets that looked like they were all part of an aerial view in a video game.

It was her first moment alone since she had arrived in Chicago three days ago. Dr. Warren's wake, funeral, and the somber party afterwards at the Warren's house had been a whirlwind. Now that Carla was alone, she felt totally drained. She struggled to sort through her thoughts.

Her biggest concern was Michael. She had to call him. But she couldn't make herself do it just yet. She was still seething that he didn't agree she should come to Chicago. She felt annoyed he had abandoned her just when they had started something big between them. It reminded her of all the men in her life. Express your love, get involved, and then they leave. He was probably just like all the rest, she thought. She had been a fool to think more of it. Todd was probably right. She'd made herself cheap. *As if Todd were one to define cheap.*

Carla figured now that she'd crossed the physical line with Michael, he would lose interest. The predator phase was over. She would be dropped eventually, so why not be the one to initiate the severing?

She felt surprisingly safer here than she'd felt in weeks. So high in the tower. Guards downstairs. At the least, it was an illusion of safety. She wished she'd come straight to her father when all this happened. But it would have been impossible without the trip to Captiva to ease some of the tension between them and Dr. Warren's funeral as the crisis drawing she and her father together.

Things weren't altogether smooth with Alexis, but Carla was working her hardest on that. When they'd picked her up from the airport, Alexis had been stone silent in the car, only listening to Max and Carla talking. Carla could see the tension all over Alexis' face. But when they'd arrived at the condo, Carla had suggested that Alexis give her a grand tour and her stepmother's face brightened. There were new draperies in the dining room, made by a designer in California. The new handmade Italian leather furniture in the library. And in the guest room, a new canopy bed was lavished in an old-fashioned lavender quilt with white lace bed skirt and pillows. Tiny violets on the carefully chosen wallpaper. Alexis' pursed red lips were softening as she elaborated on each item.

Then last night at dinner the three of them had actually sat around the kitchen breakfast table laughing. Carla had begged to have hamburgers in the kitchen, rather than a formal meal in the dining room. It was the first time she'd ever laughed with Alexis. Probably some of the laughter was tension-relief after such a stressful few days. But, maybe there was hope yet.

The phone rang to break Carla's thoughts. A bird-like chirp coming from the designer phone in the library. Carla ran across the shiny hardwood floor to pick it up. For a brief second her heart pounded. Maybe it would be Michael.

"Carla?" The voice was female and familiar, but so muffled it wasn't discernable.

"Yes?" Carla asked, hoping to figure out who was on the other end.

"Why haven't you called Michael?" the voice said tensely. "He's worried sick." The muffling was gone and Carla now recognized Amy's voice.

Carla gave a little laugh in relief. Thank God. It was Amy. She really needed to talk to someone sane. A friend.

"I don't know, Ames. You know how it is. I'm busy and the time got away from me."

"No, I don't know *how it is*." Amy snapped sharply. Carla could clearly detect now that the strange tone to Amy's voice was anger. Why would she be worked up over Carla's tardy phone call to Michael?

"Well, I'm sorry. Really. I'll call him today. Didn't you give him my message that I was here in Chicago studying the case?" Carla figured that would have sufficiently informed him of her general whereabouts and plans. Did Michael need to know where she was every waking moment? Is that was this was about?

"Sure I gave him that message. But do you think that is all you owe him? A message?"

"Wait a second. What are you talking about? I owe him something? Is he starting to talk about getting paid? Is that what has you worried?"

"No, Carla. Are you dense? He's talking about jumping off a bridge. He's beside himself."

"Wait a second. I'm confused here."

"Don't be, Carla. And don't play ignorant. No one is confused now. Not even me. Michael cared enough to tell me everything. *Everything* that happened in Florida. And I know now what a snake in the grass you are and not a true friend at all."

"Amy."

"Don't Amy, me. Don't even talk to me, Carla. You knew I loved him, and then you played with him. Now you're throwing him away and he's like a lovesick pup over you. All I can hope is that he'll come to me when it's all over."

"Amy. Listen. I'm not throwing him away," Carla said.

Silence.

"I'm in love with him."

"No you're not," Amy said. She was crying now. "You're just using him."

"That's not true."

"I don't have to listen to this," Amy said.

"No wait. Don't hang up," Carla said. "I was going to tell you all about this. But I was waiting for the right time. I knew you'd be hurt. It wasn't something we did on purpose to hurt you. It just happened."

"You and Michael didn't do this. *You* did this, Carla. And things don't just happen. They're allowed to happen. You knew I loved him for years. You knew, and you butted in, just when he was getting closer to me."

"Amy, he wasn't getting close to you." Carla hated to be so blunt, but she had to be.

"How would you know *anything* about love?" Amy said, her voice distorted now. "Just stay away from me. And when you come back to Washington, I don't want you at my house. I'll leave your things at Michael's." More muffled sobs came through the phone.

"Amy, wait." Carla was struggling with how to handle this.

"I hate you right now, Carla. I hate you. I've never hated a friend in all my life. And you are less than a friend to me now. I despise every memory I've ever had with you. And I despise myself for trusting you." Amy sobbed openly and hysterically as she hung up.

Amy's words punched Carla hard in the stomach bringing up a wave of nausea. She wanted to cry, but her tear ducts were shutting closed with molten steel. Her insides were solidifying to metal. She was willing her feelings to shut down.

###

167

"Carla? Carla, darling?" Alexis' voice was preceding her into the room. She appeared in the double doors to the library, staring at Carla who was still standing there holding the phone. "Are you all right?" Alexis cocked her perfectly coiffed head to the side. Her normally shoulder-length, shiny black hair was woven into a sophisticated updo, with ringlets falling down around her face. Her mauve lipstick perfectly matched her Jackie Onasis dress. She had several shopping bags looped over her forearm.

"Oh," Carla said, shaking her head a little to bring herself to attention. "I'm fine," she managed to say. She smiled and returned the cordless phone to its cradle.

"Looks like you've been up to some shopping!" Carla said to change the subject.

"I have!" Alexis said with a large grin, completely missing Carla's faked enthusiasm. "And if you want to see what I've got, you've got to go get freshened up. You can't simply let yourself go around like that, can you?" Alexis clicked through the library to the kitchen talking over her shoulder as she went. Carla could hear her hang her keys on the infamous labeled key hook, found in every Redfern house since Alexis had come along. Make that every Blount-Redfern house, Carla thought snidely. She was annoyed at her stepmother's hyphened name. She wished Alexis had just kept Blount, if she wanted it so badly, and left Redfern to the memory of her mother.

Carla looked down at her cutoff jean shorts and T-shirt. This was how she always dressed on a summer day when she wasn't at work. She looked up at Alexis with a blank look. After this call from Amy, Carla had little to work with in terms of diplomacy or energy.

"All right, then." Alexis said, clicking back into the library in her strappy high-heeled sandals. "I'll let you in on your my surprise before you take your shower. How's that?" Alexis put her bags down on the love seat. She dug into a Neiman Marcus bag. "How's this?" Alexis held up a silky silver pair of shorts that shimmered in the light coming through the window.

"These just had your name all over them!" Alexis said while Carla was dumb-founded. "And to go with it…" Alexis turned and dug some more in the bag. "This top." She held up a black long sleeved T-shirt that said, *"little cutie"* in silver.

"Won't this be adorable for when you go out with your friends?"

"It will be something else, all right," Carla said, trying to smile as convincingly as possible. This went past the point of comical, straight to the absurd.

"Don't be shy. Take them now. You can wear them today if you want."

Carla reached over and took the items Alexis held out. "I think I'll save them for a special occasion," Carla said. She leaned over to kiss Alexis's outstretched check.

"Just kiss *near* my cheek, honey. Not actually *on* my cheek. You don't want to mess up my makeup."

Carla kissed the air near Alexis' ear.

"Thank you," Carla added.

"Think nothing of it," Alexis said, and she clicked off again toward the kitchen. "I have this appreciation luncheon in a few minutes at the art gallery downstairs in our lobby. Marco expressly wants me to attend as one of his best customers." Carla could hear her clanking around in the kitchen, putting Carla's dirty coffee cup from the sink into the dishwasher.

"Carla, dear. Would you mind keeping the kitchen sink empty? We keep it empty in our house," Alexis said as she reentered the library. Carla's stomach tightened. This is what had ultimately caused the fight last time she'd visited. She could no longer feel at home in her father's house. Carla was struggling to grasp the reality of that concept.

"Sure," Carla said. She had so many emotions swirling in her right now, she thought she'd erupt if she said anything more than one word. She took a deep breath to help control herself.

"That's my girl," Alexis said. "Now go ahead and get your shower before noon. A girl should never be seen without her makeup, and several of my friends might stop by after the luncheon."

"I've had my shower," Carla said dryly.

Alexis looked Carla up and down. "Honey, can you do something with your hair, or at least apply a little eye shadow?"

Carla sucked in her breath and decided to do whatever it took for peace. She was stretched so thin. "You are right," she said. "The phone rang and I completely forgot what I was doing with myself."

Alexis smiled as she stood in the doorway to leave. "I'm off."

"Have fun."

"Oh, I assure you. It will be fun. Come down if you like. I'll introduce you around. But wear a dress, will you?"

"Of course!" Carla said. And Alexis let herself out the door.

Carla slumped down onto the couch. She picked up the *little cutie* shirt and held it up. Alexis had bought it in the junior section of the store, no doubt. Didn't she realize Carla was almost thirty years old? Alexis wasn't much older – somewhere in her mid- or later thirties. Alexis was in a denial bubble that magically floated her over all her cares and worries. It was a sort of a self-administered lobotomy that allowed her to survive anything unpleasant. And Max's daughters were an unpleasant reality Carla knew Alexis had struggled to make go away when she first met him. But now that they were here to stay, she was making the most of it. You had to give her that much.

Carla held the silver shorts up to her lower body. They were two sizes too small. They wouldn't fit a six year old, Carla thought. This little incident was pushing her to the brink of her expiration date for visiting. Within twenty-four hours she was going to scream if she had to hold all this in.

She had gotten some information on the case at the funeral while talking to Dr. Warren's widow and daughter. That would have to do. She had to get back to Washington. *Where was she going to stay?* Each step of the way was getting more impossible. She had to buck up and call Michael. Once again. She needed him. She was starting to hate how her need and fear drove her like a seed blowing in the wind.

Michael answered on the first ring.

"Carla," he said urgently. Obviously he knew it was her from the caller I.D.

"Hi," Carla said. She knew she owed him an apology. But she wanted to see where the conversation was going first.

"What the hell, Carla? Leave me out of the loop, why don't you. Don't you think it would be easier if we worked on this case together?"

"Yes," Carla said.

"But I haven't heard from you in days."

"I'm sorry about that. I was busy."

"This isn't about the case, anyway. Is it?"

"What do you mean?'

"You were hiding. Hell, you *are* hiding."

"Hiding?"

"Don't pretend you don't know what I'm talking about. You know damn well who you're hiding from."

Carla was silent.

"Are you afraid of me, Carla?"

Silence.

"Why should I be?"

"Then come back to D.C., and let me see your eyes."

More silence.

"Carla."

"Fine. I'll let you see them, but you won't see much."

"I won't?"

"No. I'm numb."

"Well, at least you can admit it."

More silence.

"When are you coming back here?"

"Tonight or tomorrow."

"I'll be waiting for your plane, if you let me know when it will arrive."

"I'll let you know."

"When?"

"When, what?"

"When will you let me know?"

"Today."

"Good."

He was gone so fast. Not the cozy conversation she'd hoped for. She had wanted to spill a little more of her feelings to him but her fears had held her back and the clipped tone in his voice. For a fleeting moment she felt like giving Todd a call for a little comfort.

Do you always have to run to someone? Carla thought with a bitter grimace. Why don't you learn to stand on your own two feet? Suddenly she realized that those were her mother's exact words coming back to her. When she was a child, whenever she'd complain of someone bullying her on the school playground, her mother would firmly say, "stand on your own two feet, Carla."

Carla used to laugh and think, "What other feet could I stand on, Mommy?" Maybe now that her mother was gone, this single phrase, said over and over, was a legacy of her mother's advice, downloaded into her brain to be drawn up whenever the need arose. Coming to her mind now, maybe it was a sign from her mother. Carla shook her head to shake off the idea. It was as silly as looking for her mother in a shooting star. Her mother was dead. And that was the reality of it. If her mother were alive, she'd have a place to run. Mothers are who you run to when you're scared. But she only had her own two feet now. And her own two feet were going to get onto a plane and face Washington like a grown woman. She would go deal with this – all of this — head on.

Alexis was still gone when her father came home that afternoon. She had phoned earlier saying she'd opted to go to a friend's get-together following the luncheon, rather than bring her friends home. And, the party might go from happy hour on into dinnertime. Could she and Max deal with dinner themselves? Carla assured her they would be more than happy to.

"Daddy?" Carla asked, as she leaned on the double-door entryway into the library where her father was sorting through some papers on his desk.

"Yes?" He said absent-mindedly, still looking at a paper. Reading glasses on the tip of his nose, his brow furrowed.

"I was thinking of leaving tomorrow morning early, unless you have time to take me to the airport tonight?"

Her father was still reading intently. Carla waited.

"Daddy?"

"Yes. Yes. That's fine," he said agitatedly, still looking at his paper.

Carla knew she shouldn't be so delicate. She should calmly wait until he could concentrate on what she was saying. But with all the hurts she'd already faced today, she suddenly felt childish and put off. She silently turned to leave the room.

"Carla, wait," he called out. "Where are you going? Wait a second, here, will you?"

Carla reappeared in the doorway, and he gestured her with his glasses to have a seat in one of the chairs.

"I'll be through, here, in a second."

He put his glasses back on and continued to absorb the document. After a few minutes, he finished and put the document down. He removed his glasses and sat down beside her in the matching winged-back chair.

"Now," he said. "What were you saying?"

"Daddy, I think I need to head back to Washington either tonight or early tomorrow. Which do you think would be best?"

Her father looked at her with deepening eyes. She suddenly realized he didn't want her to leave.

"I know, Daddy. I wish I could stay forever. I do. But this isn't my home and I have work to do back where I live."

"I understand all that Carla. But..." he trailed off, his thumbs rubbing the wooden ends of the arms on his chair.

"You're going to miss me?"

"Yes," he said, looking directly at her, somehow with an emotional intensity she hadn't seen in a long time.

"It was fun on Captiva, wasn't it?" she asked gently.

"Just like old times," her father agreed. His eyes were glistening. *Was he going to cry?*

"We should do more of that," Carla said, reaching over and patting his hand.

"Indeed," he said with a smile.

"Daddy?" Carla suddenly felt she should tell him about her predicament, the danger she was in. "I've been meaning to tell you something."

"What is it, Carla?"

"Well, there's this situation…" She was interrupted mid-sentence by Alexis bursting through the front door of the condo.

Carla and Max looked at each other in curiosity as they heard Alexis walk through the house looking for people. First in the kitchen. Then back down the long hall to the master bedroom. Then finally she called out. "Max?"

"In here, Dear," her father answered. There was a clatter of feet as Alexis made her way to the library.

"There you are!" Alexis let a bourbon sigh escape across the room as she leaned on the doorway. "There you are, and I'm looking high and low. Have you two had dinner? I've had dim som and lobster bisque and all sorts of yummies." She came over and sat on the arm of Max's chair and stroked his hair. "You really should have come, Maxwell," she said with a pout.

Max grabbed her hand and squeezed it. "Next time. I promise," he said.

"He never keeps his promises," Alexis said to Carla with a drunken scowl and a smile.

Carla smiled back. She wasn't about to get started on this topic, especially not with Alexis.

"Well," Alexis said with a huff. "I'm going to change out of this stiff dress and put on something more fumcurtable." Then she laughed a little with her head tilted back. "Did I just say fumcurtable? That's funny!" She stood up from the armchair and walked slowly out of the room down the hall to the bedroom, still laughing to herself.

"Daddy, can you take me to the airport tonight?"

"Honey. I really needed to work on this case tonight. It's going to go class action. That's what I was reading just now. The judge agreed with our pleading for a class action lawsuit."

"That's terrific. Isn't it Dad?"

"I suppose, Carla. It's a lot of work, I'm telling you. Simon and Simon isn't going to take this lying down."

"So, should I call a cab, then?"

"Might be for the best."

Carla felt a stab of disappointment hit her. She wasn't going to have time to tell her father about her situation, and she wasn't going to get to enjoy the few minutes with him on the way to the airport. She was starting to feel so softened up toward him. She was missing him already.

"Okay, Dad. No problem."

Steel-cold Carla left the library and marched into the bedroom. She'd already made a tentative reservation with the airline for tonight and had herself all packed. She'd have just enough time to call a cab and make the flight. She grabbed the phone in her guest bedroom and called Michael. He didn't answer so she left a message on his machine. Arrival time and airport. Maybe he would meet her. Maybe he wouldn't. At this point, she didn't even care.

Alexis was lying down with a headache when it was time for Carla to leave. Her father said she didn't want to be disturbed.

"Please tell her I said thank you for everything," Carla said as she gave her Dad a tight squeeze.

"I will," her father said, lingering longer over the hug than he had when she first saw him in Captiva.

"Will you call soon?" He hadn't said this in a long time. Carla smiled.

"Sure, Daddy. I'll call."

It was midnight, but Max was still obsessed with details about the case. After Carla left, he'd gone over the paperwork again. He couldn't get it out of his mind. It was consuming him. It could possibly be the most significant case of his career so far. He was certain of that. He could change the very health opportunities for every American with cancer if he could beat down this adversary and win. He felt his juices flowing, his adrenalin and competitive edge honing for battle. He had a hunch about some obscure laws he might pull out of his bag of tricks. He took out a legal tablet and scribbled some notes for himself. There was so much to get done. He'd need several more of the younger law partners assigned to this case with him, and he'd set that up tomorrow.

He paused for a moment and his eyes landed on the small picture of he and Ernie on the bookshelf above his desk. This one was taken years ago, when he and Carmen had been on one of their annual golf trips to Phoenix with the Warrens. He smiled. Those were good times. And now not only Carmen – the mother of his girls, was gone. So was Ernie. He rubbed his thumb over the picture of Ernie's face. Godspeed, old buddy, he thought.

By one in the morning, Max knew he needed to look at just one more folder from the office and he'd be ready to face the onslaught of Simon and Simon's attorneys in the morning. He'd just whip over to his office quickly. It wasn't far away. Alexis was out cold. She wouldn't even know he'd gone.

"Evening, Mr. Redfern," the guard said in the lobby as he let Max out. Max strode around the corner to his Mercedes, clicking the car locks opened on his way. The alarm gave a little yelp as it disengaged. He sunk into the leather seat, and the doors locked automatically behind him. As he started the engine, an arm from the back seat gripped his throat and something cold touched his temple.

"Don't even think about turning on your alarm," a monotone voice said.

Max was frozen. He was breathless, in fact. He sat thinking for a minute. Was there a reasonable way to handle this?

The man cocked the gun. "Start driving."

Max put the car in gear and pressed gently on the gas. He pulled out on to the road. The street lights were blinking red. A lone car approached going the other way. "Get a move on," the gunman said, pushing the barrel at the back of Max's head.

Max eyed the man behind him in the rearview mirror. "Which way do you want me to drive?" Max said.

"Shut the fuck up." Max was cuffed on the side of the head, a ring on the man's finger stinging hard as it gouged into Max's eye. Max drove straight along the lake road for half a mile or so. Then he was told to turn on to a deserted side street.

"Stop here," the gunman said. There were tall bushes on either side of the road.

Max brought the car to a stop.

"So here's how it's gonna be…" The man took his time.

"You rig the Simon and Simon case like a horserace. Rig it so you lose. Or your family gets hurt."

Max involuntarily shifted in his chair, tensing his arm muscles. The gunman cracked him hard across the head again, only this time with the butt of the gun. Max felt an explosion of pain and warm blood trickle down over his ear.

"You lose this case. You lose it in a way that no one, not even your best law partner could guess the case was rigged."

Max was silent staring straight ahead. His fury was so mounted he was using all he had to control the urge to fight. Warm blood was streaming down his face, but he didn't reach to wipe it with his hand.

Max felt another crack explode on the side of his head again. Nausea welling up.

"You fucking sneeze at the cops and someone dies." The man laughed hard, snorting into Max's ear. "Or better yet. We get a hold of one of your pretty daughters." Max groaned. His vision was beginning to blur.

The car door opened, then slammed shut. Max heard the gun tap on the window but he didn't turn his head. "We're *all over you*," the gunman said. And then he was gone.

13

Carla spotted Michael looking out the window of the airport as the plane taxied to its gate, a lone silhouette, legs spread military style.

"Hey there, little missy," he said, helping her with her luggage. "Had enough of flying for a while?"

"Michael, I'm so sick of flying. I'm so tired of running."

"I know you are."

His mind was distant. She could tell from the expression on his face. His eyes were focused on an invisible point beyond an invisible horizon.

"So what's going on around here?"

"You should know."

"Amy?"

"Yep."

"She let me have it on the phone this morning."

"Sorry about that."

"Why should you be sorry?"

"Should have seen that one coming."

"You can't blame yourself for everything. Amy's a big girl. She's got her mind all out of whack, that's all. She's acting crazy. Like a teenage girl."

"Well, not totally."

"What are you talking about?"

"There are a few minor details you don't know about that are coming into play, here."

"Like what?"

"Let's talk about it at home."

"Why?" Carla stopped dead in her tracks to look him fully in the eyes.

"Just because, Carla. Because it's late. And because we need a little break from everything." He looked sad and tired, a reflection of her own feelings.

"Am I staying with you tonight?" she asked.

"Is that even a question?"

It was early and Lieutenant Dirkson was out in Michael's living room talking. From the bedroom she heard them talking over details of Dr. Warren's murder. Michael was mentioning what he had told the police in Chicago. The Chicago police still wanted to pin Dr. Warren's murder on a random breaking and entering gone awry. Michael was trying to persuade Dirkson otherwise. Dirkson was asking to speak with Carla, but Michael insisted she wasn't well today. She would come by the precinct a soon as possible and talk to him. No, Dirkson said. He'd come by here. Is this where she lives for now? Yes, Michael said. Dirkson agreed her own apartment still wasn't a safe idea.

Carla rolled over in the bed with her back to the door. She didn't want to face Michael and she didn't want to face this whole town. She was trying to think of how in the world she could get any work done and keep her job, and how possibly she could get her life back. They seemed to be getting nowhere on this case.

After some rumbling around in the kitchen and the smell of toast cooking and coffee brewing, she heard Michael creep into the bedroom. The sun shining through the blue curtains made the whole room glow blue. She closed her eyes to fake she was asleep. She didn't want to get up.

"Carla?" Michael said. He was standing by the bed. "Carla, honey?" He gently touched her shoulder. She tried to keep her breathing slow and regular.

He sat down on the side of the bed next to her. He rubbed her back. "Wake up, Carla," he said. "I've got something here for you." She could smell coffee. Carla mumbled and rolled toward him, as if she were waking up for the first time. She smiled when she saw his face.

"You faker!" he said. "I knew you were awake. I could tell."

"How could you tell?"

"Because you have this soft little way of breathing when you sleep. And you were on your side. You usually sleep on your back."

"Well, aren't you 'Mr. Rhodes Scholar' on the state of sleep as shown in Carla Redfern," she said.

"I'm a scholar on a fair amount of the states of Carla Redfern," he said. He was holding a cup of coffee with lots of cream and sugar in it. He lifted it toward her.

"For example. Your cream, mademoiselle. With just enough coffee. The way you like it."

Carla laughed and took the cup. It was warm but not too hot to drink. She sat up and took a sip. She was wearing an old Marine T-shirt of Michael's, and some of his boxers.

"I like the PJs," he said.

She smiled as she sipped her coffee. Michael wrapped his hand around her ankle. "But you'd like them better off, I'd bet."

"With warm oil on my hands," he said.

Boy when she worked, she really worked, Michael thought. He hadn't seen her working like this before. Probably because all he'd ever done was play with her. Her head was down buried in the book she was reading on some project, her hair flowing over her shoulders. Should he interrupt her for lunch? It was going on two o'clock. Personally, he was starving.

"You hungry yet?" he called over to her desk.

"I guess so, what time is it?" she asked, still reading.

"Almost two."

"You're kidding me?" She turned in her chair to look at him. Her eyes were wide, her lips so full and moist. He was thinking hard about having her for lunch.

"Time flies when we're having so much fun."

She smiled. "What are we going to eat, beer and moldy cheese?"

"Studied the interior of my fridge, did you?"

"Last night when you opened it. Wasn't hard."

"I could go out for something. What do you want? A sub?"

"That sounds good," she said, turning in her chair, back to her work.

Michael walked over to her and closed her book.

"Hey!" she complained.

"Listen. What kind of a sandwich do you want?"

"Turkey"

"With everything?"

"Everything."

"You got it." Michael took his gun out of his pocket and lay it on the table in front of her. "Deadbolt the door behind me."

"Okay," she said, grabbing at her book and opening it as he left.

On the way to the deli, he realized he was whistling. Something about having her in his apartment. She had a soothing way of taming all his fears. She thought he was taking care of her. But if she only knew, it was the other way around. He wanted her to stay in his place permanently. But he couldn't dare ask her that yet. He hoped she'd get used to living with him, and when the case was over, he'd spring it on her.

Carla heard the yelping outside the building even before she heard it in the hallway. Someone had an obnoxious dog out in the hallway, and the dog wouldn't shut up. People should be more polite with their pets. The dog was yipping and making a huge ruckus. Carla unlocked the door and stuck her head out to see.

It was Michael with a big black Labrador on a leash, barreling down the hall. The dog was pulling Michael, its tongue hanging out, spit flying, eyes bright and tail wagging.

"What in the heck are you doing?" Carla said. The dog came to the doorway and jumped up on Carla, almost knocking her over. It licked her face.

"Down," Michael said, pulling the dog into the apartment as he wedged his way past Carla.

"You got a dog, Michael?" Carla was incredulous. "This dog is *huge!*"

Michael unleashed the dog and set him free in the room. The dog roamed around the whole place sniffing.

"Michael, look at the size of this dog. He's the size of your kitchen."

"I know," Michael said with a smile. He was unloading a brown bag from the Pet Club. Two large metal bowls, a big rawhide bone, a box of dog biscuits shaped like big bones, a collar with a tag, a dog brush and a Frisbee. He seemed unaffected by her questioning.

"Michael. You're crazy! What are you doing?"

Michael looked up with a big grin. "He's for you. I got him at the pound."

"For me? Michael, no. I don't want a dog."

"You'll want this guy. Look at him. He's all sugar. But other people don't know that about him. To them, he's just plain big and mean."

"Right. With tail wagging and tongue licking. He looks quite ferocious."

"He's a deterrent. He is something to reckon with."

"You honestly got him for me? Please say you didn't. Michael, a dog is a huge commitment. You didn't even ask me."

"Exactly."

"What?"

"Exactly. I didn't ask you because, of course, you would run from commitment."

Carla put her hand on her hip. My Gosh. *A dog?* She stared at the thing and the dog looked over at her, too, big eyes blinking, eyebrows raised, as if he sensed he was on trial.

Michael pulled the Camaro around to the sidewalk where Carla was holding the dog on a leash. He was wrapping himself around her and Carla was spinning to keep herself from being tangled. She was laughing her happy laugh, the one he hadn't seen lately. Sure enough, the big brute was going to help keep her safe and be good for her spirits, just like he'd hoped.

He pulled up to the corner and opened the door from the inside. They stuffed the dog into the back seat. He turned his big bulk and stuck his head out the window.

"Hey, look," Michael, said. "He looks like a captain of a ship! Let's call him Captain."

The rest of the day was more pleasant than he could have hoped it would be. It was a gorgeous summer day. Big puffy clouds in the sky. Hot, but not the sweltering hot that Washington could often be in July. They walked the entire Mall and when they came to the giant carousel, Michael begged Carla to take a ride. Carla said it was ridiculous. Finally she submitted and as long as Michael lived, he'd never forget her beautiful face smiling at him as the giant carousel came around and around.

They bought half-smoke hotdogs – Michael's favorite — from a vendor and sat down on a bench to eat for lunch. Captain wanted a half-smoke, but soon gave up and lay down beside them, glad to be in the shade. Carla teased Michael about all the onions and mustard he piled on his hotdog. Couldn't be helped. He'd done it this way since he was a child. Just like his father had before him, he told her. After they took in all the sunshine they could and wore Captain completely out, they headed back.

Carla squeezed his arm. "You were right about the dog," she said. "About Captain."

Michael smiled. He didn't want the day to end. "C'mon. Let's play some pool. I have a great little place. Besides I can watch your ass while you shoot," Michael said. Carla laughed and it was contagious. Michael laughed too. *This was a great day,* he thought.

They dropped Captain off at the apartment first. And as they were leaving, they were startled to see Amy right outside her door, holding a bag of groceries.

Michael broke the silence. "Hey, Ames."

She didn't look up, but opened her door and quickly entered, slamming it behind her.

"She's not talking to you, either?" Carla asked as they walked down the hall.

"Evidently, not. Hey. You want to lay some money down on the pool game?"

"You've got to be kidding me?" Carla laughed. "I'll wipe you clean."

"Let's see what you got," Michael said.

Sure enough the wench beat him. Beat him senseless. Where did she learn to play pool like that? She was mysterious about it. Must have been an old boyfriend. The beers they'd had loosened him up. He had been so tight and concerned the past week or so. This entire day felt great. They ordered appetizers for snacks. Carla tore into some hot wings, the likes of which he'd never seen anyone do.

"Wow. So you don't always eat with five forks?" he asked her. He could still see her at the restaurant in Captiva with the blue satin dress on and the diamond earrings.

"What are you talking about?" she said, wiping some of the Tabasco from her mouth with her hand and chugging some beer from a tall bottle.

"It's just I'm not sure I've ever seen you come down from your throne."

"My throne?" She continued chewing on the hot wing, tearing another piece off with her teeth. "You had me on a throne?"

"Close," he said. "You still are."

"Even though I eat with my hands?" She was smiling.

"Higher on the throne, now that you eat with your hands, and whipped me at pool."

Carla laughed. "You're a fool to put anyone on a throne. No one is all-perfect. No one is all one thing."

"Guess you're right. But knights like to have a lady to adore and worship," he said with a wink.

"Please," Carla laughed. She popped one end of the now-cleaned chicken bone into her mouth, to suck the last juice from it.

"I'd be careful there, missy."

Carla continued sucking the bone and looked over at him with eyebrows raised. She slowly took it from her mouth and smiled.

"Hey, Carl! Tab please."

"Sure enough, Cowboy. You got it."

It was still early but dark now when they came out onto the street from the pool hall. Walking arm in arm with her along the avenue was sweet. He felt her softness next to him. It was tearing him up. He stopped at a street lamp, backed her up to it, and kissed her hard, holding her face in his hands.

She was surprised at first. He kissed her long and hard, and she returned the kiss. A group of teens walked past and smirked. "Go get her," one said. Another whistled low.

They were careful not to talk going down the hall toward Michael's apartment. They didn't want to torture Amy, or themselves, any more than they had to.

"I'm sick about that whole thing," Carla said when Michael had closed the door. Captain was up and wagging his tail at them, eager for petting.

"Amy?"

"Yes. It ruins my happiness to have you at her expense." Carla had such a serious expression.

"I know what you're saying." Michael said, leaning down to give Captain a good rubdown. He pounded him on his sides. "Good dog, you," he said. Captain was pure emotion all over Michael. "Now go lay down," he said. To both of their surprise, Captain obeyed.

"Wow. Maybe his last owner taught him that?" Carla said.

"Maybe." Michael reached over and looped his arms around Carla's thin waist, pulling her to him. "And I'd like to teach you a few things."

Carla giggled.

He reached up and pulled her hair out of the red tie. It fell loose and she tossed her head a little. He pulled some of it out of the way and began kissing her neck. "What are you up to?" she said. She leaned her head to the side to allow him access. "That makes me into putty."

Michael laughed like a vampire in a movie and backed her into the bedroom. He fell down beside her on the bed.

They were both quiet for the first time the whole day. She was looking at him with that inquisitive probing look. Those blue eyes, deep as the sea.

"What are you trying to find?" Michael said, gently stroking her cheek with his thumb.

"You," she said. "What you are."

"You know what I am," Michael said.

"I do," she answered. "You're the last of the good guys."

"I wouldn't say all that," he said, stroking her hair. "How did you put it? No one is all one thing. No one is all-perfect."

"You're very close. Close enough for me." Her eyes were twinkling like the sky on a summer night. She smelled like sunshine.

"I love you," Michael said, his voice thick with emotion.

She smiled the smile he loved. "I love you, too, Michael. I really do."

###

Carla was in the tub soaking. She'd been in there a while. Michael was making breakfast when the phone rang. He took the portable in to her, covering the receiver for privacy.

Woah. What a sight. Long thin leg propped up on the edge of the tub, his shaving cream lathered all over it. She had one shaved stripe coming down the middle of her leg. Her hair up in some kind of sloppy arrangement, half falling down.

She looked up at him, innocent eyes, still holding the shaver to her leg. "What?" she said.

"You have a phone call. Want to take it now, or should I take a message?"

"Who is it?"

"Don't know. A man"

Carla gave him a grave look of curiosity. He knew what she was thinking. Maybe it was Todd.

"No, it's not pumpkin head," Michael said. "He doesn't have this number."

"Right."

"You want it or not?"

"I'd better take it," she said. She reached over and wiped her hand on a towel.

He uncovered the phone and handed it to her, then walked back to finish the bacon and eggs.

He could hear her tone of voice in the other room. Business. She was in business mode. The call was short.

"Well?" He called from the other room, bacon sputtering.

"A freelance job."

"You took it?"

"Yeah. I thought I should."

"Probably good you did," Michael said, turning the bacon.

"Hey, I figured out why you smell so good," Carla called from the bathroom.

"I do?"

"Heavenly," she said.

"How?"

"It's your shaving cream. It's spicy."

"You like it?"

"I love it!" she said.

That was it.

He put down the spatula with a metallic ring and turned off the burner where the bacon was frying. He walked into the bathroom, put his hand up above his head on the doorframe.

"Is breakfast ready?" She didn't look up from her shaving.

He closed the door with a deliberate click and she looked up. "No," he said. He ripped his shirt off and threw it hard against the wall, then reached for his pants buckle.

Carla laughed.

At breakfast they talked about it. She had to go to a hearing on Capitol Hill tomorrow to cover a senate hearing on teen violence for the freelance job. It would take only a couple of hours. Michael said he'd like to go along, as protection.

"Come on. I'm sick of protection. Besides, it'll be boring," she said.

"I don't care."

"Your choice," Carla shrugged.

"Always my choice to keep you safe," Michael said.

"I'm starting to go into denial again. Maybe we're making this whole thing up."

"No. We aren't. You can't let your guard down."

"I know. But I wish I could."

"Just when you let your guard down is when they'll get to us. We have to wait until the police or I figure this thing out."

"What do you think it is?"

"I still say it's the drug company. When I was up there, I talked to some underlings in Simon and Simon. Underlings of the president, but high enough to know what's up."

"And?"

"They said the entire focus of the president's office is this case. Entire focus. That doesn't sound like the course of a normal day in a top *Fortune 500* company. Unless you're trying to save your ass. Also noticed a lot of Italian names in the company roster. Not that it means anything. But you can't help but wonder if there is a mob connection."

"What did the police say?"

"Nothing. They are investigating Warren's death as any other case. If they trace a motive to his work, then fine. But until then, it's just as easy to think of it as a breaking and entering robbery accident." Michael paused for a second. "How about you, what did you find out in Chicago?"

"I talked to Dr. Warren's daughter. She said her Dad was afraid and nervous the last few days before he was killed. Not himself. She even asked him about it. He said he wasn't feeling well. But she didn't believe him. She even told her mother about it. But that was the day he got killed."

"Threat out on his life," Michael said.

"Seems to be."

"Threat to do what? Not testify?" Michael was thinking out loud.

"Probably," Carla said.

"This drug thing is huge. Haven't you heard in the news, stories of other cases where people claimed there is a cure to cancer that the government is hiding?"

"Yeah. I always thought that stuff was hokey," Carla said.

"Well maybe it isn't."

"But can a drug company be sued for not selling a product they have?" Carla asked.

"I'm not sure," Michael said. "But I'm sure that is what your Dad is trying to figure out."

"Maybe when it comes down to life and death, you have a lawsuit," Carla mused.

"Maybe," Michael said.

14

The man leaned against the phone booth and smoked. His cigarette burned fast under the long draws he gave it. He looked up M Street at the stream of traffic and shoppers in Georgetown. He had no tolerance for the rising heat. It would be hotter than hell today. He stroked his suit pants to relieve his hands of dampness. These shoppers were idiots, he thought.

"You alone?"

"Yeah, boss.

"Good. I want this to be as clear to you as your empty skull. Got me?"

"Yeah, boss. Yeah." He wiped his forehead again. Sweat was dripping near his temples.

"I want the girl. And I want her now.

"Sure, boss. No problem. We got it covered."

"Then where is she?"

"Haven't nabbed her yet. She's always with some guy. The guy that beat up Joey."

"Joey failed and learned." There was a pause on the line. "You can learn from Joey. You understand?"

"Sure, boss. I understand. You want the girl. You want her now."

"Now," the voice hissed through the phone. "No more screw-ups. You take out her guard. You do what you have to do. But you get this girl. I got pressure coming from the top on this job, and I ain't going down for something that should have been done already. Do I have to come down and do it myself?"

"No. Don't worry, boss. We got it covered."

"And one more thing, Sully. I want her alive."

"I know all dat boss. I know."

"Call me from the warehouse."

"Sure, boss."

Sully hung up the phone. A kid was waiting near the phone booth holding his skateboard and fidgeting to get his turn at the phone. He opened the door to the booth and spit on the street near the kid. Then he strode off fast down the street. He had to find Rocco and get the girl.

Carla sat at Michael's computer trying to finish another project for Janet before she headed out for the freelance job. Where was Michael? If he wanted to take her to the senate hearing, he'd better get here soon. She'd been up since six a.m. trying to finish her work. Captain was curled up on the floor beside her. She liked the sound of his slow steady breathing.

The project she was working on was tedious, a national report on the progress of various teen anti-crime associations. While she was looking under the stacks of papers on the desk, she found a small yellow note that caught her eye. It was in Michael's sloppy handwriting. "Todd Grisham," it said. And below it, Todd's address, phone number and social security number.

What is this all about? Carla wondered. Is Michael researching Todd? Stalking him? She took a deep breath in frustration and anger. Captain lifted his head and looked at her. Then sighed and put it back down, this time on her bare foot. She clicked the computer off.

She might as well get dressed. She stormed into the bedroom and searched for the skirt she would wear to the meeting. It was wrinkled beyond hope. No iron in the hall closet. She slammed the door in frustration. Not in the bathroom anywhere, or the bedroom closet. She opened the top drawer of Michael's dresser. It was filled with papers, coins, magazines, a crumpled handkerchief. She shoved it closed. She sat down on the unmade bed in frustration and tried to smooth over her skirt.

The key rattled in the door. Captain was up making a commotion. "Hey, old boy," Michael said. And she could hear him patting the dog's side. Soon he appeared in the bedroom doorway.

He was breathless. "I hurried as fast as I could. This client wouldn't shut up." He stopped when he noticed her expression. "You ready?"

"No," she said. "I need an iron."

"Right here," Michael said. He reached on top of the dresser and handed it to her.

"I didn't see it there." She never thought to look out in the open. Carla handed Michael the little yellow piece of paper with Todd's name on it. "Recognize this?" He looked down at the paper and shifted his weight. "Yes. Do you?"

"Don't get smart, Michael." She plugged in the iron at the socket by the bed.

"Why do you care if I have it?"

"Why? How can you ask me that? Because it's sneaky, that's why. Because it has to do with my life and I should know what you're doing with it."

"It has to do with *my life*, too," Michael said.

Carla scorched her finger testing the iron, then sucked on it. She started ironing her skirt in frantic motions.

"Oh, I see," Michael said. "You think I'm going to harass him and you want to protect him? Is that it?"

"No!" Carla said, her skirt was smooth now and she reached over and yanked the cord to the iron from the wall. It whipped out across the room making a crack as it hit the floor.

"Then, what?"

"I just want to know what the secret's about."

"No secret, Carla. It was there on my desk, out in the open."

"Not in the open. I found it under some stuff."

"Only because of the papers that are building up all around. Not because I hid it from you."

"Then why didn't you tell me?"

"Tell you what? That Todd called at Amy's while you were in Chicago, looking for *you* of course. And he informed me that you are "nobody's girl," but if you were anybody's, you would most likely be his. And that you give yourself away with no thought as to what it means to someone else, so I'd better not count on your affection to mean anything."

Carla was standing, but now she sat down on the bed. She stared at Michael. She felt a huge conflict of emotions. She was angry now with Todd for the same reasons she was angry with Michael. For interfering in her life.

"He said that?"

"Sure, enough." Michael crossed his arms over his chest.

"Why didn't you tell me?"

"Because I couldn't even get you on the phone when you were in Chicago, that's why."

The traffic was loud going by outside.

"I'm sorry he said that," Carla said softly. She was looking at him now and his entire stance was one of hurt and pain. She could see he'd tried to push the memory of this phone call out of his mind.

"I didn't want to talk about it," Michael said. "I'm over it. And I know he's wrong about you. About us.

"He is wrong," Carla said. "He's wrong. He doesn't know what we have."

"Carla," Michael said. "I really have to stop talking about this."

"I know," Carla said. "And we can stop now."

"Good," Michael said.

Carla suddenly felt the urge to hold him and hug him. "I'm sorry," she murmured into his chest. "I'm sorry I lost my temper and I didn't let you explain."

Michael stroked her hair. "It's okay, baby," he said. "I'm sorry I didn't reach through the phone and snap his neck."

Carla pulled back and looked him in the eye.

"You wouldn't really hurt him, would you?

Michael stiffened. "Why would you care?"

"Why *wouldn't* I care?"

"Because you still love him?

"Do we have to go around with this again? I care about him. But, I don't love him like that anymore."

"I don't know if that's really true, Carla. It's hard to know what is true. But I'm trying. I'm trying to find out." He dropped his arms and she stepped back in surprise. She hated this cold side of him. She leaned back against the dresser. This drama was draining the last ounce of energy she had left, the ounce she was going to try and use to cover this meeting and write a story. It was getting almost impossible to function.

Her eyes watered in frustration as she looked at him. His shoulders were square. She could feel his tension.

"Just tell me you weren't investigating him," she said.

"I can't tell you that, Carla. Yes. I was looking up his information. I wanted to see if he's a criminal or something. That would make me feel better. Maybe I could convince you he's nothing."

"You don't have to convince me. You already have." She was struggling for air. Tears were more near coming, now, but she wouldn't let them. She could see into the bathroom where they'd made love yesterday morning and a rush of emotion went down her body.

They stood staring at each other. Michael was the first to break down. He reached over and pulled her to him, hugging her tight and rocking her back and forth. "Let's stop talking about it, all right? Let's forget about it. I won't hunt him and I won't stalk him, okay Carla? What kind of a person do you think I am?"

"A fighter."

"And you love that about me."

She looked him in the eyes, reached up and gently played with a curl in his hair. "I do," she said. "I love that about you."

It was exhausting commuting over to the hearing, waiting in the long line to get in, and when the meeting finally started, the notes Carla took weren't all that great. She kept trying to concentrate, but nothing would process through her head. Michael was sitting by her, arms folded across his chest, pretending to listen to what the senate panel was asking expert witnesses about teen violence. Now and then she looked over and his eyes were closed. But he never dropped his head. He slept perfectly straight, sitting up, dressed in black jeans, tan jacket and cowboy boots.

When they got back to the apartment Carla flopped down on the old couch and kicked her shoes off.

"Want a beer or something?" Michael said from the kitchenette. She could hear him popping one opened.

"A coke or water," Carla said. She heard him making her an ice water. He came out and handed it to her along with two pain relievers he put into her other hand.

"How did you know?

He smiled. "Because I know," he said, and sat across from her on the tattered recliner. He put his booted feet up on the old coffee table. Captain came and put his head in Michael's lap to be petted.

"I'm so beat," Carla said. "I'm beat into the ground."

"Well, take it easy," Michael said. "You've done enough work for today." He slugged down some of his beer.

"You're right," Carla said, taking her hair down out of the bun she often wore when she wanted to look professional and also keep from getting too hot on summer days. She loosened it and let it fall. She put her stocking feet up onto the coffee table.

Michael reached over and hit the answering machine button. A series of messages proceeded, mostly clients and calls for Michael. One was from Thomas Gray, asking Carla to call immediately. Carla scowled.

"What can that be about?" she said, thinking out loud.

Michael picked up the portable and handed it to her. She dialed Thomas' office directly.

"Carla, I'm glad you got back to me," Thomas said.

"Of course, Thomas," Carla said. *Why wouldn't she get back to him? She'd worked for him for over two years.* "Did you get the work I sent over yesterday? I'm almost done with some more. I can send it tomorrow."

"Carla," Thomas said. "Hold on to it." There was an uncomfortable silence on the phone. Carla instantly knew his drift. He was letting her go.

"What do you mean?" she asked. She wanted to hear him explain.

"Carla this is very difficult," he said. "But I've decided to let you go for now. If you want to be rehired after your life shapes up, then by all means, I'll find some work for you. You've never let me down before." She could hear the discomfort in his voice.

"What do you mean?" Carla could hear herself repeating. "You are letting me go now? I turned in some work. I'm holding the line."

"Janet wasn't happy with the work," Thomas said.

Of course, Carla thought. She's never happy with the work.

"I promised her she could have a new writer."

Carla knew there was no point in arguing. Janet had broken him down and that was it. She felt a burst of disappointment and shame. She couldn't believe she'd lost her job. She was silent.

"Carla? You there?" Thomas sounded kind.

"Yes," Carla squeaked. She could hardly talk. This was hitting her hard. She looked across the table at Michael who was now leaning on his knees, looking toward her, his hand stroking Captain's head.

"Thomas," she said. "I don't know what to say."

"You don't need to say anything, Carla. Good luck. Let me hear from you."

"I will," Carla managed to say before she hung up.

Michael was looking at her with probing gentle eyes. "You'll be all right," he said. "You've got that freelance work now."

"One gig," Carla said. "One short paper on the senate meeting. I'll be done with it by tomorrow. I'm unemployed, *and* hunted now." Carla felt like she was plummeting down a never ending shoot into a giant dumpster.

"There will be more. This town has a lot of work for writers."

"Not always," Carla said. She reached up and squeezed her temples.

"Come here, babe," Michael said. "Let me hold you."

Carla looked at him resisting. He was always comforting her. Always advising her. She felt like a baby, and she wanted to fight it. Wanted to hold up her dignity.

"No," she smiled. "I'm going to forget about it for tonight." She stood up and started toward the bedroom. "How about I change clothes and fix us some dinner?" she said.

"Not much to work with, I'm afraid."

"Will you go to the market?" Carla called from the other room. "I can make this killer Italian chicken."

"Great," Michael said. Even though she couldn't see him, she could feel his smile from the bedroom. He was a sucker for a home cooked meal.

###

It was still light out after dinner and Michael wanted to go to the gym and work out. He hadn't been for days. He told Carla he felt secure leaving her with Captain on guard and he'd also talked to the building security so they'd take extra precautions with strangers at the door. He'd only be gone an hour, he said.

Fine, Carla thought. She wouldn't mind a little time alone, actually. She relished the idea of mindlessly flipping through a magazine.

Not minutes after Michael left, the phone rang. Carla glanced at the caller I.D. It was Amy. She didn't know what to do. Should she pick it up? She waited and listened as Amy came onto the answering machine.

"Carla. I know you're there. Will you pick up?"

Carla hesitated.

"Listen," Amy said. "I know I've been rough on you. Will you let me come over right now while Michael's gone? I want to talk to you." Her voice sounded tentative and questioning, but otherwise like the Ames she knew and loved.

Carla snapped up the phone. "Amy?"

"Carla. Please let me come over. I want to talk."

"Sure, come on," Carla said. And she waited at the door looking through the peephole while Amy came across to Michael's. Captain came over right away, wagging his tail hard against Amy's leg.

"You got a dog?"

"Yeah," Carla said, patting his head. "Captain."

"Cute," Amy said. "But slobbery."

"I know. But you get used to it."

There was a tense silence, then Carla put her arms out and Amy hugged her tight. "Amy, I am so sorry you are mad. I miss you so much," Carla said.

Amy squeezed her harder and wouldn't let go. "I can't make it without you," she said, muffled into Carla's shoulder.

"Don't cry, Ames," Carla said, pushing Amy away so she could see her face and wipe her tears. "We shouldn't lose each other over a man. It's not worth it."

"Easy for you to say," Amy said, flopping down on the couch. "You've got the man."

Carla sat down too. Amy shifted slightly to the side, her leg curled up under her so she could face Carla.

"Listen," Amy said. "I know I've been a crazy fool. You must think I'm so immature."

Amy looked down into her lap. "I've been lying awake, night after night, thinking over what to tell you."

"Don't tell me anything," Carla said. "You don't have to."

"When is Michael coming back?"

Carla looked at her watch. "I don't know. Maybe twenty minutes. Don't worry about him. He'll be glad to see you. He really does care a lot about you, Amy."

Amy's face was contorted as if a haze of emotions were all crossing wires. Her eyes were filling with tears. She looked confused and pitiful, Carla thought.

"I've heard all that," Amy said. "I've heard it from *him*, no less. You don't have to say it again."

"I'm sorry," Carla said, and she hung her head. She was helpless to know how this could feel better for any of them. She wanted the old threesome back, the way she, Amy and Michael used to be, before all this blew up in their faces. Times were so good then.

Amy took in a deep breath and collected herself. She wiped under her eyes. "Is my mascara smearing?" she asked Carla, leaning closer.

Carla smiled. "No."

Amy sat back. "This isn't going to be easy, Carla, but I'm just going to tell you right out."

"What?"

"The part you don't know."

"What part?" Carla asked.

There was a silence.

"Michael and I slept together once."

Carla heard a nuclear bomb lift its plumb and rain down burning ash, then her own voice responding. "Are you sure?" She choked on the words.

"I would know if I made love with somebody, wouldn't I?"

Carla winced. An image of Michael and Amy intertwined, hugging and kissing, roared through her brain like a train.

"What was the circumstance?" Carla asked. She felt prickly and crazed. She wanted Amy to say it was some kind of a bizarre accident. They were drunk out of their minds. Something. *Anything,* to make this easier to understand. Easier to take.

"When he first moved in. We sort of liked each other," Amy said.

"Wait, wait," Carla said, holding up her hand. "Why haven't I ever heard this before?"

"Will you let me finish?"

Now it was Carla's eyes that were filling with tears. She couldn't hold them back. "It's not like you think," Amy said. "I can see it on your face. He's not a playboy. He doesn't take things lightly."

"Stop!" Carla screamed as she stood up.

"Carla. I seduced him one night. *I did it*. He was lonely. He just moved in. He had broken up with his girlfriend, and I seduced him one night after he had a lot to drink."

"I don't care," Carla said. She was pacing back and forth. "I don't care about any of it."

She felt like a fool. There had been this huge secret between Michael and Amy all along, and they'd kept it from her. If she had known this information— *that her best friend had slept with Michael* — would she have even dared to get involved with him? She wasn't given the option, and now she had to deal with these facts. Amy had touched him. Felt his kiss. Felt his arms around her. Heard him moan. Carla wanted to scream and pound the walls.

"Carla. I didn't think you'd lose it like this," Amy said. "I just thought the information would help you to understand how I stupidly thought there was some hope of having him again someday."

"Amy," Carla said. She felt dizzy. "I don't know what I think about any of this. I want to go. I need to think."

"No you don't," Amy said. She jumped up and pressed Carla into the couch "You aren't going to run this time. You are going to stay here until we figure this out. Until you settle down and calmly understand what happened."

"I'm not going to calmly *ever* understand this. You understand? I want you for a friend. You want him. He wants me. You've had him. He's had me. Why don't we turn on the damn television and watch a soap opera? It would be less chaotic than this. It would make more sense than this." Carla felt her voice going raspy. She curled her knees up to her, crossed her arms over her knees and buried her face. "Amy. I can't believe you did this to me."

"You can't believe I did this to *you*?" Amy said. "How was I supposed to know you would rip each other's clothes off in Florida?"

Carla looked up. "It wasn't like that."

"Why did you think I kept you away from him for two years, never spoke about him? Didn't you think that was odd?" Amy said. "I did it on purpose. I tried to keep you away. I knew he'd fall for you. Everyone falls for you."

"That's not true."

"It is," Amy said. She stopped standing and went to sit in the chair opposite Carla. She looked defeated. She stared off at the floor. There was a silence loaded with pain and questions intensifying between them like a storm.

Carla stared at Amy. Amy wouldn't look at her. She could tell Amy was beginning to shift from diplomacy to anger. The air was electrifying.

"Amy, please don't hate me. Don't you see? He's played us both for fools."

"No. He hasn't. You still don't know him, then. He didn't do this on purpose."

"He didn't sleep with you on purpose? He didn't tell me he loves me on purpose?" Carla screamed the words.

Amy looked like a knife had just been thrust into her chest. Her breath caught in her throat. "He told you that he loves you?"

"Amy, you still lie to yourself. What the hell did you think was going on here between me and Michael?"

"A private investigation case. A protective man falling for his client, a beautiful woman in distress. A circumstance. Something temporary and fleeting."

"No," Carla shook her head. "No."

"Then what is it?"

"I don't know anymore," Carla said. "I thought he fell in love with me. I thought he wanted me. I thought I was falling in love with him."

"Either you are, or you aren't, in love with him," Amy said righteously. Carla wanted to smack the look off her face.

Carla stared at Amy hard. "I don't know anymore. I don't even know if I know *who* he is right now," Carla said. "I don't know if I even want to try and know."

The key jiggled in the lock. Captain jumped up from the rug where he was curled up and scrambled to the front door. Michael greeted him in sweats. He bent over the pounded on Captain's sides and scrubbed him under the chin. When he looked up, he was startled to see Amy. Then he smiled.

"You girls kissed and made up?" he said. Then he stepped into the room and saw Carla more fully, with her knees curled up near her body on the couch. She looked at him with red swollen eyes.

Michael stopped smiling and froze.

"Not exactly, Michael," Amy said. "We haven't kissed yet, I would say."

Carla felt jealousy roar over her head like a tidal wave when Amy said his name. She felt completely and totally irrational.

Michael stood helplessly.

"She might need some time, Michael," Amy said.

Michael snapped into reality. "Amy, what have you told her?" his voice was filling with anger. "Why didn't you let me tell her?"

"Were you going to?' Carla blurted out.

"Yes, I was."

"When?"

"At the right time," Michael said

"How about before you told me you were falling for me? How about that for some real timing, Michael?"

Carla looked at Amy. She hoped what she just had said was ripping Amy's heart wide open and hemorrhaging all the blood out of her body. She felt reckless and angry.

"I don't know what I know about friendship anymore," Carla said coldly and steadily looking at Amy. Amy had tears streaming down her face.

"And I certainly know even less about love," she said, looking over at Michael. His arms hung limp at his sides, his face utterly defeated.

"I think I'll leave you two lovebirds to sort out your roll in the hay, because I'm not up for a ménage a trois," Carla said. "I'm not up for any of this. And as of now, Michael, you are fired. I'll get my own help." She was over to the door, putting her hand on the knob.

"Wait," Michael said. He grabbed her wrist. "Carla. You can't go out there. It's dangerous."

"And this isn't?" Her voice was piercing. She shook his arm off and ran out the door.

"Let her go," she heard Amy say.

Carla kept running down the hall even when Michael called her name. She didn't look back as she heard him running after her. When she looked out the cab window as it sped away, Michael was blurred through her tears.

15

Carla didn't know where to tell the cab driver to go at first. She just wanted a place to hide. She'd like to go to a bar, sit on a stool, and drink herself senseless. Who the hell cared if there was a gunman chasing her at this point? But she realized she'd jumped into a cab, again, with no purse. She had to go somewhere where she could get money.

She told the cab driver Todd's address on Pennsylvania Avenue. When the cabby pulled up to the awning over the entrance, she talked him into waiting for a minute while she buzzed up to the apartment.

"Hey. It's me," she said into the speaker on the wall.

"Me, who?"

"*You know*," Carla said tensely.

"Sheila?"

"Todd. It's not funny."

"Candace?"

"Todd, come on. I'm serious. I need money. I'm standing by a cab and the driver's pissed off."

"Okay. I'm coming down."

Todd appeared within minutes, walking with big strides through the lobby, still in his suit pants and a starched white shirt with the sleeves slightly rolled up. He pulled his wallet out of his back pocket as he came through the glass doors. He leaned into the cab and paid the driver.

"Traveling light?" he said, turning to her when he stood up.

He stepped back from her so he could see her better in the light. It was warm out but she had her arms wrapped around herself, shivering. Her face was a mess. Something was *really wrong*, he thought.

"Come on," he said. "Let's go upstairs." He put his arm around her shoulders and guided her into the lobby.

"You got problems?" Todd asked as he pushed the button waiting for the elevator.

"Big,"

"Never surprises me." He gestured for her to enter the elevator. She stepped in lightly. He was always amazed at how light-footed she was. Like a cat.

When he unlocked his door and they entered his place, Todd realized Carla hadn't been over in months. How many months? He saw her taking the place in. He liked how she assessed and absorbed each detail. He knew what she noticed, what she approved of, what interested her. Watching her face was a pleasure to him. He could feel her mind, and respected it like the depth of the sea.

"New carpeting?" she asked.

"Last week," Todd said with a smile. He went behind the bar and began mixing up two stiff drinks, hers not as stiff as his. He glanced over at her. She was looking down and rubbing her slim sandaled foot back and forth across the carpet, a look of somber distance on her face.

He walked over to her and handed her a whiskey. She gingerly took it and sat down on his sofa, sipping the drink tentatively. Her perfume, whatever it was, reminded him of spring.

He walked with his glass to the stereo, selected a quiet jazz CD by the Bill Evans Trio, a remastered version of the 1959 *Portrait In Jazz*, and turned it on softly. He turned on a low lamp by the big chair opposite her. He'd only been home about fifteen minutes, hadn't even turned any lights on yet. When she buzzed from downstairs he had been cooking up some kind of quick garbage in his microwave.

She sat somberly on his sofa, running one hand idly across the fabric, the lights twinkling outside the window behind her.

"So tell me all about it," he said, sitting down opposite her and crossing his legs, drinking down a large portion of his drink. This might take all night, he thought with relish. What a great surprise to see her here.

She sipped more of her drink. He couldn't see her face in the shadow. "I don't really want to talk about it," she said.

He considered this for a moment. Okay. He'd play it easy. Nothing tough here. He didn't want to frustrate her.

"Fine," he said. "I was just going to eat. You care for something?"

No, she'd already eaten, she said. He wondered where she had eaten. He wondered if it had been with that gutter bum. She wondered what she was thinking and how she felt. She was so elusive tonight. He knew this mood. It was no use talking too much.

He walked over to his kitchen. The dim stove light was on and he opened the microwave door to remove the overdone dinner. Cooled now, it was completely unappetizing.

He opened the refrigerator. The light blasted out into the darkened room. He searched around for a leftover Chinese box and took it out. Opened it. It smelled okay. He took a fork and walked with it back to the chair.

"Mind if I eat in front of you?"

"No," she said, with a small smile. Her voice sounded calmer. She was gathering inner strength. He knew how she stabilized herself.

"Good," he said, shoveling some of the low mein into his mouth.

She was quiet, listening to the jazz.

"Did you need a place to stay tonight?"

She was still quiet.

He knew she didn't want to answer because she didn't want to stay. He let that question drop and changed the subject.

"Cort is acting up. Causing a real scene on the Hill. You'd love to see the brawl," he said between bites.

"Cort Goldsmith," she said with a knowing smile. "Always a gent."

"Remember how we used to wager bets on him?"

"I remember," she said with a small laugh. "Who, on his own committee, he would alienate next." She was sipping the whiskey again. That was good, he thought. Very good. She needed the relaxation. God, she had him shaking. He was getting manically excited she was here.

He pointed the fork at her as he chewed. "You always won," he said.

"Because I kept my ear to the ground," she said.

Had it really been five years ago that they'd met on the Hill? Seemed like ten. "Not me. I missed all the nuances," he said.

"No, you didn't," she said. "You just chose to ignore them."

She was still shading her face from the light by how she had her head tilted and he couldn't see all of her expression. Was she smiling? Her hair was shiny in the dark. He wanted it as his tent.

He was done eating now and set the Chinese container with the fork inside it beside him on the table and took up his whiskey and finished it.

"You need another?" he asked, standing up.

"No. Not even close."

He walked over and mixed a drink. Hell, he might as well drink straight out of the bottle. He felt crazed and knotted.

He went back to his chair with the new drink and sat down, leaning back and closing his eyes. The jazz was undulating through the room. He waited.

"I'm not using that private investigator any more," she said quietly.

He opened his eyes.

"Really?" he asked. He tried not to be too interested.

"No," she said. "It's not working out."

"I'm sorry to hear that." He was faking it, but he knew she didn't buy it. "I know you need protection right now. Are you replacing him?"

"Tomorrow."

"Need names?"

She was quiet again. Pensive.

"Maybe," she said.

"I can get some good references."

"Okay." She sounded more like a little girl now. He ached he wanted to touch her so badly.

They sat in more silence. The jazz filled the gaps.

"Will you hold me?" she asked.

He almost spilled his drink. He got up and went over to her. He held her gently so she wouldn't bruise or break.

She hesitated in his grasp at first. Stiff and unyielding. But after a minute she loosened in his arms and submitted to the closeness. She heaved a sigh and pressed herself against him.

"I'm afraid," she said.

He couldn't respond verbally to that. Too much intensity. He wished he could kiss her. Then he could show her. But he waited.

"I'm afraid and I'm tired," she added.

"I know," he managed to say after more jazz flowed by them.

"If I stay tonight, will you not try anything?" she asked. Her face was up toward him now. He could smell her sweet breath.

"I won't do anything you don't ask me to do," he said.

She was broken in his arms and he could feel it. This was the worst he'd ever seen her. It almost made him afraid.

"I want to go to sleep now," she said. She had a cold tone that sent a shiver through him. She was steel and velvet.

"Sure," he said. "Do you want my bed? I'll sleep out here."

"No, you can keep your bed," she said.

He gently stroked her arm. The tiny blond hairs were so smooth against her tan. He reached over and took her hand as he held her with the other arm.

She took his hand softly at first, and then tightly. She was fighting a battle inside. It was dark for her, that much he knew.

"I'll sleep beside you," she said. She was playing with his fingers. "I need someone close."

The music wasn't even audible to him anymore.

"I'll always be that for you," he said, and his voice came out thickly. He reached over and gently stroked her cheek. If he was lucky, he might be able to kiss her tonight. But for now, he was glad only to have her near.

"I've missed you," he said, in a surge of emotion he couldn't control.

She didn't talk. But he could feel her breath quicken. He decided he'd stop with that.

They sat listening to the jazz and breathing together. He felt they breathed the very same pattern. A siren went down Pennsylvania. The moon was rising.

"Want me to go turn down the bed?"

"Sure," she said. She sounded like a ghost. He didn't want to let go of her to go into the other room.

###

It was seven a.m. and he was already late. Todd winced as he finished his shave, nicking the same place on his chin twice. He walked out of the bathroom and through the room, securing a towel around him as he went. Carla was still sleeping hard on her side of the bed. For once in his entire long bachelor life, he wished he didn't have a king-size bed. Carla was out of grasp most of the night. And in the morning, when he looked over to see her golden hair and cupid nose, he'd found it very hard to get up for work. Very hard. She hadn't even heard the alarm, after he hit the snooze button twice.

He was almost dressed when he heard her sigh and roll over. He had forgotten how small she was. The bed engulfed her. He was tightening his tie when her eyes blinked opened. Blue orbs staring at him.

"You out the door?" she managed to say, in the gravely morning voice he just now realized had always sent a sensual thrill down his spine. She was rubbing her eyes, wearing his longest T-shirt. Her arms were lost in it.

"Big day ahead," Todd said. He knew he sounded too brief and businesslike and she would hate that. He was remembering their fight in San Francisco when he had to leave her at the hotel. Does she have any idea the sheer willpower it takes for him to leave her at all, let alone while she's lying in a bed. His bed? Probably not. She'll never know. He sat on the bed beside her, bent down and laced up his shoes.

She watched him with a small smile. She still had sleep in her eyes. Her attitude seemed calm and refreshed, but there were big black circles under her eyes.

"I wish I could stay," Todd said as he sat up from tying his shoes, looking into her eyes. He had just officially entered into a zone where he never went with women. But everything was changing now with her. All the rules were breaking. He had to tell her how he felt. He had to stick his neck out.

"I wish you could stay, too," she said. She turned her head slightly to look out the window, as if intruders were approaching at the ninth floor level, by helicopter.

"Don't worry," Todd said. "This building has the best security in the area. Top notch."

"I know," she said. She looked weak, like a sick girl in a hospital bed. He reached for her slim hand resting on the black satin bedspread.

"Thanks for everything," she said.

"What did I do?"

"Everything I wanted," she said softly. "You were a gentleman."

"I always am," Todd said.

Carla was smiling at him. Her hand was so soft. He held it and rubbed the top of it with his thumb.

"Well, I really need to go. Will you be all right? Will you be here when I get back?" He already knew the answer to that question.

"I'll be fine," she said.

"The door's opened, Carla. Totally opened."

She nodded in acknowledgment. "That means a lot to me."

There was an awkward silence and Carla began to rub the palm of her hand back and forth across his palm. Their kindred connection never waned, Todd thought. He didn't care what she said, or how she fought it. There was no question they were kindred spirits.

"You know we belong together," Todd said. The words choked slightly in his throat on the way out. But he felt he had to say this now. He might not get the chance again for a long time. Maybe never.

She was looking out the window again, but this time it wasn't with concern for danger. She was looking at an invisible point far away. She looked back at him and there were tears filling her big blue eyes. She looked down at their hands as she gently ran her finger across his palm.

"I know we do. But it just doesn't work," Carla said. "If it doesn't work, it isn't real. It doesn't matter how much you or I think we are soul mates."

"We could learn to make it work." Todd felt so vulnerable. He was aching.

"Maybe," Carla said, but she wasn't serious. Her voice was distant. She was just consoling him.

She squeezed his hand now and her shoulders stiffened, a signal that this little session of emotional display was to be brought to a close. He was lucky he got to say as much as he did.

He squeezed her hand back and tucked the covers tight around her.

"You sleep, or whatever you want," he said. "Eat anything. Drink anything. All music is yours. The Jacuzzi. Help yourself. There's a key in the ceramic pot by the microwave, if you want to leave and come back."

She smiled and nodded. He knew it was a mute point to make the offer. She had that lone look of departure in her eyes. She was scheming a plan.

Todd stood up and turned off the lamp over the dresser. The roomed dimmed down to silver morning light. Carla turned over on to her side and curled up.

"Bye," Todd said softly from the bedroom door. Lame. *Quick. Think of something.* What else could he say? He was helpless to know. So much of everything he was trying now with her, was too late.

"Bye, Todd," she said sleepily. "Have a good day."

He strode to the kitchen counter to grab his heavy briefcase. As a second thought, he left a note and some bills for her in case she needed it. If she had to leave, at least she needed a few bucks. He double-checked the deadbolt to his apartment before he went down the hall to the elevator.

Just another day in Washington, he thought. But losing Carla wasn't just another anything. It was unthinkable. His mind literally wouldn't accept that it could be so. He winced as he shook his head to make her words go away. No. He wasn't going to believe her. Not yet.

Carla dozed in and out. She couldn't find a deep sleep. She only wished she could find one that would last for weeks. The sun came brighter into the room and she was too tired to get up and pull the thick drapes, even though closing them might help her sleep. She looked up at herself in the mirror over Todd's bed. When did he put a mirror there? She looked like a scarecrow with blond hair.

She got up and went to the bathroom to find a new toothbrush. Surely in this den of pleasure there was a steady supply of new toothbrushes, she thought. She opened the closet in Todd's bathroom. A regular drugstore, all neat and organized by product. There they were. An assortment of new toothbrushes. She picked one up. Right next to it was something leopard-printed and silky. She held it up with two fingers. A woman's thong bikini. She tossed it back into the closet.

As she brushed her teeth, she looked over at the sunken tub with Jacuzzi. Todd must have added the Jacuzzi in recent months. He'd always talked about getting one. Guess he finally did it. Several candles were half burnt on the ledge beside the tub.

Looking at Todd's little Garden of Eden made her realize that she didn't miss him, or what they had. She turned on the shower in the glass stall, undressed, and stepped in. No. Todd's place, and everything in it, was making her miss Michael. Michael's tub. Michael's tattered house with love all around. Michael's laugh. His smile. His smell. *Stop it,* she said to herself. *Stop it now!* Tears were lined up ready to spill out of her eyes. She squinted and defied them then tilted her head back and let the hot water roll down her face.

In the kitchen she poured some orange juice in a small cup and opened the phone book on the counter to "Private

Investigators." She browsed through it as she sipped the juice. She found an investigator near the Federation. She called the number. A quick-speaking efficient woman took down details about her case. "You might as well come on in and talk this out with Mr. Daniels," she said. "He should be here shortly."

Carla smiled snidely. Okay, she thought. I'll go over and see Mr. Daniels. How convenient. Maybe she'd drop in and pick up her things at the Federation. Say "thanks" to Janet. At least tell Harold goodbye, and her other friends. Kill two birds with one short trip to K Street, she thought. There really shouldn't be a safety problem in broad daylight, if she took a cab. She bit her lip and looked down through Todd's big glass windows at the city humming below. Todd had left her cash on the counter. Several twenties. He had written a quick note, *"More where this came from. Call me if you need anything. Todd"* She folded the bills and put them in her pocket. "Thank you, Todd," she said softly to herself.

While she was in the bathroom the phone rang and the answering machine clicked on after the third ring.

It was Karen. Carla picked it up.

"Hi," Carla said. "How did you know I was here?"

"Good guess."

"Did Michael or Amy tell you I was here?"

"No. Amy didn't know where you were when I talked to her this morning. I have no idea what Michael thinks you're doing. But why don't you tell *me* what the heck you're doing?"

"Karen, it's such a long cheap tale, I don't even want to waste my breath on it right now. But let's just say my trust is out the window, and Michael is no longer on the case. I'm getting someone new today."

"Well, that's what I wanted to talk to you about. Have you talked to Daddy recently?"

"No. I tried calling him a couple days ago, but couldn't get through at his office."

"You can't. They won't let me through either."

"Did you talk to him at home?"

"Yes. And I'm worried about him. He doesn't sound right, Carla."

"What do you mean?"

"I don't know. He sounds distant. He sounds like he's hiding something."

"How can you tell?"

"He seems odd. He seems almost nervous."

"I wonder if this is what Dr. Warren's daughter was telling me about. She said before her father got killed, he was acting very strange and out of the ordinary."

"Like he was afraid of a threat put on him?"

"Yes," Carla said. "Exactly."

"We have to warn him."

"He won't let us. He's avoiding us."

"Maybe you could get to him on the phone by telling him you're having trouble?"

"I've tried, Karen. But I keep getting interrupted."

"Try again."

"Okay. I will. I'm going to see a new private investigator now, and after I get him all squared away and hired, I'll call Daddy and talk to him."

"Carla, be careful. Do you still have Brad's gun?"

"Yes," Carla fibbed. She had it at Michael's house, but she wasn't about to go get it.

"Well, keep it close," Karen said.

"I promise to be extra cautious," Carla said.

"I love you bumpkins."

"I love you, too," Carla said.

###

"It looks like she's gonna make a break for it soon." Sully's voice from the stakeout in the building across the street was crackling through Rocco's walkie-talkie.

"I'm on it," Rocco said. He unzipped his technician overalls and put the gun from the glove box into his pocket. Rezipped. He put a stick of gum into his mouth and pulled the van down into the parking garage, stopping at the guard's booth. He smiled. "Got a TV here for 903."

"Sure, buddy. Let me call up to the apartment and confirm."

Rocco waited, tapping his thumb on the steering wheel. He caught his reflection in the guard's window and smoothed his hair.

"The resident's not answering," the guard said.

"Listen, I just talked to the customer from my shop." Rocco raised his voice. "I got a tight schedule. You gonna let me deliver this, or what?"

The guard nodded his head in the direction of the loading dock. "Go ahead."

Rocco entered the garage and backed up to the dock, just in front of the service elevator. When he opened the rear door of the van, it hid him from the guard's view.

"I'm going up now," he said into the walkie-talkie. "She still there?"

"Still there. Should be coming out any minute."

Rocco went up to the ninth floor and stepped out of the elevator. Perfect. It was located behind an exit door with a small window looking out into the hall. He waited and watched. Nothing yet.

"She's out of my view. Do you have her yet?"

"Calm yourself," Rocco said. "Here she comes now. I'll get her."

The girl walked out of the apartment at the other end of the hall. Rocco pushed his door opened and walked toward her, tool belt jingling. She glanced up from locking the door to see him coming. He took out a large ring of keys from his pocket and stopped in front of the door across the hall from where she was, real smooth, like he was in building maintenance. She smiled a nervous smile, but it looked like she was buying it.

"Nice day, miss," he said, half turning toward her.

She nodded, then started down the hall. She was heading the wrong way.

"Oh, dammit!" Rocco cursed to himself. "Forgot my toolbox –"

He turned and followed a few paces behind her. This was going to be easier than he could have imagined.

She picked up her pace. When she got to the end of the hall, she realized her mistake and turned around with a puzzled expression.

"Lose your way?" Rocco said with a smile.

"Yes," she said. "I was staying with my friend, and I can't seem to find the way out."

"Simple," Rocco said. "Right this way," and he opened the door in front of them. "You can use the service elevator."

She looked at him, eyes narrowing. Something in her brain must have sounded the alarm, because she looked like she was going to bolt. Her mouth fell open a little, but before she could say anything, Rocco clamped one of his hands down over it, and his other arm went around her middle and spun her around. She was a featherweight. He had her through the exit door in a heartbeat.

She was screaming under his hand and trying to bite, but he had her tight enough to keep that from happening. He had her arms trapped under his grip. She started kicking hard and got him good a few times in the shin.

In the elevator, he squeezed tighter around her ribcage until he felt a pop and her scream turned into a cry. He put the elevator on hold.

He had his gun now to the back of her head and his mouth near her ear. He liked the diamond stud earrings and the way her shiny golden hair was pulled back. She struggled as he pressed his face into the hair beside her neck. She squeezed her eyes shut.

He tightened his grip on her and she moaned in pain.

"Listen up," he hissed. "Feel that metal on the back of your head?"

She blinked, staring straight ahead.

"I asked you a question." He squeezed her harder and she winced.

"That metal is a gun that I will gladly splatter your brain with if you don't cooperate. Here's what we're going to do. I'm going to let my hand off your mouth now. But one peep, and I use this gun. Clear?"

She didn't answer.

He slowly took his hand from her mouth.

"They'll hear you if you shoot me in here," she said, her voice low.

"Oh you think you know what they'll hear?" He shook the gun up in front of her face. "This is a silencer. They won't find you until they look in the dumpster."

He still had one arm tightly around her and she was breathing more heavily now. That part about the dumpster must have gotten her attention.

"You still won't try it," she said. He could see sweat beading up on her forehead.

This bitch was begging for it. He took the electric tape from his hip pocket and tore some off with his teeth. He roughly pressed some across her mouth. "Does that smear your lipstick, sweetie?" He had a good laugh in her ear. She turned her face away from him. He taped her hands together, then he opened a body-sized canvas bag and started to work it down the length of her. She squirmed as he put it on, but he flogged her one across the head.

"Shut up," he said. "You make noise; you die. Simple. Hell, you're already in a body bag!" He couldn't contain his laughter at that one.

He slung her over his shoulder with one arm, hiding the gun in the other pocket. When the elevator door opened, he threw her in the back of the van. Her head rung against the metal floor.

The girl was squirming wildly and screaming through the tape and the bag when Rocco got in the front seat. He reached back and grabbed her hair through the canvas. He yanked as hard as he could. "You shut your trap now, or you won't have your hair next time I see your pretty face. Got it?" She settled down and Rocco rolled past the guard, waving an all-clear signal. The guard smiled and waved back. They were out onto Pennsylvania Avenue.

"Why are you making me drive?" Sully's bald head turned pink when he was mad. "Because, I want to make sure this girl isn't any trouble, that's why," Rocco said. "Why you have to ask?"

"Took you long enough," Sully said.

"Didn't want anyone to hear."

"Did they?"

"Hell, no. I do things right."

Rocco unwrapped another piece of gum, folded it and put it into his mouth. Sully took a drag from his cigarette.

"This one is simple," Sully said. "We got the girl. We take her to the holding site and keep her there until we get the call."

"We gotta *wait* with her? I thought we were taking care of this and dumping her in the river."

"No," Sully said, exhaling smoke from his nose. "Frankie said she can't even be bruised."

Rocco laughed. "Too late for that."

"Don't get any more ideas." Sully gave him a sideways glance. "Frankie will cut off your hands if you mess this up."

"Yeah, sure. Frankie the Almighty."

Sully layed on the horn. *"Move, you moron!* Damn, I'll feel better when we get outta town."

"Yeah? I'll feel better when we stop for some food."

Sully looked at him. "I already ate," he said.

"Well I didn't. I say we hit up a MacDonald's drive-through."

"God, you annoy me. You know that?"

"Yeah, but you love me." Rocco reached over and scuffed Sully under the chin.

"Get off!" Sully pushed Rocco's hand away. "We'll stop when we get out of the city. I know a place where we can stop near the bridge."

Rocco looked back at the girl. She wasn't moving. She was quiet. That was strange. "You think she's all right?" Rocco asked.

"Hell if I know. I don't know what you did to her."

"I'm gonna go back and check."

"Be my guest," Sully said.

Rocco squirmed around the van seat and went to the back, kneeling by the girl. He nudged her once. No movement. He nudged her again. Nothing. Now he was wondering if he'd covered her nose with the tape, too. That would be a problem.

He reached down to the bottom of the bag and began rolling it up.

"She tied up?" Sully asked.

"No. Just bagged her and taped her hands together."

"I'd tie her up first if you wanna take that bag off."

"You seen her," Rocco said. "She can't weigh much more than a hundred pounds. She's nothing."

Sully was lighting another smoke. "Suit yourself."

Rocco unrolled the bag. Silky legs. He put his hand on one of them. Wrapped his hand around it and squeezed a little. Delicious. She didn't make a movement. Not even a twitch. She must be unconscious, he thought.

He kept unrolling. Arms limp at her sides. No movement. He whipped the rest of the canvas off her face and there she was staring at him with cold blue eyes. Blue devil's eyes that caught him off guard. She quickly lunged at him with two thumbs that she rammed right into his eye sockets. Pain roared into his brain as he lost all vision. At the same time, her knee went hard into his groin. Now he was doubled over.

He was temporarily stunned. She was feeling for his gun in his pocket. He reached down and grabbed her wrist and threw her backwards. He was still dealing with his groin, and his vision wasn't coming yet.

"Son-of-a-bitch!" Rocco said. "She lynched me." He reached over and put a knee on her chest and leaned hard.

"Told you," Sully said. "Told you. But will you listen?"

Rocco pushed down harder with his knee. He struggled to see her face, but his vision was still black and white patches.

"You don't touch her like that," Sully said. He was turning back to see. "You understand? I'm serious. You'll be floating in the Potomac River on your face."

Rocco took rope out of his pocket and wrapped it good and tight around the bitch's wrists where she'd torn the tape loose. So tight, he heard her scream from under the tape. Sully looked back.

"Hey. Her hands are blue. You can't tie her that tight."

Rocco loosened the rope. He tied her ankles. His vision was getting a little better. She curled to her side with her arms in front of her and her legs up close to her. Her eyes looked scared now. Her beautiful hair was all messed up. What a shame. He leaned over and stroked it. Soft. She winced and squirmed.

"Listen, sweetheart. Daddy Sully says I can't hurt you." Rocco looked up at Sully. He was busy merging onto the highway. Rocco put his hand on her upper thigh. Softer than velvet. She tried to fight him, but he put his knee back on her chest.

"My little viper," he whispered close to her. "I'll see what you got for fire under that hood, soon." Then he laughed. She was trying to lunge at him, but he pressed his knee on her harder.

"Hey!" Sully was looking in the rear view mirror. "What's going on back there?"

"Nothing. Just getting to know each other." Rocco laughed loud.

"Get the hell off of her and get up here. We're almost to your damn MacDonald's."

Rocco let his knee off of her and looked her hard in the eyes. She had the nerve to look at him after what she done to him?

16

The broken down warehouse on the Severn River was almost hidden by scrub. The property had been deserted for years, and trees and tall grass almost made the warehouse invisible. The van bumped around on the dirt road leading up to it.

"All campers out," Sully said as he put the van in park.

"Guess I'll lug the broad in, since you're so short!" Rocco said laughing, opening the back of the van.

There they were, those blue panther eyes, Rocco thought. Something about those eyes.

"Okay, sweetie, time to go." He'd already tied her legs, and her arms were wrapped around her chest now with tight rope, along with her wrists. She wasn't going to pull anything on him. He grabbed her and slung her over his shoulder. She didn't make a sound. Must be tired of screamin' he thought.

He wove his way up to the house through the brush, some of it caught the girl's hair as they walked. Once he had to stop and untangle it before they could keep going. She hissed at him with her eyes.

There was the warehouse. Amazed the damn thing hadn't collapsed through the winter. Sully was already inside. Had Frankie on the cell phone.

"Good clean job," Sully said. "Totally clean. We wait here until we hear from you. That's right. Yeah, boss. No problem," and Sully clicked the phone off.

###

The warehouse was dust and broken wood and glass except for the one small corner of the building that Sully had fixed up. A little wooden table and chairs by the window in the corner of the open warehouse. In the warehouse's old office, was an old spring bed he'd found at a dump. It was a little getaway for him sometimes, when he needed to get the cops off his back or hideout for a while. Should get sheets for that bed, sometime. He could see a hole where mice had started to chew on the corner of the mattress. He was glad this was the spot Frankie wanted to use for the kidnapping. Much better than being stuck in a hotel room with Rocco. At least here, you could go out and look at the river, walk around a little, get some fresh air.

Rocco stood, still holding the girl over his shoulder like a sack. Her long hair was hanging down.

"Why you standin' there like that. Go put the girl down," Sully said. "Put her in there on that bed."

Rocco raised an eyebrow to Sully. "You thinkin' what I'm thinkin'?

"Shut your yap," Sully said. "You know, you really wear me out sometimes." Sully turned to look out the window and lit another smoke. The click of his metal lighter echoed in the expanse of the big warehouse. Somewhere at the other end, a mouse or a rat, scurried in the dark.

Rocco threw the girl on the bed and walked back to Sully, dusting off his hands.

"Don't you wanna take that tape off her?" Sully asked.

"What, and listen to her bitch? You know, I need a beer real bad. You got some liquor in here Sully?"

"What do you think this is, a Holiday Inn?"

Rocco paced around. He went to look out the window. There wasn't much to see past the weeds that had grown as high as small trees.

"I'm not good at waiting, ya know?"

"Don't I know it," Sully said, sucking hard on his smoke. He wished at this point he could just watch the girl himself. Rocco was going to screw this up somehow.

Rocco paced around some more. "You think I could take the van and go buy us some beer. Maybe something for lunch later?"

Sully blew smoke out his nose. Shit, why was it so hard with Rocco? He needed food round the clock, like a baby.

"Why the hell not?" Sully said and he dropped the cigarette butt to the floor and stepped on it. "Take the van and go right about a mile on the paved road out there. You'll find a market. Rundown. The people are real nice. They don't ask no questions. Get me another pack of Camels, would you?"

"Sure. Anything else? Some caviar?"

"Shut the hell up," Sully said and he tossed Rocco the keys. "Hey, wait," he called after him as he was out the door. "Get me the paper out of the van. Something to do while I'm waiting."

Rocco came back in a minute and slapped the *Washington Post* onto the table. Sully was still standing looking out the window. Even though there was nothing to see, it made him somehow feel safer. This shit was so nerve-wracking. Kidnappings weren't his favorite day at the park.

He listened while Rocco pulled the van out and was gone. He glanced in at the girl. Her eyes were opened. She was curled on one side. Her hands still looked blue. That asshole Rocco, he thought. She was a pretty girl. Rocco was right. Pretty and young.

"If I take this tape off you, will you say stuff I don't wanna hear?" Rocco stood beside the bed.

She blinked a few times. She shook her head no.

"Okay, then. As long as you're cool. I'm cool. Deal?" He reached over and took the end of the electrical tape with his hand. He yanked hard to make it quick. The girl didn't flinch as the tape came off. She only sputtered a little, and licked her lips.

He was looking at her wrists and wondering if he should undo her. Rocco was cutting the blood off in them. And the body wrap was ridiculous, too. What was she, a death row inmate? She didn't need all this rope.

He took out his pocketknife and opened it. He saw her flinch. "Oh this?" he said, holding up the knife. "I'm only gonna cut some of this rope off you. I'm sorry my partner is such a thoughtless animal." He reached over and cut the body rope and the rope at her wrists. How far could she go with ankle ropes? He could hear her if she tried any funny business. She was rubbing her sore wrists. They were bloody where the rope had cut.

"Thank you," she said. She had a nice voice.

"Listen, sweetie. I gotta go use the can. You think you can be a good girl and stay put?" She didn't look all that tough. Rocco was just trying to rough her up so he'd have an excuse to mess with her.

She smiled at him. "I'll be good," she said. He smiled back as he took the newspaper into the can and shut the door.

Carla looked around. What a hellhole. She didn't know where this was. They had driven about an hour. The scary one, Rocco, was gone. Thank God. She had to think fast before he got back. She saw the cell phone on the table. She glanced at the bathroom door. If he was a typical man, he'd be in there a while. She looked over at the table. No way she could jump there with hobbled legs without him hearing her. She began to work on the ankle ropes. They were knotted like rocks. She dug her nails in hard and tried to loosen them. They didn't budge. She kept working them. She leaned down and looked under the bed. It squeaked.

"You okay out there?" Sully called.

"I'm fine," Carla said.

She saw a long rusty nail by the bed. She reached down gingerly and got it without making any more noise. She dug it into the knot and moved it around. It was working. The knots were loosening. She had them off. She leaned over to get off the bed. It squeaked some more.

She waited. No sound from Sully.

She slowly pushed herself up from the mattress and tiptoed across the room. She got the cell phone and dialed 911.

She heard Sully pull toilet paper off the roll.

She tiptoed back to the bed fast with the cell phone still on, and put it between the mattresses. No. She took it out. She stuffed it into the mouse hole at the end of the bed and covered it with torn-up mattress.

She started frantically tying the ropes back on her ankles.

Sully flushed the toilet.

Carla lay back on the bed.

Sully walked out of the bathroom zipping his pants.

He smiled over at her.

"You need to use the john?" he asked.

Carla said, "yes." He reached his hand down to help her up. She stood up and looked down at her feet.

"Sorry sugar, you'll have to keep those on," he said.

Carla jumped to the bathroom and closed the door. Thank God the rope didn't come apart while she was hopping. She used the bathroom. It had spiders in every corner, and the toilet water was rusted. She tied the ropes on her ankles tighter, like they were before she undid them. Then she flushed the toilet and hopped out.

Sully was out reading more of the paper in his chair. Carla hopped back and sat on the bed. Waiting for Rocco. She had the rusty nail in her pocket. She heard his van pull in.

"Got the beer, boss. Some for you, and the girl, too," Rocco said. He set a brown bag on the table. Rocco looked in at her. She folded her arms.

"You untied her?"

"Yes, you pig. I untied her. She's not supposed to be uncomfortable. Frankie's orders."

Rocco looked in at her and his eyes narrowed.

"Something about that girl I don't trust."

"You say that about everybody." Sully had the paper opened. He was still reading.

"No. It's in her eyes. She's intelligent like a shark. Got plans like a shark."

Sully lowered the paper and looked in at her. "You're full of shit," he said, and went back to reading.

"I'm cracking into this beer," Rocco said. He opened the twelve-pack of Budweiser and took out a can. "I'm wrapped so tight. I hate this waiting stuff."

"Yeah? Me, too," Sully said. He folded up the paper and lay it down. Then he looked around. "Hey. Where's the phone? I had it right here." He patted his pockets, looked under the table. "You got it?"

"Not me," Rocco said. He tilted his head back and pounded down an entire beer and crushed it with his hand. "You said I can't talk to Frankie. Why would I have it?"

Sully looked in at the girl. "You seen it, babycakes?"

"No," she answered. She kept her arms folded.

"Go check her Rocco. You ought to like that," he said.

Rocco smiled. "My pleasure."

Rocco sauntered in and looked at her. A little fear, yes. He could see it sparking up in her eyes. That was more like it

He walked over closer to her, his thighs touching the bed, and looked down at her.

"You seen our phone, princess?"

She shook her head no.

He grabbed a huge handful of her hair and yanked her head back hard.

"You sure?" he said, putting his face close to hers. "You sure you don't have it hidden somewhere?" He yanked again on her hair, just to see her wince. She wouldn't speak. Had those shark eyes on him.

"Okay, then." He took his gun out of his pocket and cocked it, aimed it right at her face. "Looks like the guard has to frisk ya," he said. She turned her head away from him.

"Rocco. You know she ain't got it on her person," Sully said. He popped open a beer.

"No. I don't know. Better safe than sorry," Rocco said. His pulse was beginning to race.

The girl stayed how she was. Arms folded across her body. She stared at him. It was a good trick, he thought. She made him feel she was putting a voodoo curse on him.

He put the gun to her head at her temple, then reached into his pocket and took out a switchblade. He opened it with a snap. Her eyes were on the knife. He smiled. Then he reached down and cut her ankle ropes. She winced.

"I wonder if you have anything hidden inside those little shorts of yours," he said, holding the gun to her.

That was good. Now her chest was heaving.

"Rocco, that's enough," Sully said. "Give it up."

"I ain't givin' it up. You think you know everything. But I'm telling you. This girl is up to something."

"Rocco, I said, back off," Sully walked into the room. He was a full two heads shorter than Rocco. He walked up to Rocco and stood beside him. "Come on man, you're losing it." He grabbed Rocco by the arm.

Rocco slammed his elbow into Sully's face, Sully collapsed forward, blood spewing from his nose. "Godammit Rocco," he said. He reached inside his coat to get his gun. Rocco was ahead of him. He rammed the butt of his gun down on Sully's head. Sully dropped. The girl gasped. Blood was pouring out onto the floor.

The shark was a mouse now. She was shaking like a leaf. Big blue mouse eyes. "Please," she started to beg. This was more like it.

He cracked her across the mouth. "No talking," he said. She reached up to touch her mouth. Tears were coming to her eyes.

He straddled her pressing both of her hands above her on the bed. "Crying for your mommy? You're gonna cry *real hard* for your Mommy," he said.

Suddenly there was a click and cold metal at the back of his head.

"Drop the gun, asshole." The voice sounded like it meant business.

Rocco dropped the gun.

The barrel pushed hard into the base of Rocco's head. "Now. Put your hands up and let go of her slowly and get off the bed. Get off slowly, or I do what my finger is just *itching* to do, you got me?" The voice had clenched teeth.

Rocco let go of the girl's hands and climbed off of her slow. He climbed real slow.

"Over to the wall," the voice directed. Rocco flinched. Maybe he could take him.

"Don't think about it. You'll be dead before you turn around," the voice said close to his ear. "Now, walk. Hands up on the wall. Feet spread."

Rocco did it. He felt the gun barrel press into his back right behind his heart as his other arm was wrenched behind him shooting pain through his shoulder. A metal ring snapped around his wrist.

Rocco turned and swung with his other hand, but that got him a knee in the stomach so hard that he doubled over. Another knee rammed into his nose. Rocco felt it break. He crumpled down. The other hand went into the cuff.

A pointy boot kicked him in the side, then kicked him again. "You. Son. Of. A. Bitch," the voice said, a kick of pain pulverizing his ribs with each word. "You don't know how lucky you are to be alive." Rocco believed him.

"You didn't read me my rights," Rocco said. "This won't hold."

"I'm not a cop," the man said. Rocco looked up and moaned. He bent his head back down. Pain was almost blinding him. The man was handcuffing his legs now. He didn't care.

"This one's not dead," he heard the man say about Sully. Then he heard cop cars. Tons of 'em. He wished he were a dead man.

Carla could smell it was a hospital even before she opened her eyes. She could smell its retched alcohol smell. It made her sick. She told her eyes to open, but they didn't obey at first. She started to sit up. Shooting pain ripped through her chest. She moaned and lay back down.

"Hold it there, little missy," a voice said from across the room. Her sight was blurry.

"Michael?"

He came to her side and took her hand.

"You saved me? How did you save me?"

"How do you think?"

Her mind was blurry. Why was she so blurry? She reached up to her head. There was a bandage on it.

"I can't think," she said. She moaned when she touched the bandage again.

"You took some knocks," Michael said.

"I did?"

"Skull fracture. Abrasions. Broken ribs."

"I didn't think I was hurt. I was just afraid of..." she thought of the terrible evil on the face of the kidnapper.

"Don't think about that ever again. *Ever,*" Michael said, squeezing her hand. "You're safe now. It's all over. The feds have enough leads to track this to the very end of the trail. Jailhouses are bulging with the arrests being made right now."

She blinked at him.

"So, I won't be stalked anymore?"

"Shouldn't be. Won't be. I can guarantee it."

She smiled softly. It hurt to smile.

She looked at him. "Michael, I'm sorry…" she wanted to talk about something. What was it? Something bad that had happened between them, but she couldn't think of the details.

"Shhhh," Michael said. He put his finger gently over her lips. "Don't think. Don't talk about anything," he said. "Just rest."

She looked at the side of the bed. Twenty-four huge long-stem red roses stood in a vase. She smiled carefully so it wouldn't hurt.

"From you?" she asked.

He smiled. "Who else?"

She squeezed his hand, but it sent a shock of pain up her arm from her wrist. She looked down at her wrist and saw dark blue bruises and slim bandages.

"It looks like I tried to cut my wrists," she said, venturing a small laugh that only caused the pain in her ribs to resurface.

"Hardly," Michael said. "You were really brave. The police got the 911 off the cell phone you hid."

Carla smiled. It was coming back to her. "Oh yeah. I hid it in the hole in the bed."

"They traced it, thank God."

"But how did you get there before they did?"

Michael smiled. "Do you require that I give away all my trade secrets?"

"Yes," she said.

Michael was only smiling.

"You trailed me?" she asked.

"You could say that," he said. He squeezed her fingers softly.

Carla was still struggling to remember what she needed to talk to him about. It was important. Her memory was temporarily downloaded somewhere else and not responding. She stared at Michael, trying to remember.

"Don't worry," he said, touching her furrowed brow. "We'll talk about it later. Right now you get some rest."

"How long do I have to stay here?"

"Overnight for observation, that's all."

Carla sighed.

"I know. Another golden cage for the songbird," he said. "But it's almost over."

Carla looked at him trying to believe it. She was confused and tired.

A nurse came in holding a needle. "Time for more codeine, Miss Redfern. The nurse turned to Michael with a look of dismissal.

"I'll be right outside," he said.

Carla turned onto her side slowly. Everything hurt when she moved.

"Just a little pinch," the nurse said as she thrust the needle into Carla's hip. It felt more like a stiletto. The nurse wiped the spot with cotton and pulled up the sheets. Carla heard Michael talking to some people. There was a great commotion coming toward her room.

"How's my baby?"

"Daddy!" Carla said. "How did you get here?"

"We came by plane, immediately," Alexis said, appearing from behind him. Michael's head was behind hers, smiling.

Carla reached out her hand and took her Dad and Alexis' outstretched hands. "I'm so glad you came. I'm so glad," She was beginning to feel the instant effects of the new codeine shot. She felt like she was talking in slow motion.

She saw her Dad looking her over. Looking at the bandage on her head, her wrists. His brow was furrowed.

"It's not as bad as it looks," she said. "Really, Dad."

"We spoke with your doctor earlier while you were asleep," Max said. "He said you'll be fine. Just need a little rest."

"You got here earlier?"

"Hours ago," Alexis said. "We just now went out for a bite to eat."

"Was I asleep?" Carla asked.

"Sort of," Max said. "You were in what they call trauma shock. They sedated you quite a bit. You dozed in and out."

"I feel very foggy right now."

"That's the codeine," Alexis said knowingly. "Trust me, tomorrow you won't even remember you talked to us, or what you said."

"Great," Carla said sarcastically. She smiled. Her Dad smiled back at her. He was still holding her hand.

Alexis went to the chair by the window and took a seat. Michael leaned against the wall beside her.

"You two have met?" Carla asked.

"Oh, yes," Alexis said, "A wonderful boy." Michael winked over at Carla. Oh brother, Carla thought.

"We can't stay long," Max said. "We just came to see you were all right. Lend our support. We're heading back up tonight."

He leaned down to her face and she kissed his cheek hard and squeezed his hand. He was visibly emotional.

"I could have lost you," he said.

"I could have lost you," Carla choked.

The room was uncomfortably silent.

"Well," Alexis said. "Thank God this terrible nightmare is under control. Max is off that case with Simon and Simon. The government is investigating the company."

Max looked down at her.

"Are you okay about it, Dad?"

"Oh, yes indeed. Carla, that was a bad deal from the start. I really anticipated some problems with that case. Let the federal government sort it all out."

"You'll still be in the paper," Carla smiled.

"I hope not," Max said. "I don't want any more excitement than the excitement of a huge fish on the end of my line off of Captiva."

"Here's to that," Michael said.

"Will you join me?" Max said, spinning to look at Michael.

"We can only hope so." Michael looked over at Carla.

"Good man," Max said, and extended his hand. Michael clasped it hard and Alexis stood up to go. She came over to the bed while Michael and Max were saying a few last words. She leaned over the bed.

"Your Dad was really worried," she said.

"I know," Carla said.

"So was I," Alexis added. Carla reached for Alexis' hand and held it. Carla truly felt something good toward this woman. A family feeling, maybe? It was some kind of a miracle.

Alexis smiled big and stood up. "Now, you don't be a stranger any more. I won't stand for it. Our house is open to you."

Carla smiled at Alexis and her Dad, now standing with his arm over his wife's shoulder.

"I won't," Carla said. "I promise to visit more often."

"I want that promise kept," Max said in his captain's scolding voice. A nurse came and shoed them from the room. Before they left, they each gave Carla one last kiss.

"Can I stay a few more minutes?" Michael asked the nurse. The nurse scowled. She looked at her watch. "Two minutes."

"That's fine ma'am," he said politely.

"I saw how you charmed her," Carla said in her drugged voice.

"Who me?"

Michael looked like he wanted to say something really big. Carla didn't want him to. She reached her black-and-blue wrist up to his face and put her finger on his lips. "Not now," she said. "Give me a chance to be codeine-free first, will you?"

Michael threw his head back and laughed.

"How did you know what I was going to say?"

"I didn't," she said. "But I guess we both have a lot to say."

Michael's eyes were looking teary-eyed. Was he going to cry? Carla stared harder at him. Maybe it was a drug-induced illusion.

He coughed and did a quick wipe job on one of his eyes.

Carla raised her eyebrows at him. She was enjoying this. Even in a stupor, it was fun watching a manly-man about to cry.

"Oh, leave me alone," he said as he shifted his weight and took a Marine stance. There. That snapped him out of it, Carla thought.

"We'll talk when I get out of here."

"Okay," he said.

"Did you want some help getting home?"

"No," Carla said. She was relishing the fact that she was finally free. "But I'll call you when I get home and settled. I promise."

Michael nodded. He reached down and gently kissed her cheek, and stood back to look at her again. His eyes seemed to be still struggling with tears. "I'll see you soon," he said, and he turned and was out the door.

###

Carla rattled the key to the door in her own place. Her very own place. She was so excited she could hardly think straight. She walked in. It smelled musty, but it looked pretty good.

"Oh no!" she exclaimed.

"What?" Amy was in right behind her with an armload of Carla's stuff.

"All my plants died!"

"Boo," Amy said. "I told you I suck at watering plants."

"You couldn't have saved them. They were orphans. That's what killed them."

"Let's get all philosophical here, shall we?" Amy said putting Carla's things on the table.

Carla walked to the kitchen. Opened her pantry. Some soup cans. Peanut butter. It felt so homey! It felt terrific.

"You all set then?" Amy said. She was dressed for work.

Carla was broken from her trance. "Sure. I'm great," she said.

"You might want to cut that hospital bracelet off," Amy said. "I think the bruises are going to attract enough attention for you." She smiled.

They stood looking at each other. It was awkward. Carla was the one to break down first. She reached out to hug Amy.

"We'll work this out," Amy said hugging her tight.

"Yeah," Carla said. "Friendship is a tight cord."

"Around your neck…" Amy said.

They both laughed.

"I've got to scoot. Will you call me?"

"Yeah," Carla said. "How about tonight?"

Amy nodded. "You going to be okay?"

"You know me," Carla said.

Amy laughed as she left, closing the door behind her.

It was so silent. Carla was stunned. Her own place. Her own life. She hardly knew what to think. She missed Captain. You know, she missed Captain a lot. She needed him over here. She'd have to call Michael tonight and see if she could get him, or at least share joint custody.

Todd was coming over and bringing dinner. Carla didn't know why she'd agreed to this. But he had pleaded so pitifully. And she also owed him money, so she told him only if he'd let her pay. He laughed at that. But she knew he was glad it gave him the chance to come over.

He was right on time. Unlike him. He carried two huge bags from the gourmet deli.

"Wow," she said. "A feast for an army."

"Thought you'd like the leftovers," he said.

He stood awkwardly at the door, looking at her.

"Come in. I'm sorry. Come on in."

"Make yourself at home," Carla said, amazed at how quickly Todd found the wine bottle opener while he was unloading the deli bags.

"Of course." He smiled as the wine cork popped off. She sat down at the table as he took the lids off of all sorts of little containers of various marinated things, salads, pasta, smoked salmon, cheesecake.

She hadn't really eaten in days, and it all looked appetizing. She held up a wine glass for him to fill it.

"Nasty bruises," Todd said, noticing her wrists.

She took a sip of the wine.

"Great wine," she said, changing the subject.

Todd looked at her with concern. For the first time he was getting a visual image of what had happened to her, Carla thought. Not a good thing to think about.

"Please don't ask about it, Todd. I'm really, honestly, trying to forget details."

"Okay," he said. He had a sad and worried look on his face that she didn't want to see there.

"Drink up," she said. "A toast."

"A toast," he joined in. He was not at all cheerful. He was breaking her heart.

"A toast to a better life for both of us."

He held his glass away from hers.

"What?" Carla asked.

"Can't drink to that," he said. "The only way for that to happen is for me to be with you."

She set her wine down.

"Todd. Please. I just got out of the hospital. I can't think about sad stuff. They told me I can't."

To this Todd laughed hard. "Who told you that?"

"Nurse Cranky."

"Well, you'd better obey then," he said.

Todd did pretty well through dinner, Carla thought. He changed the subject from the hard things, and they talked about work and where she might get another job. He was suggesting a lot of leads on Capitol Hill. She could become a press spokesperson for one of the senators.

Carla told him she was going to take up Thomas' offer to find her a job. Maybe she'd even get her old job back.

There was an awkward silence as the wine ran out and the food was eaten. Carla stood up to put some of the leftovers into the refrigerator.

"I'll get that. *Please!*" Todd said, standing up and putting down his napkin.

Carla walked to the living room and sat in her big soft chair. She was ready for Todd to go so she could enjoy her first night in peace. He had a heavy heart and it was weighing on her.

He tidied up the kitchen and came in to sit on the sofa. They sat quietly for a moment.

"I'm going to California," he said.

Carla sat up straighter. "What?"

"I got a great offer from the governor this week. And Goldsmith is going nowhere at this point, and I along with him. So...."

She looked at him. Rumpled dress shirt, tie askew, mop of golden brown hair. She loved his face. His beautiful face. This was right for him. She knew his ambitions.

"You're taking the offer, right?"

"Course I am. I've worked so hard."

"And you deserve a good break like this," Carla said.

They both sat silent. This was an awful feeling. Carla had always dreaded this day. The day they would really and truly sever their lives from one another. She gulped hard. A miserable ache was building up in her chest.

She was the first to cry. "I'll miss you," she said.

Todd choked. "An understatement." He was leaning forward in his chair, not sitting back in his usually relaxed mode.

"I'm leaving within a month. My condo sold the first day I put it on the market."

"Are you kidding?"

"Might as well make the cut clean, and with a sharp blade. Isn't that a direct quote from you?"

"Yes," she said. Now that it was happening, she wished she'd never said it.

Todd literally hung his head for a moment. Carla had never seen him so directly open about his sorrow. He looked up again. "It goes without question that I'd want you out there with me, if you'd want to be."

"I know," Carla said. She dabbed her eyes with a tissue.

"Listen. I didn't come over to stress you out," Todd said. "I don't think I should stay long, for now. I just wanted to tell you, myself, about California, before someone else did."

"I'm glad you did," she said, her eyes were swelling from crying softly. She blew her nose in the tissue.

Todd stood up and she went into his arms. They swayed for a long time, long enough for a whole freight train to go by outside in the dark somewhere. She gripped his back with her fingers. He gently stroked her hair. She didn't stop crying the entire time.

"All right, then," Todd said finally. "I'm going to go. But I'll talk to you tomorrow."

"We still have a whole month," Carla offered, sniffling. "We can go out to eat a few times."

"Sure," Todd said, downheartedly. She knew he wanted her to suggest they share more than a few dinners. But she knew that wouldn't happen. She wouldn't let it. It wasn't the right choice for her. Not for now.

She escorted him to the door and he leaned down and kissed her cheek sweetly.

He started to leave, but she reached up and hugged him one more time. She held on tight. He rubbed her back. "I've got to go," he said. Then he was gone.

17

"You've got everything?" Michael was leaning into Carla's new Jeep Cherokee, his hands grasping the door beside her. Captain was in the back seat with his head out the window. If a dog could smile, he was.

"I've got everything but the kitchen sink," Carla said.

Michael was silent looking around at the stuff she had packed. "Sure you don't need a bodyguard?"

Carla laughed. She touched his cheek. "You know I always *want* a bodyguard. But, do I *need* one?"

He looked so sad it was killing her.

"Look, it's only until the first snowfall. That's less than three months from now." If he only knew that she wished it were longer.

"You've got your map?"

She held up her pack of trip maps compiled by Triple A. "Every single iota of road between here and Lander, Wyoming," she said.

He winced as she thumbed through the maps, not careful enough to disguise the genuine excitement she felt. "This is the greatest thing that's ever happened to me," she said, hoping he'd understand.

"Not everyday someone gets a staff position on some fancy slick magazine," Michael said.

"I still can't believe it." She was going to write about Yellowstone, the Grand Tetons, Jackson Hole, the high prairie, the wildflowers and Native Americans for a full spread on Wyoming. What an assignment!

"Who ever would have guessed Thomas Gray had friends in such high places?" she said.

"And that you'd be such a great writer."

"I doubt that. I'm sure it's all Thomas' doing. He felt bad about letting me go."

"I wouldn't sell yourself short." Michael shifted his weight and looked down at his boots. "You sure it'll be safe in that log cabin you're renting?"

"More than safe," Carla said. "I've got a gun. And, my guard dog."

Michael smiled and patted Captain's head. She suddenly felt like she was taking away his child.

"You can email me, if you want to," Carla said gently, but she knew it sounded trite.

"I will. You can count on that," Michael said. His voice was growing distant, as if his thoughts were overwhelming him.

"Send me an email and tell me how your classes are going." She winced at the sound of her own removal from his life.

"Supposedly, I won't have time to even go to the bathroom, they load so much work on first year law students," Michael said, now turning his attention away from Captain and looking at Carla.

"Well, you'd better try," she smiled.

Michael smiled back. "I will write you," he said softly. His eyes were pools of sorrow.

"Well, the day's not getting any younger, and I have to try and make it to Ohio." She rubbed her hands around the rim of the steering wheel. There was an awkward silence. Finally she leaned over and gently kissed him on the lips. He would have kissed her much longer and more intensely, had she let him. But instead, she pulled away.

Michael patted the car and stepped back. "Take care, little missy."

A tear fell against her will and Carla wiped it quickly. "I'll take care," she said. He stepped back further from the jeep and she put it in gear, pulling out onto Connecticut Avenue. Captain barked.

In her rear view mirror, Michael waved. Carla stuck her hand out the window and waved back. By the time she reached the next stoplight, she couldn't see him anymore. He was gone.

She felt like a hot air balloon that had just cut ballast. She turned up the radio and the wind whipped through her hair as she merged onto the beltway heading west.

A chance to hear coyotes for the first time. To see wildflowers, not on the flat pages of a book, but bobbing their heads at high altitudes. Maybe she'd be enchanted by whirling Arapaho head dresses by firelight? Who knows what all else? She could only imagine. It was going to be a chance of a lifetime.

She smiled. *A chance of a lifetime.*

About the Author

Diana Manos is a journalist living in the Maryland suburbs of Washington, D.C. with her husband and three sons. Her articles have appeared in local newspapers, national magazines and *The Washington Post*. *Seduce Her Heart* is her first novel and a winner of the 2002 Maryland Writers' Association book contest. Ms. Manos is currently at work on her second novel.